Murder At Flaxton Isle

by
Greg Wilson

Chapter One

Nadia Kumar was too busy catching her breath to notice the unlocked door. The white stone cottage had loomed up on them as the three visitors stepped off the concrete of the funicular railway and made their way into the compound. Nadia had been focused on her feet most of the way up, trying not to drop the crate of beer she and Adam Cartwright were carrying between them. *This really is the middle of nowhere*, she thought, not without some pleasure, as they moved across to the front door of the cottage and carefully lowered the crate.

Adam was looking rather windswept in a woolly hat and thick jacket, his thin, freckled face red with exertion. He was something of a beanpole, underneath all that clothing, but you couldn't see it just now with that heavy rucksack on his back. He took a moment to recover himself and then gestured to the house. 'So, what do you think? Not bad for five hundred pounds a night!'

The cottage was a two storey affair in rough white stone. It had wooden framed windows and a wide, sloping roof.

'If it's got four walls to keep the wind out, that'll do me.' Nadia laughed. She pulled her scarf tightly around her neck. It was freezing out here. 'You wouldn't think it was July, would you?' Nadia had never been much good with the cold. She had grown up in Dubai, where the temperature rarely dropped below twenty-five degrees. But at least the low stone wall protected them a little from the bitter wind.

'I did tell you. There's no such thing as sunshine in this part of the world.'

Nadia grinned and slowly pulled off her rucksack. It was a relief to get shot of it. She slid a hand into her pocket and dug out her mobile phone. She couldn't resist taking a photograph. *Our new home, for one weekend only.*

Adam was standing by the door. He stuck his tongue out at her as she raised the camera, but then relented and adopted a suitably cheesy grin. Nadia crouched down, trying to get in as

1

much of the cottage as she could. Adam struggled to maintain his smile while she fiddled with the framing. Finally, she tapped the screen and then flipped the phone around and showed him the results.

'God, I look old.' Adam grimaced.

'Rubbish. You don't look a day over a hundred and three.' Actually, at forty-one Adam was a year younger than she was. They were an odd looking pair, she thought. He was six feet tall, ginger and as skinny as a broom handle, she was five feet one, dark haired and a little on the plump side. 'That woolly hat really suits you,' she said. 'Very chic.' Adam stuck his tongue out again. She glanced down at her phone. 'I'm going to send this to Suzy. Let her know what she's letting herself in for.' Suzy was one of the others who would be staying here this weekend.

Adam sucked in his cheeks as she tapped at the screen. 'You won't get a signal out here. Didn't you read the small print? We're miles from anywhere.'

The place was certainly isolated. Flaxton Isle was a desolate chunk of rock some miles off the coast of Scotland. It was covered mostly in grass. The only signs of habitation, apart from the cottage, were the ruins of a small chapel and the outline of an old railway track snaking down to the landing stage on the east side. And, of course, the lighthouse.

Nadia gazed up at the great stone tower. She had seen the photos on the booking website, but it was far more impressive in the flesh. The lighthouse was about twenty five metres tall, a long, thin tower made from the same white stone as the cottage. A glass-ringed lamp room protruded out from the top. The tower was connected to the cottage by a narrow corridor and the entire complex was surrounded by a rather basic stone wall. The compound itself was the only bit of flat land on the island.

Nadia took another photo and then returned the phone to her pocket. Adam was crouching down, fiddling with his rucksack, and Nadia took a moment to catch her breath. She had always considered herself a practical sort, but struggling up here from the landing stage with that crate of beer – not to mention the rucksack – had certainly knocked the wind out of her. The path was ridiculously steep. There was a rough handrail up the side of the cliff, but that was not much use when you were carrying a crate of alcohol. *I'm glad we didn't have to drag all the luggage up ourselves.* A couple of rugged looking sailors were even now dumping the rest of the supplies at the top of the cliff, about a hundred metres from the compound.

They had brought quite a lot of stuff just for two and a half days, she thought. The food alone filled two small crates.

The owner of the cottage, Jim Peterson, had met up with them that morning after breakfast. They had stayed the previous night in a B&B in Stornoway, on the Isle of Lewis. Peterson had organised the boat. He seemed a decent enough guy; good humoured if a little taciturn. He had come with them to the island and carried a fair chunk of their supplies up the slippery steps from the landing stage. He'd arrived at the compound ahead of them and had quickly disappeared inside the cottage.

Adam saw a shadow flitting past one of the windows. 'Everything all right?' he shouted through.

'Aye, I think so.' Peterson's voice was a deep grumble. He was a thick set man in his early fifties with a ruddy face and thinning hair. 'But I could have sworn this door was locked when I left it.' His head popped out through the gap. The door had apparently been wide open when he had first arrived.

'Probably just the wind,' Nadia thought, adjusting her gloves and shivering at the cold.

'Not if it was locked,' Peterson muttered darkly.

Adam gazed out, beyond the compound, at the rough, sloping grassland. 'I can't imagine you'd get many burglars out here,' he said. The island was not exactly easy to access. The northern cliffs were a good eighty metres above the level of the sea and even to the south, on the opposite side of the island, they were a good thirty metres high.

'It could have been an animal, I suppose,' Peterson said. 'Nothing seems to have been touched anyway.' He dismissed the matter from his mind. 'Come in, the pair of you. Make yourself at home.' He stepped back and gestured for them to follow him inside.

3

Nadia picked up her rucksack and exchanged an excited grin with Adam. He bowed theatrically and indicated for her to go first.

The hallway was light but functional with a polished wooden floor and white-washed walls. The lighthouse was off to the left, accessed by a heavy wooden door. A small sign declared it "For Authorised Personnel Only". That was a shame, Nadia thought. Peterson owned the cottage but the tower belonged to the Northern Lighthouse Board. The building was off-limits to visitors.

They moved right, past an elaborate spiral staircase. 'Hey, I didn't think the cottage would have one of those!' Nadia had presumed that sort of thing would be reserved for the tower. They moved into the lounge and she dumped her bag on the floor, while Adam pulled off his hat.

It was a bright, cheerful room, a pleasing mix of styles. The floor was the same light polished wood as the hallway but a carpet was laid out across it, in front of a wide stone fireplace. There was a comfortable looking sofa and a couple of armchairs. 'It looks brand new!' Nadia said. There were radiators on the walls and a television set in the corner. Most importantly, the place was warm. Nadia grinned and slowly unwound her scarf. Adam was busily disentangling himself from his rucksack.

'It's just been refurbished,' Peterson explained proudly. 'Cost a pretty penny, I can tell you. You're the first ones to see it.'

Nadia smiled. 'I wasn't even sure we would have electricity.'

Adam rolled his eyes. 'What, you didn't notice the solar panels outside?' The far side of the cottage was covered in the things.

'I haven't seen anything except my feet for the last twenty minutes. This is really lovely, Mr Peterson. The photographs don't do it justice.'

'Jim, please.' The owner stood back. 'Well, you have a look round. Make yourself at home. That's the master bedroom over there.' He gestured to a light panelled door. 'The head keeper's room, as was. The second bedroom is in the far corner

4

and there's another one at the back over there. The bathroom you've seen already.' They had passed that in the hallway. 'The kitchen's on the first floor and the dining room too. I might just pop up there and have a quick look at that.' He scratched his chin. The matter of that unlocked door was still troubling him.

Nadia unbuttoned her coat as he left.

Adam moved across to the master bedroom. 'Very plush,' he said, peering through the door. The room had the same white walls and light wooden panelling as the rest of the house. There were two windows, facing eastward, and a rather impressive double bed. 'That'll have to be for Liam and Suzy,' Adam suggested.

Nadia skipped past him and sat down on the bed. The mattress was soft and springy beneath her. 'That's really comfortable.' Adam came and sat next to her. She smiled across at him. 'This was such a good idea.'

'You think they'll like it?'

'I think they'll love it,' Nadia assured him. Despite the confident image Adam liked to present to the world, he was a born worrier. He had gone to a great deal of trouble to organise things this weekend. If it was a disaster, he would blame himself. 'It's a step up from that castle, anyway,' she added mischievously.

That was where they had held the last reunion, ten years ago. God, was it really ten years? She shuddered at the thought. *How time flies.* It had been really cold then too, in North Wales, but it had certainly been a memorable weekend. *For all the wrong reasons*, she thought, with a grin.

'I suppose we ought to grab the rest of the luggage,' Adam suggested. 'Get the food in the fridge.'

Nadia slapped her hands down on her lap. 'No rest for the wicked,' she agreed, pulling herself up. It would be nice to get everything unpacked before the rest of the gang turned up. 'This is going to be such a laugh,' she said again, as the two of them moved back into the living room.

Adam poked his head into the second bedroom. 'This one's a twin,' he called out. 'Jill can go in here and we can put the two lads in the far bedroom.' That would take care of most of the

5

group.

'I suppose I ought to share with Jill,' Nadia said. That would be a laugh. Jill Clarke was the lunatic of the bunch. She could drink any one of them under the table, even John Menhenick. 'Are you sure she's going to be all right, with John here?' Jill and John had been married at the time of the last reunion but they were now divorced.

'Well, let's hope so,' Adam said, grabbing his woolly hat from the sofa. 'I did ask them and they both seemed fine about it. Keen to catch up with the rest of us. And John's got a new girl now anyway. We can keep them at arm's length. There's another couple of bedrooms upstairs.' He gestured vaguely at the ceiling. 'A twin and a double, if I remember rightly. So you don't have to share with Jill. It might be easier sleeping upstairs, if you're planning on staying up late. Oh, I thought I might leave the double room free, though. Just in case anyone gets really drunk.'

Nadia chuckled, catching his drift. Not everyone had stuck to their allotted bedrooms the last time around. 'I think we're all getting a bit old for bed hopping.'

Adam disagreed. 'You're never too old to behave disgracefully.'

'Well, you should know.' She laughed. 'You'll be drawing out your pension any time now.'

'You before me! Come on, we'd better get that beer inside first.'

They met Peterson coming down the stairs as they made their way back to the front door. 'Everything all right?' Nadia asked him.

'Yes, it looks to be.' He managed a brief smile. 'No sign of anything amiss. I must be getting paranoid. I might open up the tower for a minute, though, just to be on the safe side.'

Nadia's eyes lit up. 'The lighthouse?' He nodded. 'Ooh, can I come and have a look? I've always wanted to climb up the inside of a lighthouse.'

Peterson hesitated. 'Ah. Strictly speaking, the tower is out of bounds, even to me. Although I do have a key in case of emergencies.'

6

Nadia grinned mischievously. 'I won't tell anyone if you won't.'

He bit his lip. 'I suppose I could stretch a point, if you promise to behave yourself.'

Adam was hovering by the front door. 'Not much chance of that,' he said.

'No, I mean, you'll have to be careful on the stairs.'

'Don't worry,' Nadia said. 'I've had a lot of practise today. I shall watch every step.'

'Well. All right then. Just a quick look.'

Adam made a pretence of being annoyed. 'So I'll just collect all the food by myself then, shall I?'

'Yes, if you would.' Nadia laughed. 'Don't worry, I'll only be a few minutes.'

Peterson had already pulled out a key and was moving across to the far door. It opened with a pleasing creak. Adam disappeared into the wind to grab the beer from outside while Nadia followed the other man into the base of the lighthouse.

It was bigger than she expected. There were a couple of small windows but even with the addition of an electric light, which Peterson flicked on, the place was rather dim looking. A few crates were piled up in one corner and there was a clatter of equipment. Almost a third of the room was taken up with an enormous generator, which looked as if it hadn't been used in decades. There were a couple of store cupboards as well and some shelves laden with bric-a-brac. 'How long has it been, since the lighthouse was manned?' Nadia asked.

Peterson scratched an earlobe. 'About forty-five years, give or take. The place was automated back in the seventies, but the lighthouse itself was built well over a century ago.' The spiral staircase certainly had a Victorian feel to it; a mesh of metal steps swirling up into the heavens. It was just like Nadia had imagined. '1906, in point of fact,' Peterson added. He nodded towards the handrail as she moved towards the stairs. 'Be careful with your footing. We're a long way from a hospital out here.'

'At least these steps aren't slippy.' Nadia grabbed the rail and placed a foot on the lowest stair. Any tiredness she'd felt had now all but evaporated. She loved seeing new things. It had been the same last time, at that castle in Wales. She had spent hours exploring the battlements. Even as a little girl, she would be the one scrabbling over the next sand dune or climbing the neighbour's fence. Her father had always teased her about it, saying how unladylike she was, but she hadn't cared.

Her parents had been born in India but Nadia had grown up in Dubai before coming to England to study. That was where she had met Adam and her other friends. She had lived in Britain for some years after that and married another Englishman, Richard Gillespie. Eventually, she had returned to Dubai and now they had started a family. But she had never lost her inquisitive streak. She didn't have the most athletic of bodies – not like Adam, who could eat like a horse and never put on a single pound – but she was never one for sitting around if there was some exploring to be done. Even if it was just a white stone tower.

The lighthouse had four storeys in all: the ground, two side rooms and the lamp at the top. Nadia stopped at the curve on the first floor and peered at the closed door. 'Is that a storeroom?' she asked.

'That's right. And a spare bunk for the keepers too, in the early days.' Normally, of course, the three man crew would have slept in the cottage. 'If there was a fog, someone would need to be up here all night, blowing the horn,' he explained.

'How did they keep in contact with the mainland?'

'By semaphore, to begin with.'

Nadia boggled. 'What, flags?'

'Aye. On a good day, you can just about see the tower from the Isle of Lewis. They had a telescope trained on the island. And then came radio, of course.' He gestured for her to continue up the stairs. 'And we've got a satellite phone now, in the kitchen, which you're welcome to use. But I'm thinking it's the lamp room you really want to see.'

He was not wrong there. Nadia all but skipped up the last few steps and then emerged happily into the glass walled room at the top of the tower. A huge central column dominated the space. Inside it was the lamp itself. Nadia took out her phone and began to take a few photos.

'It's an old-fashioned acetylene lamp,' Peterson explained. 'One of the last ones in operation. It comes on shortly before sunset each evening and sweeps around once every thirty seconds. That's four flashes a minute.'

'How far does the light travel?'

'Oh, a good twenty miles or so. You can see it from Lewis on a clear night.'

'And it's all automatic?'

'It runs itself. The board sends a boat out every three months and there's a proper inspection once a year, to make sure the equipment is in good working order. Otherwise, it's left to its own devices.'

Outside the glass bubble there was a small balcony, a walkway surrounding the lamp room, made of the same meshed metal as the stairs. 'I suppose you'll be wanting to take a look at the view,' Peterson guessed. A glass door granted easy access to the balcony.

'If that's all right. I will be very careful.'

The man considered for a moment. 'Well, all right.' He slid back the door. He probably felt obliged to be accommodating. *We're his first paying guests*. 'But do watch yourself,' he warned. 'It's quite windy out there.'

Nadia stepped tentatively outside. The wind certainly was strong. For all the fences she had climbed as a child, she had never had a particularly good head for heights. But she had no intention of looking down and there was at least a protective rail running around the edge of the balcony. She turned back to the owner and handed him her phone. 'Would you mind?'

Peterson took the mobile without comment. 'I wouldn't lean too hard against that,' he said, as she positioned herself with her back to the railings. 'That's part of the original fittings. I'm not sure it'll take too much pressure.'

Nadia pulled herself upright and gave her best smile as Peterson tapped the screen. That taken care of, she swivelled around and gazed out to sea. *That must be east, I think.* She screwed her eyes up and was pleased to make out the Isle of

Lewis in the distance. Somewhere over there, in the next couple of hours, the rest of her friends would be gathering.

John Menhenick was not impressed, peering through the plastic windows of the boat at the barren lump of rock ahead of them. 'Adam should have booked a hotel on the moon,' he said, leaning back in his seat and glancing at the blonde woman sitting next to him. 'It would have been easier to get there.'

Suzy Heigl laughed. 'I think you may be exaggerating a teeny bit.'

A special boat had been chartered to carry them out to the island. There was no ferry service from Lewis to Flaxton Isle and the craft Adam had arranged for them was a pretty rudimentary affair. Three rows of plastic seats under a covered roof with see-through sheeting either side to protect them from the spray. Not exactly travelling in style, though it was by no means the worst form of transport they had endured.

'I'm telling you,' John said. 'In the last twenty four hours, I've been in a taxi, a train, a bus and then an aeroplane from Manchester. And now this. Talk about trains, planes and automobiles.' He chuckled. 'I just need a pair of bloody roller skates and I'll have the complete set.' John was a stocky, bald man with a broad smile and a heavy Romford accent. 'It's all right for Adam. He lives in this part of the world. He don't appreciate what the rest of us have to go through. All the hassle and the expense.' That last was a genuine sore point. They had all chipped in for the cottage and the food, but the transport costs had nearly doubled their outlay; and John was not exactly rolling in it these days.

'You only came from London,' Suzy pointed out. 'Nadia had to fly all the way from Dubai.'

'Yeah, but her husband's loaded.' He waved a hand airily above his head. 'She probably flew in by private jet.'

Suzy laughed again. It was a light, pleasing chirrup. She was a great girl, Suzy. Blonde, blue eyed and as mad as a box of frogs. It had been a while since they had last met up but they kept in touch online. She was into all kinds of New Age bollocks. Vegetarian too. She'd done well on it, though. As slim as anything in her early forties but with a few nice curves.

They had met up on the quayside a couple of hours ago. Suzy's husband had been there with John's ex-wife Jill and their other friend Twinkle. John had been less happy to see Jill Clarke, but they had greeted each other politely. Well, they had exchanged good-natured insults, which amounted to the same thing. The five of them had gone for a drink together in a local café before boarding the ferry. The boat master had come to collect them. The others had decided to sit at the back of the vehicle, like kids on a school trip, but Suzy wanted to be up front, so she could see the island as they approached it. John sat next to her and at last they were able to have a proper catch up, away from prying ears.

'I have missed you,' Suzy said, placing a hand on his arm.

'Careful!' He gave her a wink 'Your husband might see.' Liam Heigl was sitting two rows behind them.

'Stop it!' she said. But she kept her hand exactly where it was. 'So did you stay with Twinkle last night?'

'Yeah, in Manchester.' Twinkle – their old mate Derek Fonteyn – was the fifth member of the group. He was sitting at the back with Liam and Jill. 'He hasn't changed. We got the flight out together this morning.'

'I love Twinkle. He's so sweet.'

'Not the liveliest of conversationalists,' John lamented. He'd had his work cut out keeping the chat going last night. Twinkle still lived with his mum in a semi-detached in Rusholme, not far from Manchester city centre. She had kept out of the way last night, thank god, while they had stayed up drinking. 'Still hasn't found himself a girl. Mind you, with a face like his, that's hardly surprising.' The poor bloke. Talk about lop-sided. One eye was a good half inch lower than the other. 'Blimey, you wouldn't want to wake up next to that in the morning.'

'You're so cruel,' Suzy said, trying not to laugh. 'It's what's inside that counts.'

'Yeah, that's what everyone says. But we all judge by the cover. You know we do.'

'At least he's not gone bald!' Suzy teased, stroking the side of John's head in apparent wonder. 'What happened to your hair?'

John rolled his eyes. 'It was starting to disappear anyway. I thought I might as well go the whole hog.'

'It makes you look like a bouncer.' She chuckled.

'Some people go for the rugged look. It works for me anyway.'

Suzy was not convinced. 'You've found yourself a new girl?'

'Yeah, Jennifer.' They had been going out for about a year now. Great looking bird, but boy did she know how to talk. 'I sent you a photo, didn't I?'

'Yes. She looks about half your age! I'm glad you've....moved on.' Suzy glanced briefly back to the rear of the boat. 'I was so sad when...when things didn't work out with you and Jill.'

John didn't really want to talk about that. 'I should never have married her. Silly bitch. I love the kids to death, but they're the only good thing that came out of that marriage.' The two of them had divorced some years ago now and John had become a weekend dad, taking the kids off to the cinema or wherever, when he could afford it. Money was a bit tight right now. John had his own business, a small garage in Peckham, but it wasn't doing well. The cost of this reunion had been a bit of a stretch. Adam had been decent about it, letting him pay what he could. Otherwise he might not have been able to come. He was glad that he had, though; even if it meant being nice to his ex-wife for the duration.

'You promise to behave this weekend?' Suzy said. 'We don't want any rows!'

'Scouts honour, princess.' He held up his fingers. 'I'll be like a little kitten.' He gazed out of the window. The boat was churning up quite a surf. The whole vehicle was bouncing up and down as they hit the waves head on. It was worse than on the train. 'So how are things going with you and Farmer Giles?'

Suzy's husband had a distinct west country accent. 'Don't

call him that!' she said. Liam and Suzy had been married for almost fifteen years now. John had never liked the bloke. Sure, he was good looking, in a bland kind of way, but he didn't have much else going for him. John couldn't understand why Suzy had married him. A girl like that, beautiful and talented, she could have had anyone she wanted. 'He's such a good father,' Suzy enthused. 'You should see him with the kids.'

'No regrets then?'

'With Liam? No, none at all.'

Farmer Giles had not been at the last reunion in North Wales. He had had to go to a funeral. 'You couldn't stop him coming this weekend though?' John teased. 'He's not going to let you out of his sight a second time!'

'He's one of the group,' Suzy insisted. 'He deserves to be here.'

John wasn't so sure about that. 'He doesn't know what you got up to last time then?'

'No, he doesn't!' She suppressed a laugh. 'He can't know. You must promise not to say a word. You know how jealous he can get. He has a fit if I even look at another man.'

John raised a finger to his mouth. 'My lips are sealed, darling. What happened in Wales stays in Wales.'

Suzy sat back in her plastic seat. 'It seems like a long time ago now,' she said.

It had been the tenth anniversary of their graduation. Adam had arranged it all, of course. He was the self-appointed father of the group, and a right old bossy boots too. Typical ginger nut. He had booked a medieval castle in Wales and they had met up for three days of fun and frolics. Lots of games and lots of drinking. Actually, it had been a good laugh. And all the better because Liam hadn't been there.

'That's why I've been so looking forward to this,' Suzy said. 'It'll be so lovely to see everyone again. It's a shame Samantha couldn't make it.'

Ah, the elusive Samantha. 'She's too high and mighty for the likes of us,' John suggested, 'swanning around in Hollywood.' Samantha Redmond was the big success story of their year. She was the one who had actually made it as an actress. She had hit the big time, since their last reunion, and was now a household name in America as well as the UK. She lived in LA these days and was a regular feature in the gossip columns on both sides of the Atlantic. You could barely open a paper without seeing her face somewhere. 'Wouldn't give us the time of day any more,' John reckoned.

'You used to say the same about me, when we first met.'

'Yeah. Because your dad was loaded. I was only teasing, though.'

'That's all you ever do,' Suzy said, with affection. 'I had an email from her, though. Samantha. Wishing us well. She still keeps in touch with Twinkle. And Nadia.' If Adam Cartwright was the dad of the group then Nadia was definitely the mum. 'It will be so good to see her again. I haven't seen Nadia in years. We're going to have such a good time this weekend. I can feel it in my bones.'

'Your little angel tell you that, did he?' John asked slyly.

'Don't mock! Yes, he did.'

He chuckled. The daft cow. 'You don't still believe that rubbish?'

Suzy had made a big thing at university about the Guardian Angel she believed was watching over her. It was ridiculous. He would hover above her right shoulder and talk to her, apparently, offering her advice. 'You only call it rubbish because you don't understand it,' she said. 'We all have an angel looking after us. You just need to be able to hear him. Then everything will work out for you.'

'Tell that to Twinkle.' John laughed.

'Oh, he'll find someone. He has a soul mate out there somewhere. Everyone does. He'll find her eventually.'

'If he listens to his angel.' John shook his head. The girl really was as mad as a fruitcake. 'Mind you, you've done well enough on it, princess. I bought one of those books of yours for my daughter, last Christmas.' Suzy made a living as a children's author. 'She can't get enough of them. Doesn't believe I know the girl what wrote them.'

Suzy beamed with pleasure. 'I'll have to sign a copy for her.'

'She doesn't like them that much.'

'Oh, you!' She punched him affectionately on the shoulder.

The books were pretty basic, from what John had seen of them. A boy, his cat and their Guardian Angel. Suzy had started out writing self-help books, but it was the children's stories that had catapulted her into the big league. They sold by the bucket load. 'So how does Farmer Giles feel, playing second fiddle to a successful author?'

'Liam's not second fiddle.'

'You're the one earning the loot. He's just living off your immoral earnings. I suppose he must be used to it by now.' Liam Heigl was a country boy at heart, from a rather modest background. Suzy's parents had been as rich as sin and she had always been able to do anything she wanted. Liam had never quite got over not being the bread winner in the family.

'He works very hard. He handles all the business side of things. He has a very logical brain.'

John chuckled. 'Can't think what he sees in you, then!'

'I can think logically when I have to.'

'I'll believe that when I see it.'

She leaned in closely. 'You won't...you won't say anything about last time? About what happened? We've never talked about it. He gets a little paranoid about that sort of thing.'

'I told you, princess. My lips are sealed. I wouldn't do anything to hurt you. You know that. You're *my* Guardian Angel.'

'Stop it!' She thumped him gently again.

'I'd do anything for you. You know that.'

Suzy eyed up her luggage, which was resting in front of the seats. 'In that case, you can carry my suitcase up to the cottage. I hear it's quite a steep climb.'

John grimaced theatrically. 'Well, *almost* anything,' he said.

Jill Clarke lifted the two plastic carrier bags and placed them on the kitchen table. Nadia stifled a laugh as all the bottles clinked together.

Some people never change, she thought.

'Four bottles of vodka. Three Bacardi. And a couple of bottles of tonic water for the wusses.' The ones who didn't want to drink their vodka neat. Jill grinned as she lifted the bottles out of the bags and lined them up on the worktop next to the kitchen sink.

'You've certainly come prepared.' Nadia smiled.

'Not half.' Jill grabbed a bottle of vodka and twisted the top. 'You got any glasses?' Nadia rolled her eyes but pulled open a cupboard.

Jill Clarke was a veritable force of nature. 'Hiya, babes!' she had screamed, from halfway up the cliff face, when Nadia had popped her head over the top fifteen minutes ago. 'You're looking gorgeous!' It was a good five years since they had last seen each other but Jill had not changed a bit. She gave Nadia a hug as soon as she reached the top, temporarily discarding her luggage. 'God, you haven't aged a day. How do you do it?'

Nadia felt a little guilty, not being there to greet them all when the boat pulled up at the landing stage. She had lost track of time, there had been so much to do. Jim Peterson had left the island mid afternoon and that had given her and Adam barely two hours to unpack everything before the others arrived. Peterson had given them a set of keys to the cottage, which Adam took charge of, but the man himself would not be back until Monday morning. Nadia was preparing a bit of food in the kitchen when she heard the horn from the boat and Adam called up to say they had arrived. He raced on ahead, to help with the luggage, and by the time Nadia got to the top of the cliff her friends were already halfway up.

Nadia couldn't help but smile, watching them all struggling on the slippery steps, without any help from the boat master, who was already making ready to depart. Once they'd got to the top, she was able to give Jill a hand with her luggage. The woman babbled away happily as they made their way across the island, giving Nadia barely any time to exchange a nod or hello with the others. Twinkle raised a shy hand, though, as they moved towards the compound.

As soon as she hit the cottage, Jill abandoned her suitcase and was straight up the stairs to the kitchen, where she was now unloading the booze. Nadia chuckled to herself as she watched her friend lining up the bottles. John Menhenick had always said Jill was an alcoholic, and he was not far wrong. Somehow, though, the woman seemed to run perfectly well on it.

Jill measured herself out a generous glass of vodka and quickly knocked it back. 'You want a glass, babes?'

Nadia grabbed a beer from the crate. 'It's too early for me.' Better to get some food inside her first, she thought. She clipped off the top of the beer bottle with an opener from the drawer and took a quick swig.

Jill was admiring the kitchen. 'They've got all the mod cons here, ain't they? It's really swish.'

'Yes, it's not bad, is it? It's just been done up.' There was a microwave and a dishwasher and plenty of glasses. 'Well, cheers.' Nadia raised her bottle. 'It's lovely to see you again.' They clinked the bits of glass together.

'It's good to be here, babes.' Jill grinned happily. She was an unusual looking woman with a thin, wrinkled face, straggly red hair and thick glasses. She was a fair bit taller than Nadia and had a nice figure, which she always made a point of displaying. Even now, as a mother of two, she dressed like a teenager. Nadia had never seen her in a pair of trousers or even a knee length skirt. Everyone else had been well wrapped up outside – apart from Twinkle, who had been content with a woollen sweater – but not Jill. She looked like she was about to head off clubbing. The girl didn't seem to feel the cold at all. She wasn't even wearing tights. It was that gleam in her eye, though, alongside the loud and rather infectious giggle, that had always ensured her popularity with both sexes, though for rather different reasons.

'We're going to have such a laugh this weekend,' she declared. 'Hey, you wait until you see the fancy dress I've brought. It's such a scream. The kids were in hysterics when I showed it to them.' Jill had two children, a girl and a boy. 'I've been practising my party piece all week.'

Adam had asked everyone to prepare a short routine. It was one of the many events he had lined up over the next forty eight hours. Something fun and light for a group cabaret, he'd told them, with an American theme.

'That's not 'till tomorrow,' Nadia said. 'I think it's just dinner this evening. And then a film show.'

'Oh, God! What's Adam put together this time?'

'I'm sworn to secrecy. How are the kids, by the way? Did you leave them with Nathan?'

'Yeah, he's looking after them.' Nathan was her new husband. She had remarried the previous year. 'Alfie's really taken to him. Julie's still a bit snotty. She's always been a daddies girl. But she'll come round.'

'I'm sorry I couldn't get to the wedding.'

'Hey, no worries. You're halfway round the world. And it was short notice.'

'I loved the dress, though.' Nadia had seen the photographs online. Jill had been positively swathed in lace. 'You looked stunning.'

'Yeah, I scrubbed up all right on the day. Tits to the fore.' She grinned and poured herself another glass of vodka. 'I wanted to do it properly this time. Big church wedding. All the razzmatazz. Rolls Royce, flowers, live band. I only had a registry office with John.'

'Yes, he was never one for splashing out.' Nadia took another swig of beer. 'You're sure you're all right, him being here this weekend?' The last thing anyone wanted was for there to be any awkwardness.

'Yeah, it's fine, babes. I see him anyway every few weeks, when he comes to pick up the kids. And he's got himself a new girl. Jennifer. Half his age.' She laughed again. 'Typical John.'

'Yes, I heard.'

'She's a right goer, so he says. Still, it takes his mind off things, don't it? He's a mean old git, but it wouldn't be the same without him.'

'No. It's good to have everyone back together. It's just a shame Samantha couldn't make it.' Their Hollywood success story. 'It would have been nice to have the full set.'

'Maybe next time, eh? Hey, how are things with you and Richard?'

'Oh, ticking along.' Nadia had met her husband, Richard Gillespie, shortly after graduating from university. She had got a job as a secretary in a property company and Richard had been her boss. She had fancied him from day one. He was quite a bit older than her, but she'd pursued him with some vigour and eventually worn down his resistance. They married soon after that – twelve years ago now – and Nadia had no regrets. Richard was a kind, intelligent man.

'You always did prefer older blokes. He doesn't mind you flying off on your own?'

'No. He's never been clingy. He knows I like to do my own thing from time to time.'

'Don't we all!' Jill chuckled. 'And he's looking after your little girl?'

'Yes, he booked the time off work. I flew up here on Tuesday. Well, to Scotland anyway. Adam put me up in his spare room for a couple of nights.' Adam Cartwright lived in a rather swish apartment in Edinburgh. 'Then we took the flight to Stornoway yesterday afternoon. Stayed in a B&B last night.'

'You and Adam.' Jill's eyes gleamed. 'The two of you have always got on, ain't you?'

'He's a good friend.' Nadia had hit it off with Adam right from the word go, in their first year at university. She had been doing a different course then – a business degree – but when she had seen how much fun Adam was having with his performing arts course, she had switched across. That had not gone down well with her father, but she had no regrets about it. And since then Adam had probably been her closest friend, even after she had moved back to Dubai. They spoke or texted practically every day.

'I'm surprised you two never got together,' Jill said.

Nadia smiled. 'Oh, we came close, once or twice. But I

think we're better off as friends. He was saying last night...' She stopped mid-sentence. There was some sort of commotion going on downstairs.

Adam was calling up to them. 'Nadia! Jill!' He sounded rather excited.

Jill polished off her vodka. 'What's he want?' she wondered, placing her glass down on the worktop.

'You might want to come outside,' he bellowed, from the bottom of the stairs.

Nadia was intrigued. 'Let's go and take a look.'

'All right, babes!' Jill called back down to the man. 'We're coming. Hey, what's that?' There was a strange whirring noise in the distance.

'I don't know,' Nadia admitted, as they moved towards the stairs.

'Sounds like a plane. Or a helicopter.'

The front door of the cottage was wide open when they got there. The others were already outside, making their way south, out of the compound. And sure enough, as Nadia emerged into the sunlight, she could see a large vehicle hovering overhead. A helicopter. She beamed at the sight of it. It was a local one, judging by the Isle of Lewis logo on the side. Another surprise from Adam? He had not said anything about this.

They followed the rest of the group down the slope. The helicopter was circling gently, its blades making quite a bit of noise and ruffling the grass all around them. There wasn't much in the way of a convenient landing spot. The ruins of a small chapel halfway down the island meant that the helicopter couldn't touch down anywhere near the cottage. But the pilot – whoever he was – knew what he was doing, and after a gentle hover he set the vehicle down on the grass to the south of the ruined building.

Adam and the others were already making their way past the chapel. Nadia followed keenly behind. She couldn't quite see who was sitting in the passenger seat, but she had a sneaking suspicion she knew who it was.

Hollywood royalty had arrived on Flaxton Isle.

Chapter Two

Samantha Redmond hefted her bag onto the top of the bed and undid the zip. She stifled a yawn and raised a hand to wipe the tiredness from her eyes. She didn't feel much like a legend this afternoon. Her clothes were crumpled, her hair was a mess and goodness knows what her breath smelt like. She grabbed a packet of mints from the bag and popped one in her mouth. Samantha had never been the glamour puss the media made her out to be. Oh, she had done her fair share of dressing up for premieres and award ceremonies; but away from the cameras she had always been more comfortable in a pair of slacks and a t-shirt. Even so, she would like to have arrived in a slightly less dishevelled state this afternoon. Despite having crossed the Atlantic hundreds of times, Samantha had still not learnt to sleep properly on a plane. It would have been better if she had flown out earlier and spent a few days back in the UK before coming on to Flaxton Isle, but her schedule had not permitted it. It was only thanks to the good graces of her producers that she had managed to work this weekend into her schedule at all. But she had been determined to make it happen and, as soon as she stepped off the helicopter and saw all those familiar faces smiling up at her, she knew she had made the right decision.

The helicopter had not been her idea. It was Adam Cartwright who had suggested it. He was far more of a showman than she was. 'Just think of their faces,' he'd texted, a couple of weeks back. In all honesty, she would rather have met up with everyone on Lewis and got the boat; but the days when Samantha Redmond could slip on a pair of sunglasses and hop on a ferry were long gone. The helicopter was the only practical alternative and if it helped to keep the media away just this once then so much the better.

She had been a little apprehensive about the reunion on the flight over. It was such a long time since she had last seen any of her friends. So many things had changed for all of them in the intervening years. How would they react? Would they be happy to see her? Even in the old days, when they were putting on plays and shooting the odd student film, she had been on the periphery of the group. On stage, she had been as much of a show off as anyone; but not in the bar afterwards or in the lecture halls. This time, however, there was no avoiding the limelight.

She jumped down from the glass bubble of the helicopter and her friends crowded affectionately around her. Despite her initial trepidation, all the smiles, hugs and good natured jibes soon began to put her at her ease. Photographs were taken, with the helicopter in the background, and John Menhenick – who seemed to have lost all his hair – did a creditable impersonation of a chauffeur. 'Can I take your bags, milady?' he asked, reaching into the helicopter. Before she knew where she was, Samantha was being led across to the cottage, while Adam received a gentle ribbing from the others for having lied to them about whether or not she would be coming.

Samantha's old room mate, Jill Clarke, a manic redhead in a sparkly top and purple miniskirt, poured out a rather large glass of vodka for her and then showed her to their room. 'You and me babes,' she said, with a grin. 'Just like old times.'

And finally, just for a minute, Samantha was left alone, and had the chance to catch her breath. She put down the glass on the bedside table.

Jill had left her luggage by the door. Samantha hefted her suitcase onto the nearest bed. She rubbed her eyes a second time and caught sight of herself in the mirror opposite. She certainly didn't look like a Hollywood sex symbol at the moment. She was tall and quite lean, in her early forties. Her hair was dark brown and a little mousy, her face finely chiselled. The papers characterised her as an "English Rose" but that was more to do with her accent than anything else. She did not come from a privileged background. Samantha had grown up on a council estate in the Midlands. Suzy Heigl was the "rich girl" of the group and she didn't seem to have changed much either, though Samantha had not had the chance to talk to her yet. Funnily enough, Suzy was a much better actress than she was, though she had channelled her talents into books rather than films. Samantha certainly had no illusions about her own abilities. She had got lucky, that was all. And Jill Clarke, despite the clunky glasses, ginger hair and rather thin face, had always been the popular one with the boys. She had had a string of boyfriends at university, while Samantha had been too shy to get involved with anyone. Not until the second year, at any rate. These days, of course, she only had to look at a man for the gossip columns to claim they were dating.

There was a knock at the door. 'Hi Sam. It's only me.'

She recognised the voice and smiled. 'Come in,' she said.

Twinkle opened the door and stood there awkwardly for a moment. He was an odd looking guy, rather tubby, with a lopsided face and untidy black hair. He had been a good friend of Samantha's at university and they had kept in touch over the years. In truth, he had seemed a little overwhelmed to see her again in the flesh. He was far too shy to give her a hug in front of the others. He had a genial aura to him, though, like a scraggy long-haired dog.

Twinkle wasn't his real name, of course. He had been christened Derek Fonteyn. "Twinkle" was a long standing joke. Samantha had always thought it a little cruel, but Derek never seemed to mind. It was partly to do with his surname and partly the fact that he had two left feet. John Menhenick had got him really drunk one night and the others had dragged him up onto the dance floor, hoping he would emulate his name-sake, the ballerina Dame Margot Fonteyn. But that evening he had stepped on just about every toe in the club and he had never lived it down. So "Twinkle Toes" he had become. Or Twinkle, for short.

He stepped hesitantly into the room. 'You sharing with Jill?' he asked, eyeing the other woman's abandoned luggage.

'Yes, back together again. She doesn't seem to have changed much. How about you? Are you in with John?'

'Aye. We travelled up together. He stayed the night with us last night.' Twinkle had a soft voice and a broad Mancunian accent.

'He doesn't seem to have changed much either,' Samantha thought. 'Apart from the hair.' John had bowed and tugged his imaginary forelock to her outside the helicopter, forever taking the piss. She didn't mind that. It was better than being venerated for no good reason, as she usually was back home.

'Yes, he's the same old John. Making a joke out of everything.' Twinkle grimaced. 'It can get a bit wearing, to be honest.'

'It's good that he came, though.' Him and the others. Adam and Nadia. Liam and Suzy. 'Everyone's here this time,' she realised in surprise. 'Even Liam.' That had not been the case at the last reunion.

'Well. Everyone except Paul,' Twinkle said.

'Yes. All except Paul.' Paul Hammond had been the golden boy of the group. Handsome and dynamic. All the girls had fancied him, Samantha included. He had come to the castle reunion ten years ago, but had died tragically a few weeks later.

'I were so disappointed when Adam said you weren't going to come,' Twinkle confessed.

'I'm sorry. I should have told you. I hated having to lie about it.' She sighed. 'But if Adam had posted anything online, even just to the others, it would have got out. It always does. We'd have had helicopters buzzing around us all weekend.' Samantha had forced herself to come to terms with all the press attention she'd received over the years – it was part of the life she had chosen – but her friends and family were a different matter. Whenever possible, she tried to shield them from the worst of it.

'You're a big star. You don't have to explain.'

Samantha smiled sadly. 'I don't really feel like a star. It's just a job, like any other. I don't think I'm any different now from how I was when we were at university together. It's the way people behave towards you that changes.' She patted the bedsheets and he sat down next to her.

'I saw one of your films on the telly the other night. That first one. *Moonlit Dawn.*'

Samantha shuddered. That movie had been released almost nine years ago now. It was the first in a trilogy of vampire action flicks which had set the box office alight. She had played the lead and the series had made her name; but it was the tight leather trousers she had worn – at the director's insistence – that had really attracted worldwide attention. From then on the press had her tagged as a sex symbol. Never mind whether the films were any good or not. 'I can't watch them any more,' she confessed. 'I'm so crap. Especially that first one. I didn't have any idea what I was doing.'

'I thought you were really good. I'd forgotten most of it. It's years since I last saw it.'

'Not really your type of film,' Samantha guessed. Twinkle was more into sci-fi than vampire fiction.

'No. I only watched it cos you were in it. You looked quite different on TV.'

'Younger, you mean?'

'No, just different,' he told her, seriously. 'Differently proportioned.'

Samantha laughed. 'That's Hollywood for you. Everything has to be bigger. It's all smoke and mirrors, though.' She looked down at herself. 'I don't really look like that.'

'Aye, I know,' Twinkle agreed. 'I've *seen* the real you.'

She blushed, catching his drift. 'So you have. I'd forgotten about that.' The two of them had shared digs together at university, with Jill and Adam. Twinkle had stumbled across her one morning, completely naked. She had forgotten to lock the bathroom door and he had walked in on her while she was taking a shower. They had both been embarrassed but Twinkle had been absolutely mortified. 'I can still see your face.' She grinned. 'You didn't know where to look.'

Twinkle was going red just thinking about it. 'It took them weeks to fix that lock. You remember, we had to put a sign on the door, whenever we went in there?'

'I remember.' *Happy days*, she thought. *Simpler days*. 'You could have sold a story like that to the papers, when *Moonlit Dawn* came out.'

Twinkle was shocked at the suggestion. 'I would never do nothing like that.'

'No, I know you wouldn't. A lot of people would though.' It was sad to think how many of her friends had cashed in on her fame. Even other stars she had dated. But her real friends had kept quiet. People like Twinkle. 'I'm so glad to see you. It's been far too long.'

'Aye. I'm glad you came.' He gazed happily across at her and there was a brief moment of silence.

'How's business going?' Samantha asked him.

'Oh, good. Moving along, you know? I don't think I'll ever go hungry.' Twinkle had made his money as an IT engineer. He was a freelancer now, but he was never out of work.

'You don't miss the theatrical life?'

'No, not really. I were always more into the technology. The cameras, the edit suites. And it's all gone digital now.'

'Strange how we've all ended up. Adam in marketing. Nadia working for an oil company. You fixing people's computers.'

'Oh, I design websites these days as well. I do do a bit of the creative stuff. But it's not where I were expecting to end up.'

'No, we're none of us where we'd thought we'd be,' Samantha agreed. They had all done the same degree course: Film and Drama at Leicester University. Each of them had had ambitions to enter into the business. Samantha had wanted to go on the stage, but there was precious little time for that now. 'And most of the group seem to be married with kids.'

'You didn't fancy having children?'

'I wanted to. I just haven't found the time.'

Twinkle smiled shyly. 'And was it true about you dating...what's his name? Your co star.'

Samantha rolled her eyes. Dan Egan, her ruggedly handsome side-kick, who was now an even bigger star than she was. 'No. That was just tabloid gossip. We're friends though. I'm not dating anyone at the moment.'

'You and me neither,' Twinkle admitted sadly. He gazed down at his feet. 'I've had a go at internet dating. Chatting to people online. But it's not easy. Suzy says there's someone out there for me, but if there is she's keeping herself well hidden.'

Samantha smiled. 'Well, if Suzy says it, it must be true. Goodness, we're a miserable pair, aren't? We should go out and join the others. Adam says they've got some pizza going.'

Twinkle stared at the luggage. 'You not going to unpack first?'

'I was. But I think I might take a leaf out of Jill's book.' She glanced across at the abandoned luggage by the door. 'Forget the unpacking. Just have a quick wash and then grab a bottle.'

The champagne cork popped and everybody cheered. *Here we all are at last*, Nadia Kumar thought contentedly. After months of planning and frantic email exchanges, the entire gang was back together and there were smiling faces everywhere. Adam Cartwright was playing the genial host, pouring out the champagne while others laughed and helped themselves to a slice or two of pizza. Adam was in his element, his narrow freckled face alive with enthusiasm. Nadia filled her plate and then held out a fluted glass, as he finished pouring for the others. 'Don't forget me!' she said.

'Too late!' Adam announced with a grin. 'Don't worry. Plenty more where that came from.' He turned back to the table and grabbed a second bottle. 'I've haven't had any yet either.'

Champagne and pizza. That had been Nadia's idea. The perfect icebreaker, she thought, as Adam unwound the stopper on the bottle and popped the second cork. People were munching and chatting away happily across the length of the dining room. She held out her glass and watched as the bubbles fizzed their way up.

Adam leaned in. 'So how do you think it's going?'

'Perfectly,' she assured him, following his gaze as it swept across the room. Despite his confident public persona, Adam was a bundle of nerves right now. Nadia's job, as always, was to provide the reassurance. 'Don't worry. Everything's going really well.' She took a sip of the champagne. 'Ooh, nice!'

Adam had poured himself a glass too. He took a quick gulp, then set it down on the table and picked up a paper plate. That was another good idea: disposable plates. It would save on the washing up; or at least, on anyone having to load the dishwasher. Adam took a mouthful of pizza.

Over by the window, Jill Clarke was shrieking with laughter at something one of the others had said. Her glasses bobbed up and down on the bridge of her nose.

'See? Someone's happy,' Nadia observed, with approval.

'She's had a skinful already,' Adam said.

Nadia laughed. 'I don't know how she does it.'

'Years of practise.'

That was true enough. 'You'll have to watch yourself this evening,' she teased. 'You know how frisky she can gets sometimes.'

'Wandering hands.' Adam shuddered. 'Yes, I remember from last time.'

'You wouldn't think she was married with kids, would you?'

'Don't worry. I can handle Jill. I am a grown up, you know.'

Nadia laughed again. 'You almost said that with a straight face.' She nudged him playfully in the ribs; then she picked up her plate and made a start on the pizza.

A warm glow of conversation permeated the room. Suzy Heigl – the author in their midst – was chatting animatedly with John Menhenick and his room-mate Twinkle. Samantha Redmond was standing a little way back, sipping tentatively on her champagne and listening quietly to the conversation. *She hasn't changed much*, Nadia thought. Samantha had always been one of the quiet ones. No wonder she and Twinkle got on so well. They were like two peas in a pod, though they couldn't have looked more different. "Beauty and the Beast" John sometimes called them. He was far too fond of nicknames. Nadia did not envy Samantha the attention she had received in the press over the last few years. Some of it had been really nasty. The girl must have developed quite a thick skin by now. But when it came to social events, it appeared, she still preferred to take a back seat. *And why not?* Nadia thought. They couldn't all be party animals like Suzy or Jill.

'Do you think she regrets coming?' Adam asked, catching Nadia's gaze.

'Not a bit of it. She's just sizing up the lie of the land.' Nadia knocked his shoulder. 'I can't believe you didn't tell me she was coming.'

'I was sworn to secrecy. I couldn't post anything online about it in case it got out.'

'You could have told me last night, though.'

'What, and spoil the surprise?'

Nadia drained her glass. 'Heaven forbid!' She smiled again. 'I still can't quite believe it. A Hollywood superstar in our midst.'

'She's not going to like what I've got lined up for after dinner though.'

Nadia coughed abruptly. 'God, no!' she exclaimed. 'There are going to be a few red faces when you put that on.' Adam had organised a rather special film show this evening.

'I might need to have a quick word with Twinkle,' Adam said. 'The video file's on my laptop, but I want to put it on the TV if I can.'

'Well, he's the expert.' Nadia had had a sneak preview of the film last night. She hadn't seen it in twenty years and it had brought all the memories flooding back. She gazed across the room and briefly met Samantha's eye. The actress smiled back at her and raised her glass. Nadia did likewise. 'She didn't come across too badly. It's our Suzy who's going to be really embarrassed.' Nadia looked across at the slim blonde woman, who was chatting merrily with John Menhenick. Suzy had a plate in her hand with a rather small slice of pizza on it. 'I'd forgotten she was a vegetarian.' It would have been embarrassing if they hadn't arranged an appropriate option. And not just for the pizza. 'It's lucky you remembered.'

'Well, some of us have to cover the details,' Adam joked. 'Otherwise nothing would ever get done.'

Suzy's husband – Liam Heigl – was banging a spoon on the edge of his champagne glass.

'Oh, bloody hell,' John Menhenick laughed. The bald man regarded Liam with mock horror. 'You're not going to make a speech are you?'

'No, nothing like that.' Liam was a handsome fellow with a rounded, boyish face and deep blue eyes. Like Suzy – and Samantha – he had aged pretty well for a person in his early forties. Unlike John, he had even managed to maintain a full head of hair. 'I just thought it might be an appropriate point to say thank you to Adam for organising all this.' Liam's gentle west country vowels flittered across the room and there were murmurs of agreement. 'He puts in all the work behind the scenes. If it wasn't for him, we'd none of us be here today drinking this rather mediocre champagne and stuffing our faces with Scotland's finest Pizza Express.' He grinned and raised his glass. 'You've done a great job, Adam. Thank you.' The others echoed the sentiment and raised their glasses.

'Somebody had to do it,' Adam said. 'And if you think the champagne is bad, you wait until you try the rum punch tomorrow!'

A rather merry bunch assembled outside the cottage at half past nine for a group photograph. The summer sun was still hovering over the horizon to the west but the lighthouse had clunked into life and the powerful beam from its huge lamp was sweeping across the sky above them.

John Menhenick had allowed himself to be dragged outside, against his better judgement. 'It'll be fun,' Suzy Heigl assured him. 'Something to look back on.'

'Yeah, of course. This is the night we got pissed and someone fell off the cliff.' John had been half tempted to grab his coat from the rack in the hallway. It was bloody freezing outside – the wind was whipping up something chronic, even within the low walls of the compound – but he had a jumper on over his shirt and Adam said it would only take them a minute.

Nadia had grabbed a coat in any case. She probably felt the cold more than he did, coming from such a hot climate. Mind you, she was fat enough to generate her own heat. Well, not fat exactly, but a bit dumpy. She had a pretty face, though. Not like John's ex-wife. *God, look at her*, he thought sourly. Jill Clarke

30

was still wearing her tight glitter top and that ridiculously short skirt. 'Christ,' he muttered quietly, 'talk about mutton dressed as lamb.'

Suzy digged him in the ribs. 'Now, now, Mr Grumpy. You said you were going to behave.'

'Don't worry, princess. I'm going to be the perfect gentleman. You'll see.'

Adam was busy organising them into two rows of four, with the shortest ones crouching down at the front. Someone had brought a selfie stick and, once the group had positioned themselves, Adam was able to hold the phone at arm's length, with the screen facing backwards so they could all see the image.

Blimey, what a sight! John cringed. Snow White and the Seven Dwarves, with the phone angled upwards so they could get the crown of the lighthouse into the back of the shot. The beam from the lamp swept over them once again.

'All right, say "cheese" everyone,' Adam instructed.

'CHEESE EVERYONE,' the group replied, reprising the old joke as the camera flashed.

'Are we done now?' John asked

'It is getting a bit nippy,' Nadia agreed, flapping her arms against the chill.

The group piled back into the house. Suzy and Nadia headed straight for the bathroom, but John moved across the lounge to the bedroom on the far side. He had put his tablet on to charge and wanted to take a quick look at it, to make sure everything was working all right. He had taken a bit of time sorting it all out, when he had first got off the boat, unpacking his luggage and neatly putting it away. Twinkle, by contrast, who was sharing the room, had simply unhooked his rucksack and tipped half the contents onto his bed. Most of it was still there. *You can tell he's never been married.* It looked a right old mess. John preferred to keep everything tidy. It was easier to find things that way. He smiled, looking across at the wardrobe to the right of the bedroom door. *All set*, he thought. Adam wasn't the only one who had a few surprises up his sleeve this weekend.

By now, there was a babble of voices coming from the

31

living room. People were scraping chairs about, getting ready for the film show. John scratched his chin. *What rubbish is he going to put on this time?* he wondered. He yanked open the door and headed out into the throng.

'I'm going to grab a beer,' he said. 'Anyone else want one?'

Liam Heigl pretended to do a double take. 'Is the pope a Catholic?' There were several other raised hands.

John clomped upstairs to the kitchen. Suzy Heigl was just coming out of the loo on the opposite side of the hall. There were two bathrooms in the cottage, one up, one down. Suzy waved a hand and followed him into the kitchen. It was a poky affair, narrow with no external windows, just the door at one end, leading out into the hallway. John headed straight for the fridge.

'So what are you doing for the cabaret tomorrow?' Suzy asked, as he pulled open the door and grabbed a few bottles.

He grunted. 'Oh, I can't be bothered with all that.'

'You've got to do something.' Suzy tutted good-naturedly, leaning up against the work surface. She was dressed in a cream sweater and black leggings. 'You have to enter into the spirit of things.'

John handed her the bottles and then grabbed a few more from the crate on the floor. 'Oh, well. I'll put on a pair of boots and do a clog dance then.' He filled up the fridge and closed the door.

'I'm serious,' Suzy said, placing the bottles down on the worktop. 'You've got to do something. I'm going to sing a song.'

John pulled himself up and pretended to shudder. 'Bloody hell. I'm going to have to break out the ear plugs.'

She laughed. 'My voice isn't that bad.'

'Nah, it's all right, princess. It's passable.' She was actually a pretty good singer. Suzy had played the female lead in a couple of operettas at university. John had been press ganged into going along to one of them. Not his cup of tea, but she had handled herself well. Better than the show tunes she normally sang, anyway. Suzy was a great girl, but she had no taste at all when it came to music. *Give me a bit of AC/DC any day,* he thought.

'I'm going to sing *Diamonds Are A Girl's Best Friend,*' Suzy gushed. 'Adam said everything should have an American theme. It's the Fourth of July tomorrow.'

John pressed his back against the kitchen units. 'Yeah, but that's for the Yanks. Nothing to do with us, is it?'

'It's just a bit of fun. I've got the music for it. And the dress too.' She grinned. 'And a big feather boa.'

John's eyes widened. 'You're going to do the full Marilyn Monroe?'

'Absolutely!'

'Blimey! What, standing over a hot vent?'

'No, I'm not going that far. I don't think Liam would approve.'

There were footsteps clunking up the spiral staircase. *Talk of the devil.* Liam Heigl popped his head around the door. 'I hope you're not getting up to anything untoward with my wife,' he joked, seeing the two of them together. 'I know all about kitchens and parties.'

'Give us a chance,' John shot back, moving forward to grab the beer bottles. 'I've got to get her drunk first.'

Suzy blushed at the suggestion. 'I am here, you know!'

John handed one of the beers to her husband.

'Just came up to get the vodka for Jill,' Liam explained.

What a tosser, John thought. *Can't leave us alone for five minutes.* Liam always made a pretence of being friendly – laughing and cracking jokes – but there was invariably an edge to the humour. Behind closed doors he was a right bastard. Jealous of anyone who said so much as 'hello' to his wife. John couldn't stand the sight of him and he was pretty sure the feeling was mutual. 'Couldn't you have left Farmer Giles at home?' he hissed, as the two of them followed Liam back downstairs with the drinks.

Twinkle was busily fiddling with the television set as they returned to the living room and John handed out the beers. Adam had asked their resident IT wizard to connect up his laptop, so they could watch the big show on a proper screen. John passed around the bottle opener and grabbed himself a chair. 'Wake me up when it's finished,' he whispered to Suzy, as she sat down next to him. He wasn't holding out much hope for anything interesting. It was probably going to be a slide show. A load of soppy old photos from their university days he had no desire to see again. What was the point? If something was worth remembering, you remembered it. You didn't need to see the photos. Suzy felt differently, however. She bombarded him with pictures online every week; snaps of her kids, snaps of her lunch and all sorts of other rubbish. Still, it was good to keep in touch.

'That's it,' said Twinkle, stepping back from the television set. 'All ready to go.'

Nadia was standing in the far corner by the light switch. At a nod from Adam, she flipped off the lights. The laptop screen popped up briefly on the TV and Twinkle upped the volume; then he clicked twice on the video file.

All at once, swirling music filled the air. An archaic black and white title sequence flashed up on the screen, complete with artificial fluff and scratches. *Oh, bloody hell.* John rolled his eyes. It was Adam's graduation film.

Suzy was clapping her hands in delight. 'Where on earth did you find that?'

Adam grinned. 'I got in touch with one of our old lecturers at university.' Each of them had directed at least one film or play as part of their degree course. It was an integral part of their final assessment. It was either that or writing a dissertation. John had directed a play. Most of the productions had been a load of old rubbish, but everyone had mucked in, helping each other out. That had been a manic few weeks, John recalled. Adam's film had been the biggest of them all, of course. He never did anything by halves. He was such a show off. A forty minute black and white film noir musical. *I ask you!* He had always been a pretentious twat. John had been cast as the barman in some seedy New York dive. He'd helped build the sets as well. In return, Adam had taken the lead in his play. 'They still had the original reel of film locked away somewhere,' Adam explained, 'and they finally agreed to let me buy it. I got a friend of mine to digitise it so we could watch it on TV.'

Twinkle had found a seat next to Samantha Redmond, their Hollywood star. 'Hey, that's you!' he observed happily, pointing to the screen. The actress shuddered, catching sight of herself. The younger Samantha was walking down a cobbled street, in glorious black and white, but a sinister man with a cigarette was waiting for her on a street corner. The music soared menacingly as she approached her doom.

'Who did the music for this?' Nadia asked.

'Paul Hammond,' Adam said. Their late lamented friend. 'You'll see him in a minute. You remember, he played the piano in the bar room sequence?'

The young Samantha had reached the street corner and a hair raising scream echoed from the speakers as the sinister figure produced a knife and stabbed her to death. 'Blimey, you're making a meal of that,' John thought.

Samantha covered her eyes in embarrassment. 'God, I'm awful. If my agent ever saw that, I'd never work again.'

John chuckled, enjoying her discomfort. 'And barely two minutes in.'

To his left, Liam Heigl was also laughing. 'It's a disgrace, Adam. You've got a Hollywood star and you kill her off right at the start. She should have got top billing.'

Samantha disagreed. 'Not in a musical I shouldn't. I can't sing a note.'

'And it is a film noir,' Adam pointed out. 'The lead actress has to be a blonde.' He nodded across to Suzy Heigl. 'That's how these things work.'

'Even if she is out of a bottle,' John threw in cheekily. Suzy smacked him on the shoulder.

The screen cut to an illicit speakeasy in downtown New York. A young Suzy was standing on the stage in a dazzling velvet dress, belting out a languid, boozy song. God, she'd been something back then, John thought. The kind of girl who would stop traffic. The real Suzy nudged him in the ribs and pointed to the corner of the screen. A young John was standing over by the bar, making a complete fool of himself, pretending to prepare a cocktail. 'Oh, blimey!' He groaned.

Liam had already spotted him. 'Hey, you've got hair!' He chuckled.

'And a moustache,' Suzy observed.

'I grew that especially. First and only time.' Adam had talked him into it. It looked dreadful.

The camera slowly tracked across the nightclub before settling on the pianist. The blond haired, blue eyed Paul Hammond was sitting at the piano, his eyes closed, confidently playing along.

'He looks so young, don't he?' Jill Clarke breathed. She was sitting furthest from the screen. She took a sip of vodka. 'God, he was so handsome. Poor babes. I should have married him when I had the chance.'

John rolled his eyes. 'I wish you had,' he muttered.

Derek Fonteyn had grown rather attached to the nickname Twinkle, even if no-one outside of his university friends ever used it these days. He sat back happily on the sofa and glanced down at his watch. It was almost midnight now. Nadia and Samantha had gone to bed and Adam looked set to join them shortly. The rest of the group were getting quietly stewed. There was still some food on the table – a pretty good spread – but most of them had moved across to the sofas at the other end of the room. This was the time of day Twinkle liked the best. Having a quiet beer with your mates and chilling out into the early hours. He didn't mind all the daytime theatrics – this group was never knowingly quiet – but there was something to be said for a gentle after hours pint and a slow wind down before bed.

Twinkle hadn't realised how much he had missed his old mates. He felt a sudden surge of affection for them, even for John Menhenick, who was forever taking the piss. John was whispering something in Suzy's ear and making her laugh. Those two had always been good friends. Liam Heigl was sat on the adjacent sofa, with Adam and John's ex-wife. Jill Clarke was laughing like a drain. She had always been the loudest of the bunch. The last time Twinkle had seen her was at her wedding last year. He smiled at the memory. It had been a lavish, fairy tale affair. There had even been a live band at the reception. And the dress Jill had worn had left nothing to the imagination. Twinkle hadn't known where to look when he had offered the happy couple his congratulations. Her new husband seemed like a nice bloke, though. Nathan. Solid and reliable. A good contrast to John. He hoped the two of them would be happy together.

Jill had had a rough few years. Her divorce from John had been really messy. Twinkle was friends with both of them and he hadn't wanted to take sides. The writing had been on the wall for years, though. Thankfully, the marriage was now well behind them. Twinkle had been a little worried about how they would get on this weekend, but John had been adamant: 'I have no interest in her or her new bloke. I've moved on.' He had someone else in his life now, another redhead, but a younger one. John had never been one to want for female company.

Twinkle had not been so fortunate in his love life. He had only had a couple of relationships and neither of them had lasted. His looks were against him, of course – it would be daft to pretend otherwise – but there was more to it than that. He was just too shy to put himself forward. He didn't know how to take the initiative with people. He did have a few female friends, but they all treated him like a brother rather than a potential partner. Not that he minded too much. It was nice to have someone to talk to.

The conversation drifted towards Adam, their de facto host, and his work promoting various acts at the Edinburgh Festival. Adam was a really nice guy, relaxed and in control. He had a few wrinkles now but he was still the beating heart of the group. Him and Nadia. If it weren't for them, it was unlikely the rest of the them would have stayed in touch. Jill was sitting to Adam's right, her body twisted firmly towards him, hanging on his every word. 'Babes, you must have met some amazing people,' she slurred, her eyes fixed on his face.

Adam took a sip of beer. 'All sorts,' he agreed. 'It's always a fair mix. Actors, comedians, a few variety acts. We had a couple of ventriloquists last year and an escapologist. A fire eater the year before that.'

'That sounds so cool!'

'He certainly showed me a few tricks.' Adam grinned. 'I nearly lost my eyebrows the first time. I was lucky I didn't lose my hair as well.'

'Babes, you've got lovely hair,' Jill gushed, her hand brushing his shoulder. 'I like it short like that.'

He coughed good-naturedly and changed the subject. 'What about you, Twinkle? How's business?'

Twinkle put down his beer. 'Oh, not too bad, you know. Building up gradually. Word of mouth.' He had worked for a big software company for many years, but had branched out recently and now had his own web design business.

Suzy, who was sitting to his left, placed a hand on his arm. She was quite a tactile person. 'You did such a good job on our website. Liam was very pleased.'

'Glad you liked it,' Twinkle said. Suzy's previous author website had been pretty rudimentary. It had been kind of her to think of him when she wanted it redesigned. 'It were good fun doing it.'

'It was excellent,' her husband agreed. Liam was sitting next to Jill, on the opposite side of the sofa from Adam. 'Much better than the lash up we had before. I think it could have done with a bigger photograph of me, though,' he joked. 'It's not all about Suzy.'

John Menhenick nodded. 'Yeah, anyone can write children's books,' he agreed facetiously. 'Money for old rope.'

Suzy thumped him on the shoulder. 'I'll have you know it takes great skill and talent.'

That was true enough. Twinkle had brought a couple of Suzy's books, as presents for a cousin's kids. He had flicked through them when he was wrapping them up and they looked really good. Suzy had done all the illustrations herself as well as writing the text. He was proud to know such a talented person. Mind you, they were a talented bunch. Not just Suzy and Samantha but Adam too. He could have been a first rate actor if he'd wanted to be. He'd been smashing in John's play at university. And Liam was pretty good too. He had played the lead in a production of *Oedipus Rex*. Samantha deserved her success, but the truth was any one of them could have hit the big time. *Well, anyone but me*, Twinkle thought. He might have made a decent director, though. He'd always had a good eye for the visuals.

Paul Hammond had been the best of the lot, however, God rest his soul. He could sing and dance as well as act. Seeing him again in Adam's film had brought the memories flooding back. Paul had been a good mate of his, back in the day. He had only made a brief appearance in the film, but he had acted them all off the stage. 'It were strange, seeing Paul again, after all these years,' Twinkle declared sadly. Apart from a few photos, there was not much left of his old friend. It pained him to realise just how long he had been dead.

Adam nodded. 'I'd forgotten how good a pianist he was.' Adam had been close to him as well. Paul had been best man at his wedding.

'And some fantastic songs too,' Jill Clarke declared. Adam had written the lyrics but Paul had composed the melodies. 'You two made such a great team,' she said, gazing drunkenly at Adam. 'You could have been a fantastic song writer.'

'Oh, I still dabble a bit.' Adam extricated himself gently from the sofa, before Jill's hands could wander any further. 'Anyone want another drink, before I head off to bed?'

John Menhenick laughed. 'You're such a lightweight! Yeah, go on.' He whispered something in Suzy's ear and she chuckled again.

Twinkle was still thinking about Paul. 'You know, I can't help feeling responsible for his death, even after all this time.' He had been there, the night Paul had died, all those years ago. They had been out on the town together, a few weeks after their last big reunion. They had both got very drunk. Twinkle was only half a mile from home and he was going to walk it. 'I should never have let him drive that night. I should have called him a taxi.'

Jill wagged a finger at him. 'It wasn't your fault, babes. You weren't to know what would happen.'

They had been laughing and joking as the car stopped and started. Then, when the vehicle had built up a head of steam, Paul had lost control of the wheel and the car had ended up wrapped around a lamp post. Paul had been killed instantly but Twinkle had walked away with barely a scratch. He had stopped drinking for a time after that.

'At least it was quick,' Liam Heigl said.

Adam had returned from the kitchen with the beers, which he handed across.

'So what's the plan for tomorrow?' Liam asked him.

'Well, if you're going to stay up half the night talking, a late breakfast, I think. Then, when you've sobered up, we can see about doing the cabaret.'

John Menhenick groaned. 'Do we really have to?'

'It's compulsory,' Adam insisted, with a grin. 'You're going to have fun this weekend, John, whether you like it or not.'

Samantha Redmond was having some difficulty getting to sleep. It was funny. She had barely been able to keep her eyes open after dinner, but as soon as she retired to bed and flopped down onto the mattress, her mind refused to switch off. It had been such a hectic day. She closed her eyes and plumped up her pillow but sleep would not come.

The door creaked open. 'Only me, babes,' Jill Clarke whispered. A narrow sliver of light illuminated the room.

'What time is it?' Samantha asked, rubbing her eyes. She must have dozed off without realising it. It couldn't be early if Jill was coming to bed.

The woman shut the door behind her and staggered across to the far side of the room. 'Don't know. About four.' She hiccoughed and then giggled at the sound. 'God, I've had a skinful.' Her voice was certainly slurred. She had been knocking back the vodka all evening. Samantha had no idea how she managed it. And she would be up at the crack of dawn, too, if she was anything like her younger self.

Jill groped for her bed and pulled back the duvet.

Samantha watched her in silhouette as she took off her glasses and fumbled for the bedside table. Then she removed her heels and unzipped her skirt. That was as far as she got, however. At this point, she collapsed backwards onto the bed.

Samantha craned her neck. 'Are you all right?' she whispered, after a few seconds of silence. But Jill had already started snoring. Samantha dropped her head back onto the pillow. It really was just like old times.

They had shared a room together back in Leicester. The same digs as Adam and Twinkle. Not that Jill had spent much time in the flat. She had been out all hours partying, while Samantha had spent her time at the library, fretting over her latest essay. The two of them could not have been more different, but they had always got on. No matter how gloomy or stressed Samantha was feeling, Jill could always raise a smile, just by saying something daft. She had thought motherhood might have tempered her a little, but apparently not. Apart from a little extra weight, Jill was the same crazy girl she had known twenty years ago. Or even ten years ago, come to that.

The castle reunion seemed a long time ago now. That was the last time Samantha had seen Paul Hammond. It was odd seeing him again on TV, at the piano, looking so young and handsome. It had prompted quite a few memories, not just of university but of events at the castle. More than a few people had swapped beds that weekend. Mind you, it had been easier in North Wales. There were more rooms to tip-toe around, more nooks and crannies. And no journalists watching her every move. Not that Samantha had done anything that she regretted. Not like some of the others. She smiled at the thought. Twinkle had got very drunk and declared his love for her at the foot of her bed. She wasn't sure if he remembered that. But it had been so sweet. She felt really sorry for him that night. They had crashed out together on the bed, but nothing had actually happened. It was better that way. Nicer to stay as friends, she thought. Her behaviour had been positively nun-like compared to the others. Jill and John were still married then, but you wouldn't have known it from watching them. And Suzy Heigl, unshackled by

41

her husband, had completely disgraced herself. Yes, what a strange weekend that was. Her last moment of freedom. Funny how you never realise it at the time. A few months later, she was offered the lead in *Moonlit Dawn* and had never looked back.

The lighthouse lamp briefly cut through the curtains and illuminated the room. She gazed across at Jill. The girl was sprawled on top of the duvet, her boobs half out of her top and her skirt halfway down her legs, snoring away for all to hear. Samantha felt a wave of affection. Why did she waste her time in Hollywood, listening to vacuous people telling her how wonderful she was, when she could be here with her real friends? *I mustn't leave it so long next time*, she decided.

'I don't want to go to bed.' A shrill voice could be heard vibrating through the far wall. Suzy Heigl was moving into the master bedroom.

'I think you've had enough,' Liam Heigl told her.

'That's for me to decide.' Suzy's voice had a bitter edge to it, quite unlike her usual light tone.

'Not when we're with other people. I'm not having you behaving like that.'

'Don't you tell me how to behave!'

Samantha let out a quiet sigh. That was another thing that hadn't changed. Liam and Suzy rowing. They had been married for something like fifteen years now and they were as nice as pie in public. But they had always rowed ferociously behind closed doors. Every other day, it seemed. It was inexplicable. They clearly loved each other dearly, but for some reason they were always at each other's throats. It was not the sort of relationship Samantha could ever envisage being a part of.

'Somebody has to,' Liam snapped back angrily. 'What were you saying to John in the kitchen this evening?'

'Nothing at all. We were just getting a few beers.'

'Why do you have to encourage him, Suzy? You know how he feels about you. He's fancied you since the year dot.'

'We're friends, that's all. I wasn't encouraging him.'

'You sat next to him on the boat.'

'Oh, for god's sake, Liam. There were only a dozen seats

on there. I had to sit somewhere.'

'You didn't have to sit next to him.'

'We're old friends. Why shouldn't I sit next to him? He's always behaved like a perfect gentleman to me.'

Liam scoffed. 'He's not a gentleman. John Menhenick is a poisonous toad. He just squats in the corner, spewing out venom to anyone who'll listen.'

Suzy was outraged. 'Don't you dare talk about him like that.'

'Why not? It's true. And you only encourage him.'

'What about you and Jill?' Suzy countered. There was a clunk; maybe a cupboard being opened. 'She couldn't take her eyes of you all evening. Chatting you up at every opportunity.'

'Only after Adam had gone to bed. In any case, she was drunk.'

'That's no excuse. She'd have had her hands all over you, given half a chance. Rekindling the flames.'

'I didn't give her the chance, did I?'

'Only because I was there.'

'Look, Jill and I had a brief fling at university. But that was twenty years ago, before you and I got together. And it was a mistake. I wouldn't touch her now with a barge pole.'

'You didn't do anything to discourage her tonight.'

'I was trying not to be rude,' Liam insisted. 'In any case, at least I wasn't snuggling up to her on the sofa, like you and John. What did you say to him? What was he whispering in your ear?'

'That's none of your business!'

'Tell me!'

'Oy, keep the noise down!' The raised voices had briefly roused Jill Clarke from her slumber. 'Some of us are trying to sleep.'

There was a brief, embarrassed pause from next door. Samantha glanced across at the darkened shape on the bed opposite. Had Jill heard the "barge pole" remark, she wondered. Probably not. The girl was too far gone to make out anything more than a general din.

43

'Sorry, Jill,' Liam called out at last. 'You sleep well.'

'You too, babes,' Jill mumbled. And the snoring quickly resumed.

Chapter Three

'You've got to see the costume,' Suzy Heigl said, when Nadia bumped into her outside the bathroom the following morning. 'I'm going to try it on, before I get dressed.' Nadia had been busy with Adam organising breakfast. She had come downstairs from the kitchen to round up any stragglers. She didn't want anyone missing out. They had laid on the works: bacon and eggs, cereals, toast, orange juice. Adam had planned everything to perfection.

It was a bright sunny morning. The light was flittering in through the large windows of the cottage and Nadia felt on top form. She had been a bit of a wimp, going to bed early last night, but her batteries were now completely recharged and she was raring to go. *This is going to be a day to remember*, she thought. A cabaret, lots of daft games and then on to disco night. There was no question of her going to bed early this evening; not when there was a lethal rum punch in the offing.

Suzy shuffled her across to the master bedroom.

'You sure you want me to see it?' Nadia asked. Everyone was meant to be doing their own thing for the cabaret and the surprise was half the fun.

'I don't think there's any harm in a sneak preview,' Suzy said. She had a towel wrapped around her head, firmly covering her blonde locks, and another around her body. She seemed in a surprisingly good mood this morning, considering the blazing row she and Liam had had last night. Nadia was sleeping in the bedroom above them and the sounds of their voices had briefly roused her. *Probably woke everyone up*, she thought, with a smile. Hearing the two of them at each other's throats again, she had struggled not to laugh. The couple were always arguing and then making up. It was part of their dynamic. And the daft thing was, they never seemed to realise everyone else could hear them.

Liam Heigl was up already. Nadia had bumped into him coming down the stairs from the kitchen. Jill Clarke, who had drunk a small swimming pool last night, had headed out even earlier to do her morning exercises. Nadia was suitably

45

impressed. If she had drunk half as much as Jill had she would barely have been able to walk this morning. But no matter how much the red-haired woman put away, she was always up and fresh as a daisy the next morning with no sign of a hangover. *Lucky sod*, Nadia thought. *How on earth does she manage it?*

She followed Suzy into the bedroom. The large double bed had been neatly remade. Suzy was always one of the tidy ones. You would barely know anyone had been in the room, apart from a couple of items on the bedside table. Nadia watched as she strode over to the closet and pulled out a long white dress. It was elegant and beautifully tailored. She brushed her hand down the length of it. 'What do you think? Isn't it great?'

'Very nice,' Nadia agreed. It really did look like the dress in the film. Mind you, despite the blonde hair, Suzy was far too skinny to make a convincing Marilyn Monroe. She had the bust but not the hips. 'You'll raise a few eyebrows with that.'

'That's the idea.' Suzy laid out the dress carefully on the far side of the bed and then opened a drawer in the bedside table, pulling out a silver hair dryer. She sat down on the edge of the duvet and looked across at Nadia. 'What are *you* going to do for the cabaret. Or is it a secret?'

'Not a secret exactly. Adam's written a couple of sketches. No singing, thank god. Just lots of appalling jokes.'

'Sounds fun!'

'Taking the mickey out of everyone. Ourselves included.' They had rehearsed it all thoroughly back in Edinburgh. 'I haven't got much of a costume, but his is quite elaborate.' Nadia chuckled at the memory of it.

'He's not going in drag again, is he?' Suzy asked, her eyes lighting up at the thought. At the castle, Adam had given a show-stopping rendition of *Sweet Transvestite*, complete with black lingerie, tights and suspenders. It had brought the house down. Adam was a different man in front of an audience; and he had something equally eye popping up his sleeve this time.

'You'll have to wait and see,' Nadia teased. He had shown her the full costume the other night, back at his flat. Even his partner, Judith, had boggled when he had walked into the room.

Nadia had got off lightly in comparison. She was dragging up too, but only as a man in a suit. They had rehearsed the routine to within an inch of its life and she was sure it would be warmly received. 'Anyway, I'll leave you to get dressed. Breakfast is ready, as soon as you want it. Bacon and eggs. Oh, well, eggs in your case.' She kept forgetting Suzy was a vegetarian. 'And plenty of toast.' At least the girl wasn't a vegan, she thought. That would have made things really complicated. Happily, Adam was always on top of those kind of details.

'Do *you* eat bacon?' Suzy asked, unwrapping the towel from her head and grabbing a hair brush. 'Isn't it against your religion or something?'

Nadia shook her head. 'That's Muslims.' Her family were Hindu. Eating meat was frowned upon but not prohibited. 'Anyway, I've never been much of a one for religion.'

Suzy put down her brush. 'Everyone needs a little bit of the spiritual in their life, Nadia. It's good for the soul.'

'You're probably right.' Suzy had always had something of a spiritual bent. Her Guardian Angel was a standing joke among the group. 'Adam's my angel at the moment. I'd have messed everything up, if he had left all this to me. You'd be having bread and water for breakfast.'

'You and Adam, you make such a good team.' Suzy shot her a mischievous grin. 'And I hear you're sharing a room together this weekend.'

'A twin room.' Nadia coughed in mock embarrassment. 'Just for the sake of convenience. But I'll have you know it's entirely innocent.'

'I'm sure it is! Did you stay with him in Edinburgh?'

'Yes, at his flat. They have a spare room.' Adam and Judith had put her up for a couple of nights. It had been like sharing digs again; although come to think of it she had never actually shared with Adam.

'What's his wife like?' Suzy asked. 'I didn't get the chance to speak to her at the wedding last year. She was very pretty, though.'

'Judith? Yes, she's great. Very down to earth. You'd like

47

her. I think there may be a kid on the way too, at long last. Oh! Don't tell Adam I said that.'

Suzy smiled. 'My lips are sealed. Tell Liam I'll be up in five minutes,' she added, as Nadia moved towards the door.

'Oh, he's not having breakfast. I think he's gone out for a walk. Stretching his legs. I saw him heading off out the door a few minutes ago.'

Suzy frowned and looked down at the hair dryer.

'Is everything all right between you?' Nadia asked. 'I...er...I heard you talking last night.'

'Shouting you mean. Yes, everything's fine,' Suzy said, with apparent sincerity. 'You know what we're like. It always blows over. It's my fault, spending too much time with John yesterday. Sorry if we woke you up.'

'Not a problem,' Nadia said with a grin. 'It made me feel quite nostalgic.'

John Menhenick stifled a yawn and took another drag of his cigarette. He had stayed up half the night once again, talking bollocks with Twinkle. By the time they had staggered back to their room it was almost dawn and it was scarcely worth going to bed. Twinkle had crashed out anyway and wouldn't be up again for a few hours. John had made the most of his free time. He'd had a few things to sort out, while the house was quiet. He could always have a bit of a siesta later on. He smiled to himself and let out a puff of smoke. He had come a little way out of the cottage and was leaning against the outer wall of the compound, looking down the length of the island. *Blimey, what a dump*, he thought. Just grass and rock. Bleak as anything. At least it was warmer this morning. He had grabbed his thick black coat from the rack but he didn't really need it. The sun was out in force and the bright light was glittering off the sea in every direction. Typical Adam, choosing a spot like this. The back end of beyond, but not too far from his own home. It had been the same last time. He had had a house in Wales back then; and, lo and behold, a Welsh castle had been booked for their reunion. Now he lived in Scotland and everyone jumped to his tune once again. Mind you, the location did have its advantages.

His thoughts drifted idly back to last night. Jill had been an absolute disgrace, as usual. *Stupid cow.* What did she think she was doing, throwing herself at Adam like that? And then at Liam, of all people. With Suzy sitting opposite them. That girl needed a good slap. Not that he was surprised at Jill's behaviour. *She'd drop her knickers for anyone, the little tart.* She was probably just doing it to make him jealous, trying to reignite the old flame. But she was wasting her time. If this weekend had proved one thing, it was that John now had no feelings at all for his ex-wife. He had more important things to worry about.

The smells of breakfast were wafting up from the cottage. He'd had his fill of bacon and eggs already. *Perfect start to the day.* Adam had got that right, if nothing else. John dropped his cigarette and stubbed it out on the concrete. Bacon and eggs and the first fag of the morning. It didn't get much better than that.

A bird fluttered up from the roof of the derelict chapel, halfway across the island. John gazed idly down at the building. It was a rough looking place, shabby and overgrown. From the edge of the compound, you couldn't see how much of the roof had caved in, but the hefty stone walls were covered in bits of grass and other weeds. *Bloody stupid place to build a chapel.* Nadia had said the building was hundreds of years old. She had asked the owner about it, apparently. Before the lighthouse, the island had been used to graze sheep. *Blimey,* John thought. What a bleak, miserable life that must have been.

He rubbed his face and another bird flew away. Two birds, actually. Something had spooked them. The ghost of a shepherd, perhaps? He grinned at the thought. That's what Suzy would think, anyhow. The daft cow. More likely it was one of the others, out for a stroll. Who hadn't he seen this morning? He couldn't think. Not that it mattered. He was in a rather mischievous mood right now. Whoever it was, he would creep up on them and give them the fright of their life. It would be worth it just to see the look on their face.

He stepped away from the wall and moved onto the grass.

The slope of the island was steeper than he expected and he almost lost his footing in the mud before he was halfway to the chapel. *Oh, sod this for a laugh,* he thought, about to turn back. But then he heard a shrill voice up ahead; a woman giggling. He scowled in disappointment. It was his ex. He would know that laugh anywhere. The stupid cow was out here doing her morning exercises. He should have guessed. Jill had always been an early bird, no matter how much she drank the night before. That was about the only thing they had in common.

John turned away from the chapel. The last thing he wanted was to stumble across his ex-wife spread out on that stupid green exercise pad of hers. *Hang on a mo.* He stopped as a sudden thought struck him. Why would she be laughing if she was out here on her own? She couldn't be on the phone; there was no signal. Which meant there had to be somebody with her. He listened carefully. Yeah, there *was* someone else there. He could hear a low murmur just above the whirl of the wind. *Who the hell is that?* he wondered. It was definitely a man.

He crept to the back wall of the chapel but hesitated for a second, wondering if he really wanted to see what was going on. From the sounds he had heard, he already had his suspicions and they were not pleasant. His curiosity got the better of him, however, and he made his way slowly around the side of the building. There was a gap for a window, overgrown with weed. He ducked down and peered over the solid stone lip. *Oh, Christ!* He was right. There was his ex-wife, on the opposite side of the building and with her was Liam Heigl. Jill had her back pressed against the far wall. Her skirt was hitched up around her waist and her legs were wrapped tightly around Liam's solid hips. He had his trousers around his ankles. His naked backside flashed in the sunlight and Jill moaned with pleasure.

John looked away. It was a repulsive sight. His ex-wife with her eyes screwed shut. God, how many times had he seen that expression? But he had never expected to see it again. *What the hell do they think they're playing at?* He had always suspected there might be a bit of hanky panky this weekend – in fact, he was banking on it – but not between those two. Well, Jill perhaps; she

50

would shag anyone. But Liam Heigl – bloody hell, in broad daylight, a couple of hundred yards from the house. What was he thinking? Suzy would have a fit if she found out. It was one thing, playing away from home. John wasn't going to take the moral high ground over that. But it was another thing doing it when your Mrs was just round the corner.

A wicked thought struck him then and, with a silent smile, he fumbled in his pocket for his mobile. He flicked on the phone, unlocked it and took careful aim. A couple of quick shots, that would do it. *You never know when they might come in useful.* He grinned. He was not about to tell tales but it never hurt to have a little something in reserve. And Suzy certainly deserved a lot better than this prick.

He pocketed the phone and was about to creep away when Jill opened her eyes and caught a flash of movement in the vacant window frame. She let out a yelp and John stopped where he was. There was no point pretending he wasn't there. She had seen him now. He stood up and gave a regal wave. Liam flinched, sensing something was wrong but unable to see what it was. Jill whispered something in his ear and Liam clumsily disengaged, almost tripping over as he fumbled for his trousers. Jill quickly patted down her skirt, her eyes flashing with fear as she gazed across the chapel at her ex-husband.

'It's not what you think, babes,' she called out, lamely.

John laughed at the brazenness of that. *If in doubt, deny everything.* 'Of course not,' he said. 'It never is.' He moved around the crumbled edge of the wall into the low frame of a door. Jill was hastily getting herself dressed. He moved into the chapel and regarded the pair of them with undisguised contempt. 'God, what a sight.' Liam was zipping up his flies. 'I'd expect this of her, but I thought better of you, Liam. A married man.' John tutted theatrically. Now that he was here, he found himself rather enjoying their discomfort. He hadn't thought Liam would be this stupid, rutting away so close to home. Anyone could have stumbled across them.

Liam was frozen to the spot, not knowing what to say or do.

51

'You're not going to say anything, are you, babes?' Jill asked.

'What, to your new husband?' John smirked. 'Why not? It's about time he knew what sort of girl he was married to.'

'It wasn't her fault,' Liam stuttered.

'Oh, *now* he's being the gentleman.' John laughed. 'Now he's got his pants back on. Don't worry, darling.' He addressed his ex-wife. 'I couldn't give a toss about you. No skin off my nose who you shag. But Suzy, that's another matter.' His eyes narrowed on the husband. 'What would she think if she knew you were screwing around behind her back?'

'I didn't...' Liam stammered. 'I didn't intend...'

'You didn't intend for it to happen.' John snorted. 'No, of course not. She jumped on top of you. I'm sure Suzy will understand.'

'You're not going to tell her?' Liam was horrified. 'She'd never forgive me.'

'You should have thought of that before, mate. Perhaps it's time she found out what you're really like.' John raised his hands. 'Oh, don't look so worried. It's your birthday. I'm not going to tell on you. And you know why? Because I know how much it'll hurt her. And she deserves better than that.' He gazed across at the other man. 'She deserves better than *you*.'

Liam riled at that, his fear abruptly giving way to anger. 'Oh, and you're a saint, are you?' he spat back. 'You're such a hypocrite, John. Don't you dare preach to me. You were never faithful to Jill here, even when you were married.'

'Babes, don't...'

'No, he's right,' John agreed. 'I was no saint.' He gestured contemptuously to his ex-wife. 'I was every bit as faithful to her as she was to me. But never on my own doorstep. I never rubbed her face in it.'

'I'm not talking about Jill. I'm talking about Suzy.' Liam was going on the offensive now. His eyes were blazing, his hands bunched into tight fists. 'Don't think I don't know what's going on between you and her. Between you and my wife.'

John gave him a blank look. 'I don't know what you're

talking about, mate.'

'I'm not your mate.'

'No, you're not. Your wife is my mate. We've been friends since way back. Good friends. And friends look out for each other.'

'Friends! Lovers, more like!'

John snorted again. 'Don't talk bollocks, Liam. She ain't interested in me. Not in that way. She never has been.'

'I think she is,' Liam asserted.

'I don't care what you think.'

'Don't deny it. You're having an affair with my wife. You slept with her in Wales, didn't you? And you've been meeting up with her ever since.'

John shook his head. 'Mate, you're deluded. I'm not sleeping with your wife. And you're in no position to lecture me. Not after this. One word from me, mate, and your marriage is over.'

Liam stepped forward, his fists raised. 'You little...'

'Ooh, tough guy. Come on then.' John lifted his hands. 'Give it your best shot.'

Jill regarded the two men in horror. 'Liam, no!'

'You stay away from my wife!' the taller man snarled.

John was more amused than threatened. 'Why don't you make me?' This little tosser couldn't do him any harm. He was tall, sure, but he had no muscles to speak of.

'Babes, don't! Don't hurt him!' Jill rushed forward and grabbed hold of John's arm, trying to restrain him. He whipped his hand up and slapped her hard across the face. There was a moment of shocked silence.

'This is between me and him,' John told her bluntly.

Liam could see the mark on the side of Jill's face. 'You shouldn't have done that, John.'

'I'll do what I bloody well like.' It was his turn to show a bit of anger. 'She deserves it. Christ, she can't keep her legs crossed for five minutes.'

'That's no excuse. You're an animal. You're not fit to be around other people.'

John smiled sourly. 'So what are you going to do about it?'

'I'll show you.' Liam moved forward once again.

'Liam, no! He'll kill you! I'm sorry, babes. It was all my fault. Just leave him alone.'

'Give it a rest, darling!' John raised his hand a second time. 'Sod off back to the cottage and leave us alone. This is between him and me. Oh, and keep your mouth shut.' Jill nodded tearfully and quickly dipped down to gather up the last of her things. John watched contemptuously as she rushed away through the door. 'Jesus!' He shook his head, looking after her. 'What did I ever see in that?'

'If you'd treated her with a little more respect, the two of you might still be together,' Liam said. 'Don't take it out on her. All Jill ever wanted was a bit of affection. I don't think you've ever really understood her.'

'What, and you do?' John laughed. 'I know everything I want to know about that little tart. I was married to her for seven years. So come on then.' He spread his arms wide, opening up his chest. 'First one's for free.'

Liam was having second thoughts. 'Look, John. I don't want to fight you. What's the point? It won't change anything.'

'You're right,' he agreed. 'It won't change anything.' John made to move away, but then turned back and thumped Liam viciously in the stomach. The man rocked backwards under the force of the blow, losing his footing and smacking to the ground. John smiled down at him. 'I've been wanting to do that for a long time.' He turned to the door.

'Please don't tell Suzy,' Liam mumbled after him. 'It'll break her heart.'

'Yeah,' John agreed, looking back. 'It will. Don't worry, mate. I have no intention of telling her anything. Well.' He grinned. 'Not before lunch anyway.'

Nadia Kumar was taking a moment to run through the lines in her head. She was sitting at the dinner table upstairs, her lips silently forming the words and her hands miming the gestures they had worked out together in rehearsal. Everyone had been a bit subdued at lunch – probably a few hangovers still being nursed – but hopefully the cabaret would liven things up a bit. Adam was sitting on the opposite side of the table, with a pen and a pad, writing out the order of events. 'We'll have Suzy as the opening number,' he suggested. 'Then the first sketch. And then maybe Twinkle?'

'What's he doing?' Nadia asked, drawing back in her chair.

'I don't know. He didn't say.' Twinkle had never been much of a one for dressing up. He was a good sport, though, and would doubtless come up with something suitably entertaining. 'I think he wants it to be a surprise. No music, though, so it won't be a song.'

'Probably just as well.' Nadia laughed. 'His singing voice is worse than mine.'

Adam scribbled down the name. 'Then maybe Jill, another sketch, then John.'

'Oh, haven't you heard? The word on the grapevine is, he's not doing anything.'

Adam lifted his pen with mock severity. 'He's going to do something. Even if I have to drag him up on stage myself.' He chuckled for a moment; then he put down the pen and frowned. 'Is it just me, Nadia, or is there a funny atmosphere here today?'

So Adam had noticed it too. 'It's not just you,' she said. 'Everyone seems a bit distracted.' Adam and a few of the others had arranged a game of poker before lunch, but it had proved a bit of a damp squib. The conversation at the dinner table had been equally subdued. 'I think it may be something to do with John and Jill.'

Adam's eyes narrowed. 'Why? Has something happened?'

'I'm not sure.' Nadia drew in a breath. 'Just having the two of them in the same building was asking for trouble. It sounds like there may have been some friction this morning.' Nadia wasn't too sure of the details. 'Samantha was telling me about it, just before lunch. Jill was a bit upset, she said, when she came back to their room first thing. She wouldn't say why. A few barbed comments maybe. But she was all right after breakfast.'

Adam frowned. 'Do you think maybe I should have a word with John?'

'It's probably nothing. You know what he's like. All mouth and no trousers. It's funny. They're all right with each other when they're drunk. It's when they sober up that there are problems. But I'm sure it'll be fine.'

'I hope so,' Adam fretted. 'We can't let them sour the mood for everyone else.' He paused for a second, taking in the sounds of the cottage. 'Mind you, the place seems completely dead at the moment anyway.'

Everyone had scattered after lunch. Suzy and a couple of the others had organised a second game of cards, but that had fizzled out after an hour or so. The rest of the group had gone off to try on their costumes or to rehearse in private.

'The calm before the storm,' Adam reckoned.

'The calm before the cabaret.' Nadia grinned. She was really looking forward to the show. It was bound to cheer everyone up. 'I can't wait to see their faces when you walk out in that bunny girl costume. It'll bring the house down.'

'Yes, I'm looking forward to that,' Adam dead panned. He had even got a pair of fake breasts to stuff down his front 'Just so long as no one sees me getting changed. Don't want to spoil the surprise.'

'Not much chance of that.' Nadia had got off lightly in comparison. She would be playing the President of the United States. The male president, in one of Adam's cast off suits, which was about three sizes too big for her. 'You do realise people are going to be taking photographs?'

'I don't care.' Adam laughed. 'I have no shame. And besides, my arse looks great with a pom-pom on it.'

Nadia flicked her eyes to the ceiling. 'You keep telling yourself that.'

'I'm not the only one, though. From what I hear, Samantha's got something pretty kinky lined up too. Something her fans would pay good money to see.'

Nadia raised an eyebrow. 'Sounds like fun. What's she doing?'

'I'm sworn to secrecy.' He glanced down at his pad. 'I'll think we'll save that for the finale. But we might have to ban any photographs at that point.'

Nadia chuckled. 'God, what is she doing? A striptease?' That would be a first. Despite her sex bomb image, Samantha Redmond was famously reticent about disrobing in public.

'No, not a striptease. Not this time. That's Liam's job.'

Nadia boggled. 'Liam?'

'Yeah.' He grinned. 'In a pair of star-spangled underpants.'

Nadia almost exploded with laughter.

'Well, there has to be something for the girls too,' Adam said. 'It's only fair. Don't tell him I let on, though. Oh, do you think we should bring that second crate of beer in? Before we get started?'

Nadia rose to her feet. 'Yes, good idea. I'll do it.' She pulled out her phone and checked the time. 'We'd better start moving the chairs, too, if we're going to get started by four o'clock.'

'I'll take care of that. You see to the beer.'

'And then we'd better get the costumes out. Make sure you haven't crushed your pom-pom.'

'Or the bunny ears.' Adam grinned again. He rose up and navigated around the edge of the table.

The stage area would be on the opposite side of the room. They had already set up the stereo for the musical numbers. Twinkle had transferred all the tunes onto Adam's iPod, which he had connected up to the stereo. The dining chairs would be positioned in the middle, for the audience, but there were a couple of sofas that would need to be moved out of the way first. Adam set to work.

Nadia made her way down the spiral staircase into the lower hallway. The front door was wide open as she headed towards it and there was a bit of a breeze blowing through. *John's probably stepped out for another fag*, she thought. Or perhaps he was busy rehearsing his lines, if he was going to do something for the show. She wondered idly what he had said this morning that had so upset Jill. Probably just the usual off-hand comments. John was pathologically incapable of biting his tongue.

The second crate of beer was just outside the front door. Nadia was about to step out when she spotted Jill Clarke moving in the opposite direction, her cheeks looking rather flushed. The woman stopped abruptly at the sight of her friend and put her hand to her heart theatrically. 'You frightened the life out of me, babes, for a minute there.' She flashed a grin. 'Just collecting my exercise mat. I left it outside this morning.' She had the mat rolled awkwardly under her arm.

'You're lucky it didn't blow away.'

'Nah, I always peg it down if it's windy. You not in costume yet?'

'No, I was just coming out to grab the other crate of beer.'

Jill glanced down at the booze. 'Do you want us to give you a hand?'

'If you like. It's not that heavy.'

She stowed her mat by the coat rack and then helped Nadia to grab the crate. The two women took an end each and manoeuvred the crate through the door into the hallway.

'How are you this afternoon?' Nadia asked. 'Samantha said you were a bit upset this morning.' If there were any problems, it was better to get them out into the open.

'Oh, it was nothing, babes,' Jill declared breezily. 'I'm fine.'

'Just John being a dick again?'

'Yeah. He don't change, do he?' She grinned, but this time her expression seemed a little forced. 'Oh look!' She stopped in her tracks, gazing at the far end of the corridor. 'I thought the lighthouse was off-limits.' The door to the tower was hanging open.

Nadia followed her gaze. 'It is.' *That shouldn't be unlocked*, she thought.

'Must be Adam, having a look round. He's got a set of keys, ain't he?'

'To the cottage, yes, but not to the tower. In any case, he's upstairs, sorting out the furniture.'

Jill shrugged. 'Must be someone playing silly buggers then. You sure it was locked up?'

Nadia was certain. She had seen Mr Peterson do it, when they had come down together from the lamp room yesterday afternoon.

'Maybe someone's found a key in a drawer or something, wanted to have a look round.'

'I suppose so.' But the front door had also been unlocked when they had first arrived at the cottage. 'I think I might just take a look,' Nadia said. She remembered how concerned the owner had been about it all.

They lowered the beer crate to the ground.

'You want me to come with you?'

'No, no. I'll just pop my head around the door. You sort your mat out. I'll take the beer upstairs in a minute.'

'It's all right, babes. I'll do it.' Jill bent down again and lifted the crate with surprising ease. The girl had quite thick, muscular arms. That exercise mat had clearly been put to good use.

Nadia moved across to the far door and into the storeroom at the base of the lighthouse. 'Anyone in here?' she called out. The room was dark and musty, piled high with boxes and rusting equipment. She didn't bother to switch on the light. She moved straight to the staircase, grabbed the handrail and made her way up. 'It's only me,' she called ahead. If someone was here, it was most likely John or Liam. Or maybe Suzy. The blonde woman had been disappointed to learn the tower was out of bounds. But there was no sign of anyone about. Nadia tried the door to the side room on the first floor, but that was firmly locked. She moved on up to the lamp room. Again, there was no sign that anyone had been up here since yesterday. Nadia took a moment to catch her breath. It took some effort, climbing those stairs. She hadn't expected to be tromping up here again quite so soon.

She gazed across at the glass door leading out onto the balcony. The sky was starting to cloud over now, the sun disappearing from view. The horizon had been much clearer when she had come up here yesterday. She pulled the door back and moved out onto the balcony. The wind whipped through her dark, shoulder-length hair. But there was no-one about. The lighthouse was empty.

So who unlocked that door? she wondered. Had somebody found a key or had they had managed to pick the lock? She smiled at that idea. *Adam would know how to do it.* One of the clients he had promoted at the Edinburgh Festival had been an escapologist. She had shown him a few tricks, apparently. But if Adam had been that desperate to climb the tower, he could have come up with her yesterday afternoon. Perhaps the door hadn't been properly locked after all. That was the most likely explanation. Maybe the wind had blown it open. The front door had been unlatched since breakfast and there was always a bit of a breeze coming through.

Nadia decided to take another quick circuit of the balcony. She would never tire of the view up here. Flaxton Isle was a beautiful place, green and raw, tranquil against the blue of the sea. She grinned as she noticed a lone figure wandering about somewhere down south. At this distance, she couldn't make out who it was. *Somebody out for a walk, anyway.* She gave a wave but whoever it was wasn't looking up. She peered at the horizon instead. Try as she might she could not make out the coastline. Not this time. *At least it's not going to rain,* she thought, glancing up at the clouds. Peterson had assured her the weather would be fine the whole weekend. She put her hand lightly on the rail and moved round to the other side of the lighthouse.

Taking a quick breath, she peered over the edge, straight down at the sea below. It was only a short distance between the bottom of the lighthouse, the edge of the compound and the northern cliff edge. She shivered, taking in the long vertical drop. Perhaps it wasn't such a good idea, peeping over the edge like this. Nadia had never been particularly good with heights. There was a small line of almost vertical steps to one side of the cliff, crude and badly worn. *They look pretty lethal*, she thought. Not like the ones leading up from the landing stage. Perhaps these had been carved out for the workers, when the lighthouse was being constructed. There was a tiny pebble beach at the bottom of the cliff where it was possible boats might once have landed. It was a pretty small beach though, a thin sliver against the lashing waves, and there was no landing stage there.

Nadia screwed up her eyes. *What's that?* she wondered. She had caught sight of something spread out across the pebbles; a black something. *Bin bags, maybe*? She frowned. Surely no one would be dumping rubbish down there.

The lamp room had a pair of binoculars. Her curiosity getting the better of her, she went back inside to grab them. Then she returned to the balcony, got down on her knees and peered once again over the edge. It took her a moment to find the beach through the glasses. She panned across and the black object suddenly came into view. She adjusted the lenses to resolve the image and then almost dropped the binoculars.

There was a body lying at the bottom of the cliff.

Chapter Four

Samantha Redmond was grateful for the distraction. The sofa was heavier than it looked and the castors were snagging a bit on the carpet. It was easier just to lift the thing. 'Back a bit your end,' Adam directed. 'That's perfect.'

Samantha dropped the corner to the floor. They had already moved the dining table up against the far wall and pulled out the various chairs. The "stage" such as it was would be on the east side of the dining room.

'Anything else I can do?' she asked.

There were clunks from the adjacent kitchen. Jill Clarke was emptying out a crate of beer, stowing some of the bottles in the fridge. No doubt she would be helping herself to a glass of vodka as well.

'Just line the chairs up at the front there,' Adam suggested.

Samantha was grateful to have something to occupy herself with. It helped to keep her mind off the forthcoming "entertainment". Truth to tell, she was feeling a bit apprehensive about the cabaret. Her choice of routine was not ideal. It had to be something risqué – Adam had insisted on that – but it had been left to her to decide exactly what. She had chosen a short comic monologue. It was her choice of costume she really regretted, however: a St Trinian's schoolgirl, complete with straw boater, short skirt and jolly hockey stick. It had seemed like a good idea back in LA but now she was having second thoughts. Samantha had never been particularly comfortable showing off her body in public. She had been lucky in her professional career. The first *Moonlit Dawn* film was more of an action flick than a traditional vampire movie and its success had given her enough clout to pick and choose her subsequent roles. She had been able to insist on a no-nudity clause for each new contract, which was a rarity in this day and age. She did not think of herself as a prude, however – in her profession, that was simply not possible – and she was anxious to show off a lighter side to her friends. Perhaps she could have chosen something a little less kinky than a schoolgirl, though, on an exchange trip to America. But it was too late to worry about that now. Better just to focus on the lines.

Rumour had it that Liam Heigl might be doing a full on striptease, so there would be something for the girls too. Samantha was looking forward to that. With his boyish face and puppy dog eyes, Liam had always been the best looking member of the group. Samantha had had such a crush on him at university. Sadly, his attentions had been focused on Jill back then and Suzy soon afterwards.

'Did Liam find that belt?' she asked, absently, as she tidied up the line of chairs. Liam had been tearing his hair out earlier on, trying to find the last piece of his costume.

'I think he borrowed one,' Adam said. Adam Cartwright had aged a little less well than Liam. He still had a full head of hair, cut fashionably short, but there were lines on his face and a few bags under his eyes. He had lost none of his poise or enthusiasm, though. He took a step back, taking in the entirety of the room. 'That's the seating done, I think, but I want to decorate the stage area a little. It's a shame we haven't got any proper lights.' The windows behind the stage were a little distracting.

'I've got a lamp in my room, if that's any help,' Samantha suggested. 'A free standing one.'

Adam smiled. 'I think we'll give that a miss.' He was right. It probably wouldn't help. 'We'll use the spare room over there for costume changes. I'd better pin up the running order. Where is everyone, anyway?' He looked at his watch. 'We're starting in twenty minutes.'

'Jill's in the kitchen. Perhaps I should go and round the rest of them up?'

Adam shook his head. 'No, leave that to me. Better sort yourself out. Get your costume ready.'

'All right.' She moved past him and headed for the stairs. She had folded everything up neatly earlier on so she could smuggle it up here without anybody seeing it. Even the boater and the hockey stick.

She stopped outside the bathroom. Nadia was huffing and puffing up the staircase. 'Hi,' Samantha said, as the plump woman arrived at the top. 'It looks like we're all set. Hey, is something wrong?'

Nadia took a moment to catch her breath. 'I need to speak to Adam.'

'He's just in there.' Samantha let go of the bathroom door and followed Nadia back into the main room. 'What's the matter? Has something happened?'

Adam was coming out of his bedroom, carrying a large American flag. He sensed immediately that something was wrong. 'Nadia, what is it?'

The woman's face was grim. 'I think there's been an accident.'

Samantha followed them out of the cottage and into the compound. Adam thought they would get a better view from the cliff edge, rather than clomping up to the top of the lighthouse. They moved swiftly past the storehouses and around the tower before heading out onto the short patch of grass between the compound and the drop. Nadia had filled them in on what she had seen but Samantha had no idea what to make of it. Could it be one of them? she wondered, with a shiver. Had somebody slipped and fallen?

'Hey, be careful,' Nadia warned, as they drew near to the edge. 'Watch your feet, Adam.' The grass verge only extended a few metres beyond the compound wall, before plummeting away to the sea.

'Don't worry, I'll be careful,' he said.

Nadia handed him the binoculars but then moved back to the compound wall. She had obviously seen all she wanted to see. Adam dropped to his knees and shuffled forward cautiously. Samantha followed his lead and crawled up beside him as he popped his head over the edge of the cliff.

'What can you see?' she asked.

'I'm not sure yet.' He fumbled for the binoculars, which were now hooped around his neck. 'Oh, yes. I see it.' He drew in a breath. 'It's definitely a body.'

Samantha shuddered. So Nadia had been right. She peered over the lip of the cliff. 'Is it one of us?' That was the most important question right now.

'I don't know.' Adam hesitated. 'I can't see his head.'

It was a hell of a drop down to the sea, she thought. A good eighty metres or so. Luckily, Samantha had no particular fear of heights. She had done a bit of mountaineering a few years back, in preparation for a film role, and she was well used to vertical drops like this. The beach was a thin sliver at the bottom, barely a beach at all, just a few pebbles close to the base of the cliff, with the sea bashing away at them. And there, sprawled out across the rocks, was a dark, broken figure. Samantha shivered again. She could make out the arms and the legs – even without the binoculars, her eyesight was pretty good – but the head was obscured from view and there was no way to tell who it might be. She tapped Adam on the shoulder and he handed her the lenses. She secured the loop around her neck and then brought the binoculars up to her face. Adam had already adjusted the focus and it took only a couple of seconds for her to locate the body. Trousers and a heavy black coat, wet through. Samantha swallowed hard. That looked like John Menhenick's coat. *Oh, please God, don't let it be him,* she thought.

Adam had got to his feet and moved back to the compound wall, where Nadia was hovering anxiously.

Samantha kept her focus on the beach. How long had the body been down there? she wondered. Everyone had been at lunch, so if it really was one of them, they must have fallen in the last two or three hours. The body was almost certainly that of a man. *Please God, don't let it to be John,* she thought again.

Nadia and Adam were discussing the matter over by the wall, though the wind cut across their voices and Samantha could only make out the odd muffled word. She let the binoculars drop and pulled back from the edge. The knees of her trousers were green with grass and mud as she lifted herself up.

'The door was open,' Nadia was saying as she moved back to them. 'What if there's someone else on the island?'

Adam scratched his head. 'The body can't have been down

there more than a few hours. Otherwise the tide would have washed it away.'

'What door?' Samantha asked, brushing some of the grass from her knees.

'The door to the cottage,' Adam explained. 'It was unlocked when we arrived here yesterday afternoon. Jim Peterson, the guy who owns the place, he swore he locked it when he was out here earlier this week. Nadia thinks there might be someone else on the island.'

'And you think *they* might have fallen down there?'

Adam shrugged. 'We don't know.'

'I hope so,' Nadia said. 'It surely can't be one of us. Nobody would be that stupid, jumping around on a cliff edge.'

Samantha was not so sure. She gazed up at the tower looming above them. 'And you say the door to the lighthouse was open as well? So you think whoever it was might have fallen from up there?'

Adam didn't think so. 'You'd have to jump out a fair way to get past the cliffs. And you can see the handrail up top, surrounding the lamp room. That should prevent any accidents.' He bit his lip. 'But it's not impossible, I suppose.'

'Surely we'd have seen an intruder,' Nadia thought. 'The compound isn't that big. And how would they have got out here to the island in the first place without anybody noticing?'

'Well, that's the question. Look, first things first,' Adam said. 'We need to find out if everyone is okay.' It was not for nothing that Adam was considered the father of the group. 'We have to make sure none of us are missing.'

'We'll need to phone the mainland too,' Samantha suggested. 'And call the police.'

'Agreed. Nadia, can you get the satellite phone? It's in the kitchen upstairs.'

'Yes, of course.'

'Dial 999. Tell them what's happened. And do a head count too. Everyone should be upstairs by now, for the cabaret.' It was almost four o'clock. 'See if anyone's missing.'

Nadia shuddered. 'Let's hope not, eh?' She moved back

into the compound.

Samantha watched her go. 'How long do you think it will take for them to get out here?' she asked Adam.

'I don't know. An hour or two maybe. Less, if they come by helicopter. We're lucky it's the middle of summer. They'll have plenty of time to recover the body before it gets dark.'

Samantha was not so sure about that. 'I think the tide may be coming in. Adam, he could be washed away before anyone gets here. Did you...did you see the coat?' Adam nodded grimly. 'It might be John.'

'Yes, that thought had occurred to me.'

'He might have come out for a cigarette and lost his footing.'

'Well, somebody certainly lost their footing,' Adam agreed sadly.

Nadia's mind was in such a whirl as she made her way back into the cottage that she almost collided with Jill Clarke a second time. The red-haired woman was heading for the stairs, having returned to her room briefly to pick up her costume. She stopped on the bottom step as Nadia pulled up. 'Everything all right, babes? You look like you've seen a ghost.'

'You might not be far wrong,' Nadia said. 'Is everyone upstairs?'

'Yeah, I think so. I heard Suzy and Liam go up.' Jill dropped her eyes briefly. 'And I think Adam's up there as well. We're going to be starting in a couple of minutes.' She began to climb the stairs.

'I think there might be a slight delay,' Nadia said, grabbing the railings and following her up.

Jill didn't seem to hear. She reached the top of the stairs and passed through the hallway into the dining room, intent on stowing her costume.

Nadia arced right, into the kitchen. Liam Heigl was grabbing a beer from the fridge. He frowned at the sight of her. 'Nadia? Is everything all right?'

'No. No, it isn't.' She glanced back at the hall. 'There's been an accident. We think someone's fallen off the cliff.'

Liam blanched. 'Someone? Who do you mean, someone?'

'We don't know.' Nadia scanned the work surfaces and pulled open a couple of drawers. 'Where's the phone?'

Liam reached down to his pocket. 'You want a phone?'

'No, not a mobile. The satellite phone. Adam said it was in here.'

He shrugged. 'I haven't seen it. Somebody's fallen, you say?' It was taking a moment for his brain to properly register what Nadia was saying. 'What, are they injured? A broken leg or something?'

'Not injured. Somebody's been killed.' She met his eye then, unable to hide her distress. 'Have you seen John anywhere?'

'No, not...' Liam hesitated. 'Not since lunch time, anyway.' He hadn't joined them at the card table afterwards.

Nadia opened another cupboard, then growled and threw up her hands in despair. 'Where's the bloody phone?' She moved out of the kitchen.

'Is everything all right?' Suzy Heigl asked, observing her with some concern as she moved into the dining room. Suzy was sitting on one of the chairs that had been set out in the middle of the room.

'You haven't seen the satellite phone, have you? I can't find it in the kitchen.'

Suzy shook her head. 'I didn't know there was one. Nadia, what's going on?'

'I think it's John,' she replied grimly, recalling the heavy black coat she had seen at the base of the cliff. 'I think he's dead.'

It had never occurred to Samantha Redmond that anything like this might happen. Oh, she had been a little apprehensive about the reunion, to be sure, but it had never crossed her mind that anyone might die. The group were in good health, after all, and still relatively young. And they were in Scotland, not the wilds of Antarctica. It should have been a fun, relaxed gathering; a chance to catch up with old friends. At worst, somebody might have got drunk and banged their heads. But dying? Nobody had expected that. Nobody had prepared for it. And now they were stuck here, miles from anywhere, and help would not be immediately forthcoming.

Adam crawled up next to her. 'The sea looks pretty rough,' he observed, as the waves crashed against the pebble beach below.

It did look pretty grim. 'Who do you think they'll send?' Samantha wondered. 'The coast guard? Or the police?' The sooner the authorities arrived and took charge, the better for everyone.

'I don't know,' Adam admitted. 'One or other. But you're right about that sea. I'm not sure they're going to get here in time.'

That thought troubled Samantha greatly. 'If he's washed away, we might never recover the body. Adam, we can't let that happen. Not if it is John. Or whoever it is.'

Adam dropped the binoculars. 'I'm not sure there's anything we can do to prevent it. We can't climb down a sheer rock face.'

Samantha had already taken a good look at the terrain. 'There might be one way. Did you see those steps over there?'

Adam shot her a puzzled look. 'Steps?'

Samantha pointed along the line of the rock to the east. 'Just over there. There's a set of them, do you see? Right the way down the cliff.'

Adam squinted, following her direction. 'Are those *steps*?' He peered blankly across. There were a few indentations in the rock but they could barely be described as steps.

'They're quite rough,' Samantha admitted. 'It's not a good angle to see them from. But they're definitely steps of some kind.' She had taken a close look earlier on through the binoculars. 'They're a lot cruder than the ones running up from the landing stage, but they do go all the way down to the beach.'

Adam lifted the binoculars and quickly focused them. 'They look more like a....well, a sort of ladder.' The descent was practically vertical. 'And some of them are pretty thoroughly worn away.'

'They're probably decades old,' Samantha said. 'It may have been a short cut for some of the workers, when the lighthouse was being built.'

'Well, it's certainly not for paying guests. It looks absolutely lethal. I don't think any of us could get down that way.'

I probably could, Samantha thought, *if it came to it*. But she kept that thought to herself.

There were voices coming from behind. She turned her head and saw Nadia Kumar moving through the gap in the compound wall. The rest of the group were following closely behind her.

Adam pulled himself up to greet them.

Liam Heigl's boyish face was cracked with concern. 'Nadia says there's been an accident.' Suzy Heigl was clutching his arm in bewilderment.

Jill Clarke, appearing behind them, looked utterly devastated. 'Is it...is it really John?' she breathed, her hands clasped together fearfully. Tears were already flowing down her narrow face. Despite the divorce and the events of that morning, Jill still had a great deal of affection for her ex-husband.

Adam moved across to her. 'We think so. I'm so sorry.'

Jill let out a strangled sob. 'Oh, my baby! My poor baby!'

'Hey, hey. It's all right,' he breathed, quickly embracing her. Jill was shuddering now. He patted her gently on the back, trying to calm her. 'It would have been quick, if it is him. He wouldn't have felt anything.'

Suzy, standing to their right, was too shocked even to cry. Her husband was looking distressed too. None of them wanted this.

'I loved him,' Jill sobbed, her shoulders shuddering awkwardly in Adam's embrace. 'The miserable bastard. I loved him so much. No matter what he did.'

'I know you did,' Adam cooed gently.

Nadia was hovering awkwardly behind them.

'Did you get through to the mainland?' Samantha asked her.

'No. I couldn't find the phone. I've looked all over the place.'

Adam pulled back and cast her a perplexed look. 'You couldn't *find* it?'

'Not in the kitchen. Or the living room.'

Liam could not see the problem. 'Why can't we use our own phones?'

'There's no connection out here,' Adam explained.

'There's wi-fi in the house. Or some sort of network, anyway,' Liam said. 'I'm sure there is.'

'Not here,' Adam insisted. 'We're off the grid. We're too far away from Lewis. That's why we need the satellite phone. There isn't a relay point for mobiles.'

Liam frowned. 'I was sure I saw something.' He dropped his arm from Suzy's waist and dug into his pocket. Suzy moved across to comfort Jill, while Liam retrieved his phone and tapped gently on the screen. 'Yes, there, look, you see?' He held the device up, displaying a set of bright connection bars. 'There's a network in the house. It's password protected, though.'

Adam and Nadia exchanged a look. 'But Mr Peterson said...'

'It must be a local network,' Adam concluded. 'Connecting up the TV or something like that.' He shrugged, dismissing the peculiarity. 'Whatever it is, it's no use to us. Even if we had the password. It can't be connected to the internet.'

Samantha was more concerned about the disappearance of the satellite phone. If they couldn't contact the police then they were in real trouble. 'That phone must be in the house somewhere.'

'I had a pretty good look,' Nadia said. 'Are you sure it was in the kitchen?'

'It was there when I was cooking breakfast this morning,' Adam said.

'I'll have another look.'

'What if we don't find it?' Samantha asked. She gestured

to the cliff edge. 'We can't leave John down there. If the police aren't out here in the next hour or so, it may be too late.'

Liam peered across. 'Is he right at the bottom? Of the cliff, I mean?'

Adam confirmed that with a nod.

'We're going to have to do something ourselves,' Samantha suggested. 'We can't leave him down there.'

'But what can *we* do?' Liam scratched his chin. 'There's no way we can get down there, is there?'

'There *is* a set of steps hacked into the rock over there,' Adam said, gesturing eastward. 'But they're practically vertical. And half of them look to have been worn away. I don't think anyone....'

'I could get down there,' Samantha asserted quietly.

Adam did not attempt hide his surprise. '*You* could?'

She nodded firmly. 'I've done a fair amount of rock climbing. I did six weeks training in Namibia once, for a movie.'

'Yes, but...'

'You mean the free climb sequence?' Liam asked. 'In *Moonlit Dawn 3*?' Samantha gave a nod. 'I remember seeing that.' He grinned. 'I thought it was a stunt double. You really did that yourself?'

'Pretty much,' Samantha admitted. 'It wasn't actually a free climb. I was in a harness. They painted all the wires out afterwards. But yes, I was hanging on my own halfway up the mountainside.'

'That must have been a few years ago, though,' Adam pointed out, diplomatically.

'About four or five, I think. But I've done a bit of climbing since then. I got the bug for it.' The previous summer, she had gone mountaineering in Italy. It had been all over the papers. She'd wanted a bit of peace and quiet, up in the mountains, but somebody had hired a helicopter and taken lots of snaps.

'Even so...' Adam said. 'Samantha, there are no wires here. And it has to be an eighty metre drop. It's too dangerous. You might get yourself killed. And that won't help anyone.'

'And even if you did get down there,' Nadia said, 'how would you get him back up here? John, I mean. You wouldn't be able to carry him.'

That was true enough, Samantha thought. 'I might be able to find a way to secure him, though, to stop him being washed away. Until we find that phone and get the police out here. We can't just leave him down there.'

'I don't think we have a choice,' Adam said.

'Hey, there might be a bit of rope in the lighthouse somewhere,' Nadia thought.

'Not long enough for this. We'd need...' Adam stopped, a new idea flickering across his face. 'Hang on a minute. Nadia, you remember when we arrived? Mr Peterson gave us a quick tour. Didn't he say there was a winch in one of the storehouses?'

'Yes, that's right.' The woman nodded. 'For the railway. It's not attached to anything, though. Not any more. But there is a wire cable in there.'

That got Samantha's attention. 'A cable? How long is it?'

'I don't know,' Nadia said. 'But it must be fairly long. The old railway runs all the way down to the landing stage. It must be several hundred metres.'

Samantha looked back to Adam. 'What if we used that? I could take it with me, as a safety line. We could let it out a bit at a time. And if we could find a bit of rope as well, then we might be able to tie the end of it to an arm or a leg. At the very least, we'd be able to stop the body being washed away.'

Jill Clarke let out a sob at the unfortunate choice of words.

Adam took a moment to consider. 'We'd have to unwind the cable by hand. That's the winch room there.' He pointed to a small outhouse nestling in the near corner of the compound. 'We'd have to run it out the back window. It wasn't intended to play out in this direction. And there'll be no give in it. It's not like a bungee cord. It's metal. If you slip, it could slice your neck off.'

'I'm sure I can handle it,' Samantha said. 'We can't leave John down there, at the mercy of the elements. He's our friend, Adam. He deserves a decent burial.'

Jill wiped her eyes and nodded emphatically.

Suzy Heigl had been following the debate carefully. 'Poor John,' she breathed. 'I can't believe he's really dead.'

'Who's dead?' a rough voice called out from behind them.

Samantha started in surprise as a dark figure popped up between the stone walls of the compound; a bald man in a heavy winter coat. 'What are you all doing out here?' John Menhenick said. 'I thought we were going to put on a show?'

Jill let out a gasp of astonishment. 'John!' It took her another moment to fully take the man in, and then there was no holding her back. She rushed across and took him in her arms. 'Oh baby! Oh, my baby!'

John Menhenick struggled to free himself. 'Get off me! What the bloody hell are you doing, woman?' He quickly disentangled himself, only to find the rest of the group staring at him in shock. 'What? What is it? What's going on?'

'There's a body at the bottom of the cliff,' Adam said. 'We thought it was you.'

John scratched the top of his head. 'Why would I be at the bottom of a cliff?'

'We thought you'd fallen.'

'Don't be daft.'

Liam Heigl looked from John to the cliff edge. 'But if it's not him...' he said.

Samantha's heart skipped a beat. She scanned the small group of friends. If it wasn't John then there was only one other person it could be.

It was her turn to let out a cry.

'Where's Twinkle?' she said.

Chapter Five

The winch room was situated on the near side of the lighthouse. It was a damp and musty place, with cobwebs filling the cracks and corners. John Menhenick pushed open the door and stepped inside. Suzy Heigl was not far behind. John was surprised the blonde girl had volunteered to help out. She hated creepy crawlies. 'Watch yourself, princess,' he said, stepping across the uneven floor. 'There's some broken glass down there.' Suzy followed him in through the low doorway.

There wasn't much in the way of useful equipment in here – most of it must have been cleared out a long time ago – but the winch itself was still in position, an enormous metal drum laced around with wire, like cotton on a reel.

'I don't think anyone's been in here for decades,' John grunted. 'Blimey, what a dump.' There was a small window on the far wall, which was too grimy to let in much more than a token light. The frame looked rather solid too. 'I don't reckon we'll get that open. We're probably going to have to smash the window if we want to get a line out.' That would be fun, he thought. They had already had to jemmy the lock on the door. 'Always assuming we can unwind it.' The plan was a pretty dubious one. Clambering down the side of a cliff. What was the point of that? It would be different if Twinkle was still alive, but going down there just to recover the body was a complete waste of time. 'She's a mad bitch, that Samantha. She'll break her bloody neck.'

He glanced back at the doorway. Suzy was staring quietly across at him. She was still in a state of shock. That was hardly a surprise. It had been a bit of a shock for him too, finding out everyone thought he was was dead. Blimey, what a stupid mistake to make. And the look on their faces, when he had popped up suddenly, alive and well. He wished he had taken a photo. It was a classic. But then the realisation had dawned on everyone: it was Twinkle who had really died.

Suzy was still reeling from the confusion. 'I really did

think you were dead,' she whispered.

John tried his best to make a joke of it. 'I'm surprised people weren't breaking out the champagne.'

'It was the coat that did it,' Suzy explained, her voice wavering as she gestured to the chunky black jacket he was wearing. 'Nadia said it was yours. We didn't know Twinkle had a similar one.'

'Yeah, same make,' John said, looking down at it. 'No, you wouldn't have done. He didn't wear it on the way out.' On the boat, Twinkle had made do with a sweater and a woolly hat. 'You wouldn't think it to look at him, but he could be quite vain. Didn't want to turn up wearing the same jacket as me. The daft pillock.'

Suzy closed her eyes. 'I can't believe he's gone.'

John could not believe it either. Twinkle had been alive and well the last time he had seen him. 'It's daft, ain't it? He was fine when I spoke to him after lunch. Well, in good health, anyway.' He grimaced, thinking back over that last conversation. 'He must have slipped or something. Afterwards, I mean. He was a clumsy bastard at the best of times.'

Suzy acknowledged the truth of that with a nod.

It didn't help that the two men had argued. John had been talking to him, out there on the cliff top. *Bloody hell*, he realised, *I was probably the last person to see him alive.* That had been a couple of hours ago now. Perhaps that argument had contributed to his fall. *Not paying attention to what he was doing.* But John refused to feel guilty about that. *It was his own bloody fault.* And now they had a dead body on their hands. *Christ.* There would have to be an inquest. The police would be all over the place. *That's all we bloody need.* A perfect end to a perfect weekend.

Suzy looked up. 'So you were over at the chapel, rehearsing? When Nadia found him?'

'Yeah.' That was what he had told the others, anyway. 'Had to find somewhere quiet, didn't I?' There were a couple of steps on the far side of the chapel, out of sight of the compound. He had settled down there and had a smoke, while he got a few things organised. 'It's all your fault,' he joked. 'You insisted I had to do something for the cabaret. I was trying to remember that monologue I did at our graduation do. You remember?' John had played a thief, pleading to a judge to be let off. Talk about type casting. 'I needed somewhere quiet to run through it all. See if I could drag the lines out of my head. Then I had a bit of a wander down south.' Away from prying eyes.

Suzy nodded, accepting the explanation.

'So were you really upset then?' John gazed at her slyly. 'To think I might be dead?'

'Yes, all right.' A twinge of humour resurfaced in her eyes. 'I admit it. And Jill too. She still holds quite a torch for you. Can't think why!'

'We were married for a long time.' John crouched down by the winch and tugged at the metal cord, searching for the end piece. 'Samantha must have a screw loose, if she thinks we can lower her down there using this.' The cord was tightly wound around the drum. Originally, there would have been an engine to wind and unwind it, but that had long since been stripped away. 'It's never going to work.'

Suzy was more optimistic. 'I think she knows what she's doing. I certainly wouldn't want to try it. But she's right, John. We can't leave Twinkle down there. He'll be washed away in a couple of hours.'

Samantha Redmond had been pretty shell-shocked when she'd realised it was Twinkle at the bottom of the cliff, rather than John. The two of them had always been good mates.

Suzy was gazing at her feet. 'I was talking to him last night. Twinkle. Before dinner. He said...he said he was trying his hand at a bit of internet dating. He'd met a girl online that he quite liked. They were going to meet up for a meal in a week or two. He had hopes something might come of it.' She was starting to cry now. 'It's horrible. So horrible to think he just slipped...'

John moved back from the winch and took the girl in his arms. Suzy was right. It was difficult to believe he was gone. Twinkle could be a right pain in the arse sometimes – and this weekend more than ever – but John would never have wished him dead. 'It's all right, princess. It would have been quick.' He held her tightly for a moment. *If only the stupid idiot...*

Liam Heigl popped up at the far window, the proverbial bad penny. He saw the two of them together and tapped on the glass.

John maintained his grip but raised a hand to the husband. 'She's upset,' he called out, by way of explanation.

The other man nodded grimly. 'We all are,' he said.

Samantha Redmond did not want to think about what she would find when she reached the bottom of the cliff. Instead, she was doing her best to remember everything her instructor had told her. *One step at a time,* he had said. *Concentrate on the feet and the hands.* It was good to have something simple to think about. *Always keep one hand secured and take it as slowly as you can.* The metal cable was proving to be a significant handicap, though. It ended in a thick metal hook which she had attached to the belt at her waist, but it would be no use at all if she slipped. In all likelihood, the belt would simply snap. *Just keep calm,* she thought. *Deep breathes. There's no hurry.* She had a length of rope with her as well, wrapped around her body, and that was even more of an encumbrance.

Anxious faces were observing her every move from the top of the cliff. John Menhenick, of course, had treated the whole thing like a game. She had been shocked at his cavalier attitude. He had wanted to video her descent on his phone but Adam had put his foot down. 'You're mad,' the bald man protested. 'We've got a Hollywood star descending a cliff face on an errand of mercy and you don't want to take any photographs? We could make a fortune with these.'

'We're not taking photos,' Adam insisted, through gritted teeth. John was banished to the compound wall, where the steel wire was trailing out from the winch room. Liam was on the other side of the window, with Suzy, letting out the cable a bit at a time. The wire was wrapped around another heavy steel drum they had manoeuvred out onto the grass from one of the ancillary storerooms. Everyone was wearing gloves now, of varying provenance. Samantha's were thick and robust but Liam – who had to help feed out the cable – was sheathed in barely more than a pair of mittens. Adam Cartwright lay at the cliff face with Nadia, looking down at the steps and anxiously shouting out instructions to the others, directing the gradual release of the cable.

We make a good team, Samantha thought, glancing up at them. *Even after all these years.*

She had managed to convince them that the wire was an effective safety line, but she suspected Adam knew the truth: it was no help at all. She had almost lost her nerve when she arrived at the top of the steps; not because of the height but because of the degree of risk involved. Samantha would have no backup if she made a mistake. She remembered the horror stories her instructor had told her about people who had not prepared properly for a climb and had died as a result. Luckily, the steps had proved to be in a slightly better state of repair than they had appeared from the side. Each was barely a few inches across, however, and the angle of descent was alarming.

Keep calm, she told herself again, *and focus on the moment.* Fortunately there was almost no wind, the cliff face serving as an effective break. *Take your time. Better to be safe than sorry.* And, with these thoughts occupying her mind, she inched herself slowly downwards. A bit of spray hit her back, telling her she did not have much further to go. Unfortunately, the steps here were rather more slippery than the ones higher up. She would have to take special care. Finally, after several more minutes of careful exertion, Samantha reached the bottom step and placed a foot on the pebble beach.

It was narrow, not more than three metres across with the tide as it was at the moment, but stretching a good ten to fifteen metres along the base of the cliff. Even here the terrain was not even and she would have to scramble over some nasty looking rocks, with the spray drenching her clothes all the while. She unclipped the wire from her belt, shivering in the cold and the wet, and gestured upwards for Nadia and Adam to let out a bit more cord. She stepped away from it as the metal wire wobbled and the hook finally touched the ground. She motioned a stop and, after the inevitable four second delay, the wire was left dangling and still.

Derek Fonteyn's body was lying a few metres from the steps, sprawled out across the pebbles. His clothes were saturated, his black coat torn and wet through. A dark woolly hat covered the top of his head. That and the angle of the body had made it difficult to identify him clearly from the top of the cliff. But, moving in now, Samantha could see that it really was Twinkle. She fought down the lump in her throat. A small part of her had hoped, somehow, that they might be mistaken; that some other person might have met their end this way. But as soon as John Menhenick had appeared behind them outside the compound, she knew it had to be him; and her resolve to come down here and recover the body had only strengthened. Adam had realised he could do nothing to dissuade her, and had set about helping her as best he could.

Samantha made her way across the jagged rocks towards the body. She stopped a few feet away from him, looking down at his plump torso and the grotesquely twisted limbs. She shuddered. Samantha had known Twinkle forever. Even when they were continents apart, they had messaged each other regularly. Not a week would go by without some exchange or another. She had been planning to invite him over to LA for a holiday next year. But it was too late for that now. She would never see that sad smile again. She closed her eyes briefly and then steeled herself for the task ahead.

First things first. She unhooped the rope she was carrying and placed it down on the rocks next to him. Small pools of water were already beginning to form around his lifeless body. The waves were crashing in, not violently but with some persistence. Another half hour and he would be loosened from his position and swept away. Samantha was not going to let that happen.

It was going to be an awkward job, though, lifting a literal dead weight all the way up the side of a cliff. There was no elegant way to do it. The rope would be wound around Twinkle's body and then attached to the far end of the cable, which would be used to haul him up. The others would take care of the hard work and Samantha would stay down here to watch. In principle, a bit of reverse abseiling might not have been a bad idea, but not with this equipment. The winch was designed to drag a cart up a hill, not to lift a human being; and, besides, she did not want to add to the weight. Samantha would have to make her own way back up the cliff, this time without even the pretence of a safety line.

She looked down sadly at the body of Derek Fonteyn as she started to attach the rope. *Let's get you home*, she thought.

Nadia Kumar had some difficulty grasping the arm as the body drew near the top of the cliff. She was already struggling to contain her revulsion. This was Twinkle they were dealing with, not some random lump of plastic, being inched slowly towards them. The vertical cliff face and the eighty metre drop did not help matters. Nadia tried not to think about how close she was to the edge. She kept her eyes focused on the shoulder and tried to hook her arm underneath it as he reached the top. Adam had already grabbed the other arm. The wire cable was no use to them at this point. The body had to be lifted manually the last couple of feet onto the grass. The call had gone out to stop winching and Jill Clarke was on hand to keep the cable steady as they hauled Twinkle back onto dry land. With some effort, Nadia and Adam managed to get the top half of his body over the lip of the cliff and onto the grass. Then they shuffled back on their knees and pulled the rest of him over the top. Adam unclipped the end of the wire.

Nadia took a moment to catch her breath and then shuddered as she finally took in the battered face of her old friend. There was no blood – that had all been washed away – but Twinkle's puffy face was broken and twisted, and there was something unnatural about the angle of his head as it flopped down onto the grassy bank. Jill saw that too. She let go of the cable and turned away, clutching her stomach and retching all over the grass. Nadia, who was struggling to contain the bile in her own throat, knew exactly how she felt.

Adam had taken off his jacket and gloves. Once the body was secured a safe distance from the edge of the cliff, he draped the coat over Twinkle's head. It was the best any of them could do in the circumstances.

Jill was wiping the spittle from her mouth. She replaced her glasses with some embarrassment. 'Oh, babes, what a day!' she lamented.

Nadia nodded sympathetically. And it wasn't over yet. Samantha still had to return safely. She was a real dare-devil, that girl, on the quiet. Nadia could not help but admire her nerve. *I certainly wouldn't have had the guts to do it.* It was one thing, abseiling down the side of a cliff for fun, with proper equipment. But to do it like that, without any back up. Samantha must have nerves of steel.

The actress had remained on the beach while they finished hauling Twinkle up. It was sensible for her to wait down there, even with the tide creeping in. Better to concentrate on one thing at a time. Now the body had been recovered, they could keep a proper eye on her as she clambered back up the steps. Not that they could do anything if she got into trouble; but Samantha seemed to know what she was doing.

Liam helped Adam to lift up Twinkle's body and carry it through to the compound. Nadia remained where she was. She would stay out here for the time being to keep an eye on Samantha. Jill was happy to keep her company. It was difficult to know who was providing moral support for whom. The two women shuffled over to the top of the steps and laid themselves out quietly on the grass. It was rare for Jill to be less than animated, but for once, like Nadia, she was lost in her own thoughts.

The sight of Twinkle's body had upset them both. In life, he had had such a warm, kind face, for all its unfortunate lopsidedness. He had been a lovely guy, the last person anyone would have wanted to die. Ida Fonteyn, his mother, would be devastated when she found out. What had he been doing out here, Nadia wondered, so close to the edge? Just admiring the view? It would be like him, she supposed. A quiet moment alone, contemplating infinity. And then a misplaced foot and perhaps a sudden gust of wind. Nadia shuddered. It would have to be something like that.

Her thoughts wandered back to the lighthouse, where she had recently grabbed the rope. It was odd that the door should be open like that. And the front door on Friday afternoon. Probably neither of them had been locked up properly. But now the satellite phone had gone walkabouts too. Their only link with the outside world. It was all very odd. Adam was worried too, she could tell. He was hiding it from the others, but they both had a sense that something was not quite right here. It wouldn't have been so bad if they were able to contact the mainland. The police would sort everything out. But without that satellite phone they couldn't summon anybody at all. And Mr Peterson wasn't due back until Monday morning, the day after tomorrow.

Jill was observing her quietly. 'You all right, babes?'

'Yes. Just thinking.' She turned to face her friend. Jill had had a hell of a day too. 'How are *you* doing?'

'Bit shaky.' The woman attempted a grin. 'God, what an afternoon. What are we going to do, eh?'

'I don't know. We're going to have to find that phone, somehow. When Samantha gets back. It's bound to be in the cottage somewhere. We can't wait until Monday morning to pass on the news.'

'We'll find a way, babes.'

Samantha was within earshot of them now. Nadia gave her a wave, but the intrepid movie star was concentrating too much on the task at hand to notice anything going on above her. As she grew close to the top step, Nadia rose to her feet, crouched down and held out a gloved hand. Samantha looked up then, as she clambered onto the grass verge and took a moment to catch her breath.

'You did a good job there, babes,' Jill said, with a smile.

Samantha shrugged. Her cheeks were flushed and her face was grim. 'I didn't really have much choice.' She brushed down her trousers, which were wet through. 'Did you have any trouble, getting him up?'

'No, no trouble,' Nadia said. 'The boys have taken him inside. I think we should probably go in as well.' She pulled her scarf tightly around her neck. The cold had penetrated right through to her bones. 'I think I've had enough of cliffs for one day.'

Samantha glanced briefly back down the steps. 'Yes. You and me both.' She lifted her hands to examine her top and grimaced at all the dirt. 'I'm going to need a long, hot shower.'

Jill Clarke was already heading back to the compound. Nadia was about to follow her, but Samantha gestured for her to wait a moment.

'What is it?'

'I...er...I found something else, while I was down there,' Samantha said.

'You found something?'

'Yes.' She hesitated and reached into her pocket. Nadia watched as she pulled out a small bit of plastic, a set of numbers on a key pad.

Nadia peered at it curiously. It looked like part of a mobile phone. 'Is that the satellite phone?' she asked, incredulously.

'I think it must be. It was smashed to pieces, I'm afraid. The bits were scattered across the rocks, not far from...from where I found Twinkle.' She regarded Nadia sadly for a moment. 'I think he must have been trying to phone someone when he fell.'

There was a long queue for the shower, but Samantha was given first dibs, after all her hard work. Her mind was racing as the hot water flowed over her. She had kept her cool up and down the cliff side but her hands were shaking now as the reality of the situation began to bed in. *Twinkle, of all people.* The most inoffensive man in the world. Adam and Liam had laid him out respectfully on the floor in the spare room. The body was still too wet to lay him on top of the bed. Suzy Heigl had grabbed a couple of sheets to cover him over with and had put a pillow under his head. It had seemed appropriate, somehow. No-one had any idea who Twinkle had been trying to call when he had slipped, but with no mobile signal it was hardly surprising he had resorted to using the satellite phone. And now he was dead; a tragic and pointless accident.

Samantha flicked off the tap, stepped out of the shower and grabbed her towel from the rail. The bathroom was awash with brightly coloured towels – a pink one for Suzy; a green and white one for Jill. She grimaced, catching sight of Twinkle's dark brown towel hanging forlornly between them. Despair bubbled up in her throat and she struggled to contain herself as she worked to dry herself off.

Adam had taken control of the situation, as always. The reliable pair of hands. But even he could not stop the group from fretting about what would happen next. They couldn't call the police. They couldn't raise the alarm. It would be days before anyone got out here. Samantha felt a little more sanguine about that than some of the others. Twinkle's body had been recovered now, so it didn't matter that much if they had to wait for help. There was plenty of food and drink to tide them over. In some ways, the delay was a blessing. It would take them some time to come to terms with what had happened. Better to do it in private, while they still could. As soon as the authorities arrived, there would be no peace for any of them. The media would descend en masse. There would be helicopters and journalists of every description swarming across the island. And the whole focus would be on her. Never mind Twinkle; he would barely get a mention. It would all be about Samantha Redmond. And that was not fair. Twinkle did not deserve to have his death turned into a circus.

She wrapped herself up and unlocked the bathroom door. Suzy was waiting patiently outside on the sofa, the next in line for the shower. The two women exchanged nods but said nothing as Samantha moved across to the far room.

Jill Clarke was lying on her bed on the other side of the door, flicking distractedly through a magazine. 'All right, babes?' she mumbled, looking up.

'I'm fine,' Samantha said, though she didn't really feel it. She sat down on her own bed and regarded her room mate sadly. 'How are *you* managing?'

Jill eye's were still red from where she had been crying. 'I don't know.' She flipped the magazine closed. 'It makes you think, don't it? When someone dies. How short life is.' She swung her legs over the side of the bed and sat up for a minute. 'All the mistakes you've made. How quick it can all be over.'

'I know.' Samantha was struggling to hold back her own tears. 'At least he was here with his friends. He had a good evening last night. He was looking forward to...' She trailed off. It all sounded far too lame. 'It was just so pointless,' she gulped at last, unable to stop the tears from flowing. 'He was so kind, so sweet. Such a loyal friend to me.'

Jill came over and sat down next to her, putting an arm around her shoulder. 'He loved you, you know. He was devoted to you, babes.'

'I know. I often thought...' Samantha sighed, raising a hand to wipe her eyes. 'He would have made someone a good husband. But it's too late now.'

They sat in silence for a moment.

'What are we going to do, babes?' Jill asked at last.

'There's nothing we can do. Just sit tight and wait until Monday. It'll be all right,' she asserted, half-heartedly. She squeezed Jill's hand and the other woman smiled. 'Anyway, I'd better get dressed.' Samantha rose to her feet and wiped her eyes again. Jill got up and returned to her magazine.

Samantha pulled some underwear from a drawer and slipped into it, discarding her towel and moving across to the wardrobe. She pulled out a fresh pair of trousers and a jumper. Something dry at last. As she closed the wardrobe door, she caught a brief glimpse of herself in the mirror. 'Goodness, I look a sight.' Her eyes were red and puffy now, just like Jill's.

Her room mate disagreed. 'You look gorgeous, babes. You always did. You could pass for twenty-five.'

'I wish.'

Jill was insistent. 'You've aged better than anyone. No

wonder you're all over the papers. And the gossip mags.' She tapped the magazine she was reading.

Samantha pulled a face. 'I don't know why you read that stuff. Not a word of it is true.'

'I know. Load of old rubbish. But it's fun to read.'

Samantha zipped up her trousers and then pulled her neck through the head of the jumper. 'I suppose so.' She glanced at the mirror again. The wardrobe behind it was a basic affair with a crude decorative twirl at the top. She looked up momentarily and something odd caught her eye. A small black object was peeping out from behind the decoration. 'What's that?' she wondered, craning her head up as best she could.

Jill glanced across at her. 'What's what?'

'I don't know.' Samantha lifted herself on tiptoes to take a better look. It seemed to be some sort of reflective material. 'I'm not sure.' She grabbed a small chair from over by the window.

Jill chuckled. 'Babes, you've done enough climbing today.'

Samantha was already clambering onto the chair. There was not much dust on top of the wardrobe. Like most of the fixtures and fittings, it was almost brand new. A small black hemisphere nestled silently behind the decorative frontage, peeping unobtrusively through a gap in the design. Whatever it was, the tiny object did not seem to be attached to anything. Samantha picked it up and held it in her hand for a moment.

'What is it?' Jill asked.

Samantha peered at the thing closely. It had a small circular lens on the front, taking up most of the space. It looked rather like... 'I think it's a webcam,' she concluded, with some surprise. 'A miniature camera.' She glanced back at Jill, who was staring up at her from the bed. 'I think someone's been filming us,' she said.

Chapter Six

Liam Heigl was absolutely hopeless when it came to peeling spuds. Nadia watched with some amusement as he managed to lose half a potato amid the first peel. 'Here, like this,' she said. 'Just gently scrape the edges.' The man's mind was clearly on other things, and she could not blame him for that. They were all in a state of shock. It had been an awful day and nothing was going to change that. But Nadia would take a leaf from Adam's book and try to stay positive; keeping people's minds occupied and away from the events of that afternoon. That's what friends were for, after all. 'So is it true you were going to strip off for the cabaret?' she asked him, with an impish grin. If that question didn't distract him, nothing would.

Liam smiled self-consciously. 'Yes, I was. It was Suzy's idea.'

'What, the full Monty?' Nadia's eyes sparkled, looking up at him. He was a good head taller than she was and had a handsome, puppy-like face.

'No, just down to my boxers. I don't think anyone would want to see more than that.'

Nadia flicked her eyes downwards theatrically. 'Ooh, I don't know. I think Jill might have appreciated it.'

She was expecting him to laugh at that, but instead Liam grimaced. 'Yes, I suppose so.' He gazed at the potato in his hand and scraped the peeler roughly along the edge. 'Like this?'

'Yes, that's better,' Nadia said. 'Hey, what's happened to your hands?' Now that she looked closely, she could see his fingers were a little ragged.

'That cable earlier on. I should have got some thicker gloves. How many of these should we do?'

'About thirty, I reckon.' One spud down, twenty-nine to go.

It was Adam who had suggested preparing an early dinner. He and John Menhenick were hard at work poking around in the basement of the lighthouse, to see if there might be a radio in there or a second satellite phone. A bit of cooked food would do them all the world of good, he said. Nadia had been pleasantly surprised when Liam had volunteered to help out. She hadn't envisaged him ever mucking in in the kitchen. He had always struck her as more of a changing-plugs type of guy; but Suzy had assured her he was thoroughly domesticated. Not that Nadia was much of a whiz in the kitchen either. In Dubai, they employed a cook to take care of that sort of thing. But Nadia did like to dabble on occasion and Richard was always appreciative of her efforts. *I wish he was here*, she thought. Her husband knew how to keep everybody focused. He was a fair few years older than her and was the most level headed man she had ever met. Adam was doing his best but Nadia could see the strain under the surface. He liked everything to run smoothly and when it didn't he could become agitated very quickly. She grinned, remembering that student film they had watched last night. Nadia had operated the boom microphone for that and it had kept dropping into shot. Adam had been tearing his hair out. But it served him right for picking the shortest girl in the group to hold it. He had seen the funny side afterwards, however.

Liam was not smiling. The mention of Jill had discomforted him for some reason. He put down the freshly peeled potato. 'You know....when I thought John was dead...' He pressed his lips together briefly. 'A part of me was glad. Isn't that awful?' He looked down at the worktop in embarrassment. 'I just thought...I didn't care at all. And he's my friend. I mean, I know we...'

'It's all right,' Nadia said. Perhaps it was better to talk about it. Get it all out into the open. She reached a hand up to his shoulder and gave it a gentle squeeze. 'When something like this happens, it pulls you all over the place.'

'But I would never...I would never have wished him dead. At least...' He stopped, unwilling to finish the thought. 'But then, thinking he was...and then to see him standing there, smirking, alive and well.' Liam's voice had taken on a decidedly bitter tone.

'You really don't like him.'

'No. No, I don't. But it's not....' He sighed again and

abandoned the potato peeler. 'Something happened this morning.' His eyes flicked cautiously to the door and he kept his voice low. 'I...made a mistake.'

'A mistake?' Nadia wasn't sure what he was getting at.

'I was up early, before breakfast. I went for a walk, to clear my head. Suzy and I had a row last night. You may have heard us.'

Nadia suppressed a laugh. 'I think the whole house heard you. But she said you'd made up.'

'Well, yes, after a fashion. But not really. Not a proper talk, like we usually do. I was still fuming, to be honest. I walked down to the chapel and Jill was there. She'd brought a mat out to do her exercises. In the freezing cold. She's always the first one up.'

That was true. Mad as a hatter, first thing in the morning and last thing at night. And seemingly impervious to the cold.

'I told her about...about the row,' he continued, in a monotone now, but still keeping his voice low. 'She told me it would be all right. She gave me a hug. And then things...things got out of control a little bit.'

Nadia boggled, nearly dropping the potato in her hand. 'Oh, Liam. You didn't...?'

'I...didn't intend to. It just happened.'

'God.' Nadia frowned. 'Are you sure you should be telling me this?'

'Well, that's the thing.' He glanced across at the door again. 'I wouldn't have told anyone. It was a stupid, stupid thing to do. We went out together, you know. Jill and I. At university.'

'I remember.'

'But it was just...I was so angry. With Suzy. She can be so unreasonable sometimes. And then...and then it happened. I know there's no excuse. And...and while we were...while we were together, John Menhenick turned up. Caught us at it.'

'Christ.' Nadia grimaced. No wonder Liam was upset. Caught in the act, and by John of all people.

'I tried to explain. I pleaded with him not to say anything. Not to tell Suzy. But you know what he's like. He delights in causing mischief. He'll tell her what happened. I know he will. And that'll be it. Fifteen years of marriage gone in a shot.'

Nadia was thinking fast. 'Do you want me to have a word with him? With John?'

Liam baulked at that. 'No. Lord, no. I think that would make it worse.'

'He might not tell her. They're good friends. He wouldn't want to upset her like that. He'd know how badly she'd take it.'

Liam disagreed. 'He doesn't care who he upsets.' The bitter tone had returned. 'He enjoys lording it over people, disrupting everything. And those two. They've always been so *close*.'

That, by the sounds of it, was the crux of the matter. The green eyed monster was showing its face again. Liam had never been able to conquer his jealousy. He had married a rich and very beautiful woman and he was terrified of losing her. It was so stupid. Suzy was devoted to him and always had been. But she would hit the roof if she found out what he had done. 'There's nothing going on, you know,' Nadia said. 'Between John and Suzy. Nothing at all. Whatever you may think, they *are* just friends. Like Samantha and...and Twinkle.'

He gazed down at her in surprise. 'You don't think they've ever...?'

'No,' she told him firmly. 'Trust me, I'd know.' Nadia prided herself on always being up to date on the gossip. People had a habit of confiding in her. She really was the mother of the group.

'It's just...you hear things sometimes. About what happened at the castle, at the last reunion.' The gathering Liam had not been able to attend.

'That was a long time ago...'

Liam tensed and Nadia scowled at herself, realising how badly she had phrased that. 'Something happened? Did they sleep together at the castle? Her and John?'

'Not to my knowledge,' she assured him hastily. 'I certainly didn't see them hooking up. Look, Liam, I'm not going to lie to you, there was a bit of bed hopping that weekend. Things that some people might regret. Like what happened between you and Jill this morning. But that's ancient history now. Have you...spoken to her about it?'

'Jill?' His eyes widened. 'No, I...I've been avoiding her. And then all this....' Liam lapsed into silence.

'It has been a hell of a day,' Nadia conceded. 'But as to the last reunion...' She placed a hand on his arm. 'Best not to worry about it. It's in the past. Done and dusted. If there was ever anything between John and Suzy, there certainly isn't now. They haven't seen each other for years.'

'That makes no difference,' Liam grumbled. 'Things can start up again. I know that, more than anyone. But it's not just...' He gritted his teeth. There was something else that was bothering him. 'My son, Paul. He was born in April, the following year.'

'Yes, I remember. After the reunion.' The boy had been named in memory of Paul Hammond. It took Nadia a moment to grasp the implication. 'You don't think....?'

'He was born nine months afterwards.'

Nadia started to laugh. She couldn't help herself. 'And you think...?' She shook her head. 'That's absolutely ridiculous. God, Liam, you've been worrying about that for the last ten years?'

'I haven't...I was never sure....'

Nadia was quick to put his mind at ease. It really was absurd. 'Look, I went to the christening. And I've seen the photos online.' Suzy had bombarded everyone with pictures of her kids as they grew up, the boy and the two girls. 'He's the spitting image of you. Trust me, he is definitely your son.'

'You really think so?'

'Of course I do. Of course he is. Look, Liam, even if...even if something happened ten years ago – and I'm not suggesting for a moment that it did – Suzy's a grown up. She'd have taken precautions. Believe me, you have nothing to worry about. That boy is definitely yours.' She grabbed another potato from the pile and shuffled the pot across towards him. 'Now, come on. Pull yourself together. We've got to get these potatoes on the boil in ten minutes.'

'You must be some sort of jinx,' John Menhenick asserted good-naturedly, as he helped Adam Cartwright to manoeuvre the crate to the floor. The storage room at the base of the lighthouse was crammed full of junk, a lot of it in boxes and most of it covered with thick layers of dust. Every time they shifted something the air would explode. John coughed as another cloud engulfed him. 'Every ten years,' he continued, warming to his theme. 'Paul Hammond last time, in Wales.' Paul had died in a car accident a few weeks after their previous meet up. 'Now Twinkle in Scotland. If the next reunion is in Northern Ireland I don't think I'm going to bother.' He grinned and squatted down in front of the crate they had just lowered to the floor. There wasn't much of interest inside: just some more rope, coiled up, and a couple of metal lamps. *Oil lamps. Blimey.* The place was even older than he had thought. There was a spanner, too, and a couple of mallets, but nothing of any great use.

'I don't think there'll be another reunion,' Adam said quietly, gazing down at the open crate. The ginger haired man seemed to have lost any semblance of humour in the last couple of hours. He seemed to be taking Twinkle's death as a personal affront. *Doesn't like his plans being mucked about,* John thought. He could sympathise with that. 'This is going to cast a shadow over everything,' Adam said.

'Not something to tell the kids,' John agreed. 'The castle was fun though. If only Paul hadn't popped his clogs a few weeks later.' That really *had* cast a shadow. 'Blimey, it's going to be the same this time, ain't it? A reunion followed by a funeral.' He dug a hand into the crate, to see if there was anything else buried underneath. 'Makes you think, though, don't it? How short life is? You know, I think this is a waste of time.' He pulled out his hand and stood up. 'There's nothing in there. You're not going to find a radio in these old crates.'

Adam was not to be discouraged. They had barely scratched the surface of the room so far. 'We need to get in touch with the mainland somehow. We can't wait thirty six hours to inform the police.' He bent down in front of the second crate – the one underneath the box they had just shifted – and pulled open the lid. This one was stuffed full of flags, in all manner of bright colours. Adam pulled one out and held it up for John to see.

'There you go.' John grinned. 'Semaphore. We can send them an SOS.'

Adam finally managed a smile. 'I only wish we could. I don't think anyone's likely to be watching the island that closely. Not these days.'

John grabbed a flag himself and waved it about. 'Is that how they did it? With flags?'

'So Nadia said. She had a chat with the owner. Apparently, they used to have a telescope trained on the lighthouse. If there were any urgent messages, the keepers would use the flags to communicate. Before radio of course.'

'Fat lot of use they are now, though,' John said, dropping it back into the box. ''Course, there is one easy way to attract their attention.'

Adam was all ears. 'What's that?'

'Well, the lighthouse itself.' John spread his arms to indicate the tower as a whole. 'It's all automated, ain't it? There must be a plug somewhere. If we cut the power, they're bound to notice.' He chuckled. 'The lighthouse goes wonky, they'll realise something's up and send someone out to investigate.'

It wasn't a serious suggestion, but Adam still took a moment to consider it. 'They have some pretty expensive equipment in here,' he said. Not the bric-a-brac they were sorting through; the modern electrics. 'If we damage it, there'll be hell to pay. And it might be a safety hazard, if a ship comes by and doesn't see the light.'

John scoffed at that. 'Have you seen any ships today?'

'Yes, one or two. In the distance. We can't risk an accident. It wouldn't be fair.'

'One day won't make any difference. Besides, all the ship have got GPS these days. Radar. You name it. I don't know why they even need lighthouses any more.'

'Not every ship has GPS. No, if it's a choice between

switching off the lamp and waiting thirty six hours then I think it's safer to to wait.'

'Yeah, I suppose so.' It was a mark of Adam's distraction that he had taken the idea seriously at all. He wasn't usually this dense. 'Anyway,' John said, 'Twinkle's not going anywhere, is he?'

'No. But it would be better to have someone in authority out here sooner rather than later.' Adam rummaged further into the second crate. 'Just to calm everyone's nerves. Instead of waiting another day. Oh. But there may be a third option,' he added in surprise.

'What's that?' John watched as Adam pulled something out from underneath the flags. A chunk of metal. 'Blimey, what is that?' There was a hand grip and a long, fat tube. 'Some sort of gun?'

Adam peered at it thoughtfully. It didn't look like a regular pistol. 'It could be a flare gun,' he guessed.

'What, like a firework?'

'Something like that. Yes, I think it is.' He dug deeper into the crate. 'Look, these are the cartridges here.' There was a small box of them. 'You load them into the barrel at the back, I think.'

'There you go then!' John beamed. 'We can have our own Bonfire Night. Beats the Fourth of July.'

'Better than that,' Adam said. 'If we wait until after dark, we might be able to attract some attention.'

Suzy Heigl was grinning from ear to ear. The blonde woman had all but raced up the lighthouse steps, not even grabbing a coat. It was just the kind of distraction they needed this evening. She took the flare gun from Nadia and examined the mechanism with undisguised glee. 'I've always wanted to let one of these off!'

Nadia was happy to let her do the honours. She placed the box of cartridges carefully on the ledge. 'You'll have to go outside, though. You can't fire it in here.' The lamp room was hardly the place for fireworks.

Suzy stuck her tongue out. 'Spoilsport. God, that's bright!'

95

She brought her free hand up to cover her eyes. The lamp was spinning around above their heads and every fifteen seconds it would almost blind them.

'You're not meant to look at it!' Nadia laughed.

But Suzy could not contain her enthusiasm. The events of the day were briefly forgotten. She was like a little kid in a sweetshop, gazing in awe at the splendour of the Edwardian lamp room. 'This is so cool. I've always wanted to see the inside of a lighthouse. A working one too.'

'It's great, isn't it?'

'Twinkle would have loved to see all this. All this ancient technology.'

'Yes, I think he would,' Nadia agreed sadly. 'And the view as well. Although I think he might have struggled with the stairs.'

Suzy gazed out through the surrounding glass. The sky was darkening now and the stars were beginning to pop out, but there was still enough residual light to make out the line of the horizon and the white of the sea as the beam of the lighthouse swept across it. 'You could get vertigo up here, we're so high up.'

'About a hundred metres above the sea line,' Nadia reckoned. 'I wish I had Samantha's head for heights.'

'It must be a fantastic view during the day time.'

'It is. Mind you, it looks pretty good even now. Look, you can see the chapel over there.' She pointed inland, across the island, as the ancient stone monument was momentarily bathed in light.

'Oh yes! There it is!' Suzy grinned. 'Oh, Nadia, this is such fun! I'm so glad Adam suggested this.' She glanced down at the pistol in her hand and fumbled for the catch to open up the barrel.

'Careful where you point that!' Nadia laughed, as Suzy inserted a cartridge into the stubby tube. Nadia stepped past her, casting her eyes down briefly as the light flipped around again, and then opened the glass door which led out onto the circular balcony. She pulled her scarf tightly around her neck and gestured the girl forward. 'Be careful!' she warned.

Suzy stepped out onto the balcony. She had a thick jumper

on but leggings rather than trousers and no jacket. Nadia was dressed – as John Menhenick had put it – for the Antarctic, with gloves and a thick woolly hat. Suzy stood for a moment, mesmerised by the view and by the wind that whistled across her face. Then she looked back at Nadia and grinned again as she lifted the flare gun in her right hand.

John had been sceptical of the idea, but Adam thought it was worth a try. Set off a flare and see if that attracted the attention of the mainland. Suzy had volunteered to take charge of the expedition. She had been raring to go, but they'd had to wait for the sun to set first, in the late summer evening, before clambering up the inside of the tower. Suzy was like a little girl with a new toy. Her pretty rounded face was glowing with pleasure. That was Suzy all over, bless her. Enthusiastic to the point of overkill. Nadia liked to have fun too and to try new things, but nobody bounced up and down quite as much as Suzy Heigl. No wonder the kids loved her books so much. She was on exactly their wavelength.

Dinner had been a strange affair. Everyone had tried desperately hard not to be gloomy. A kind of forced bonhomie had become the order of the day. This had gradually developed – with a little alcoholic lubrication – into a more sincere good humour. It was odd the way people behaved in the face of tragic events. Sometimes the only way to deal with it was to put it out of your mind. Better to laugh than cry, Nadia had always thought; and Adam had agreed with her. But still, there was an awkwardness there, even in this little adventure. They were all of them trying a little too hard.

Nadia grabbed the binoculars from the side of the door, looping the cord over her head and then stepping out to join her friend.

Suzy had the pistol raised and was aiming it vaguely out to sea. 'Which way is the mainland?' she asked. 'I've lost my bearings completely up here.'

Nadia pointed straight ahead. 'Lewis is over there, I think. Look, you can see a few lights. That must be where you caught the boat.'

97

Suzy aimed the pistol in that direction. 'This way?'

'Yes, but you probably need to point it straight up. As high as it can go.'

Suzy raised the gun as instructed, then closed her eyes and pulled the trigger. Nadia grinned and watched as a ball of light leapt from the barrel. Suzy opened her eyes to see it flare high above them. For several seconds the whole of Flaxton Isle was laid out before them; then the beam of the lighthouse swept round, and for the briefest of moments the flare was upstaged.

'This is so cool!!' Suzy exclaimed. 'It worked first time!'

'Careful!' Nadia warned her, as the girl jumped up and down in excitement. 'I don't think this balcony is made for acrobatics.' The floor was a maze of metal wires and the handrail was more than a hundred years old.

Suzy was grinning again. 'I didn't think it would work! Shall we try another one?'

'Why not? Give it a minute, though.' The miniature sun was still hovering way above them. Nadia gazed out across the sea. The flare was working far better than she had hoped. If anyone happened to look out from the mainland just now they were bound to see it.

Suzy had already nipped back inside the lamp room to grab another cartridge. She loaded it up with apparent professionalism, then stepped outside again and pulled the trigger. This flare did not shoot straight up, despite the perfect vertical aim. Instead, it skittered sideways and plummeted into the ocean. Suzy giggled.

'That was a bit of a damp squib,' Nadia thought. More like a poorly made firework than a flare. Mind you, it was remarkable the gun worked at all. *How long is it since the last keeper was out here?* Forty years or so. Wasn't that what Mr Peterson had said?

Suzy grabbed another cartridge and loaded it up.

She was right, this really was good fun. It was great to step away from the events of the day for a few minutes, even if there was a serious point to the exercise. 'I wonder if anyone will see it.' Nadia lifted her binoculars and shivered at the cold. She waited for the lamp to go past and then focused on the Lewis coastline in the distance. Suzy was about to fire the third flare but Nadia waved at her to hold off. 'Hang on a minute!'

'What is it? What can you see?'

'I don't know.' She squinted slightly at the lens. 'There looks to be something happening over on the mainland. Lights or something.'

'What sort of lights?'

'I'm not sure. In the sky, above the...' It took Nadia a moment to determine what she was actually looking at. 'Fireworks. Someone's letting off fireworks. On Lewis.' That was odd, she thought. 'It must be some kind of display.'

'A fireworks display?' Suzy frowned. 'In July?' Then she jumped up and down. 'Of course, it's Independence Day. The Fourth of July.'

Nadia dropped her binoculars. 'Not in Scotland.'

'No, not normally. But there were some Americans on the plane out here,' Suzy explained. 'They told us they were staying on the island for a few days. Perhaps they're having their own celebrations.'

'Maybe,' Nadia agreed. The timing was a bit awkward, though. 'Let's just hope nobody thinks we're a part of it. Come on,' she said, flapping her gloves against her arms. 'It's freezing out here. Better make this the last one.'

Chapter Seven

Nobody felt like staying up late that evening. Even Jill Clarke, who had knocked back the vodka at dinner, had retired to bed before eleven. Samantha was grateful for the peace and quiet. Adam was still up, however, and she sat with him for a time, chatting about nothing in particular. She had never been particularly close to him, despite sharing digs at university, but she had always admired his organisational skills. Adam seemed to be able to keep a level head no matter what fate threw at him, though he could be every bit as outrageous as Jill when he was up on stage. Nadia said he fretted a lot about things, but Samantha had never seen any sign of it. He had certainly handled himself well today, when she had forced her hair-brained scheme on him to rescue the body of their friend.

'You were very brave this afternoon,' he said, placing his empty beer bottle down by the side of the sofa. 'Not many people would have had the guts to do what you did.'

'Foolhardy, more like,' Samantha admitted ruefully. She poured herself a small glass of wine. 'Anyway, it was a team effort. I wasn't the one hauling the body up the cliff side.' *The body.* How easy it was to talk in those terms and how disrespectful it felt. This was Twinkle they were talking about, not some anonymous corpse. She shuddered, thinking of her friend, and fought back the wave of despair that threatened to overwhelm her. 'I hope someone did see those flares,' she said, changing the subject slightly. 'We can't leave him lying here for two whole days.' She had changed her mind about that over the course of the evening. Whatever circus it might entail, it was better if someone in authority arrived sooner rather than later. 'He needs to be properly taken care of. His mum needs to know what's happened to him.' Samantha took a sip of wine. 'Did you ever meet her? Ida Fonteyn?'

Adam scratched an ear hole. 'I'm not sure. I don't think so. I suppose she must have been at our graduation.'

'Yes, she was. Quite a short woman. A little tubby, but

very nice. And devoted to Twinkle. She'll be devastated.'

'He was still living at home, wasn't he?'

'Yes. He never managed to move out.' She put down her glass on the coffee table. 'I suppose we ought to...collect up his things in the morning.'

'It might be better to leave that for the police,' Adam suggested.

'I suppose.'

Twinkle had shared a room with John Menhenick. The bald man had decided to stay where he was for the night. It was too much hassle to move, he said. The body was laid out in the spare room, anyway.

Samantha sat back on the sofa. The time had come to broach another subject; something that had been troubling her for some time now. It was a triviality in comparison to the death of her friend, but it was still rather unnerving and she wanted to find out what Adam thought. 'Do you think there's something....I don't know...something odd going on here this weekend?'

'Odd?' He gazed at her curiously.

'Yes. I didn't want to say anything over dinner. I didn't want to worry anyone. Well, any more than they were already.' She reached down into her pocket and pulled out the miniature camera she had found on top of the wardrobe. 'What do you make of this?' She handed it across to Adam.

He looked down at it briefly. 'What is it? A webcam? It's very small.'

'It's tiny. I found it in my room this afternoon. On top of the wardrobe.'

Adam's brow furrowed. 'A camera?'

'Yes. It had a grandstand view of the whole room.'

He turned it over in his hands. 'Was it connected to anything?'

'No, not that I know of. It doesn't have any kind of socket.'

He placed the device on the coffee table and pulled out his mobile.

'You did say there was no internet here? No signal or

101

anything like that?'

'No, there's no internet,' Adam confirmed. 'But look at this. Liam mentioned it earlier on.' He leaned across to let Samantha see the screen of his phone. A possible connection – *"Home1"* – had popped up in the bottom right hand corner. 'There is some kind of network here in the house. A wi-fi connection. Not online, just joining up a few local devices. There must be a hub somewhere.'

That was strange, Samantha thought. 'Did the owner mention anything about that?'

'No. And it's password protected, so I can't find out anything more about it.'

'Twinkle would be able to,' Samantha reflected sadly. This was his area of expertise. She leaned forward and retrieved the webcam from the table. 'So if this camera transmits wirelessly, it could be connected up to another device somewhere in the house. A laptop or something?' That was exactly what she had feared. 'Someone could be spying on me and Jill?'

'It's possible,' Adam agreed, with some concern. 'Without an internet connection, they couldn't stream it online. But it could be recorded easily enough. Maybe stored for a later date. And if there is a hub somewhere, there might be any number of devices hidden away. It might not just be you.'

Samantha shuddered, glancing across the room. It was a worrying thought, that they might all be under surveillance. But why would anyone want to do that?

Adam pocketed his phone and retrieved the camera from the coffee table. 'You say you found it on top of the wardrobe?'

'Yes.'

'Did you find any others?'

'I...didn't really look. Do you think it might be the owner of the house? What was his name?'

'Peterson. Jim Peterson.'

'Do you think he could be behind it? Recording us all. Could he be some sort of pervert?'

Adam shrugged. 'He seemed a nice enough guy when I spoke to him. But you never can tell. And this place *has* just been refurbished.' He twisted the webcam around in his hands. 'But there is another possibility. Did Nadia tell you? The front door was open, when we first arrived here. It should have been locked up.'

'Yes, I remember her saying.'

'The owner thought somebody might have broken in. Maybe students or something. Although the lock wasn't damaged.'

'So somebody could have come out here before us and set all this up?'

'The network and the camera in your room,' Adam agreed. 'It's possible.'

'But who would do that? And why? Why would anyone want to film a few old friends at a reunion?' Samantha picked up her glass thoughtfully. 'I suppose it could be something to do with me.' That was the most obvious explanation. 'Somebody looking for gossip. I have had journalists going through my bins before now.'

Adam bit the top of his lip. 'I have a feeling it may be a little more salacious than that. Don't forget, it's not just sound. It's full on video.'

That thought had also occurred to Samantha. 'You mean someone was hoping I might jump into bed with someone and they could film it all?' She shuddered at the thought.

'Well, it could be. But the odd thing is, nobody knew you were coming here this weekend. Well, nobody apart from me.'

'Some of my people knew,' Samantha said. 'You weren't the only one I told.' Now she came to think of it, there were several people who had known Samantha would be here.

'But Peterson certainly didn't know. He couldn't have had any idea who was coming. In any case, if you were being targeted, how would they have known what room you were going to be in? Nadia and I didn't start allocating beds until after we got here.'

That was true. Perhaps it wasn't anything to do with her after all. She certainly hoped not, anyway. 'Do you think some of the other rooms might be bugged?'

'I don't know. We'll have to check in the morning. It's too late now. Look, have you told anyone else about this?'

'Only Jill. She was there when I found it. She thinks it's a practical joke. She says John must have put it up there.'

'I don't think it's a joke,' Adam said, gravely. 'You don't think....' He hesitated, an uncomfortable new thought occurring to him.

'What?'

He shifted in his seat. 'Twinkle was always the technical one among us. He'd know how to set something like this up.'

Samantha was appalled. 'That's ridiculous, Adam. Twinkle wouldn't spy on us. And he certainly wouldn't record anything to...to sell to anyone. If he'd been that way inclined, he could have cashed in on me years ago. He knew all sorts of private things. And anyway, you couldn't sell that sort of material. Not video footage. Filming without consent in a private residence. You could get sent to prison for that. Even the tabloids wouldn't touch it.'

'He may not have been intending to sell it,' Adam suggested quietly. 'You know how fond he was of you, Samantha. And he never had much success with women. He might just have done it...well, for himself.'

'No. No, I won't believe that.' She shuddered. 'Not Twinkle. He would never do anything like that.' He would never abuse her trust in that way.

'A lonely middle aged man...'

'No, that's absurd. Adam, I knew him better than anyone here. It's not in his nature.'

Adam sat back. 'You're probably right.'

'It's much more likely to be somebody we don't know. The owner. Or an intruder, if the place was broken into.'

'Well, that is the most likely explanation,' Adam agreed. 'But it still doesn't explain how the lighthouse door came to be unlocked this morning.' He scratched his chin. 'Unless there's somebody else here on the island with us.'

John Menhenick yawned and checked the time on his phone once again. It was a quarter to three in the morning. He had switched the bedroom light off when he had gone to bed but had sat up for the first hour, with the light from his tablet illuminating him, having a beer and finishing off a few things. It had been a hell of a day, all things considered. He hated having to change his plans like this, at the last minute, but he hadn't had much choice. It was all Twinkle's fault, poking his nose in where it wasn't wanted. That bloke could be so pig-headed sometimes. But he had paid the price for it, the poor sod. John could still see him, standing on that cliff edge, his cheeks flushed with anger. That had been the last time he had seen the man. It couldn't have been much after that that he had slipped.

John had dozed off for a couple of hours after midnight. He had set his phone to vibrate at 2.50am, in case he missed the deadline, but as it turned out he had woken well ahead of time. He switched off the alarm and lay for a moment, listening to the sounds of the house. The beam of the lighthouse swept briefly across the window, but the light was heavily muted by the thick curtains. A slight creak sounded from somewhere nearby. Probably just the floorboards adjusting themselves. *I'll give it five minutes anyway,* he thought. He didn't want to bump into anyone at this hour, even if they were just popping out to the loo.

Yep, it's been a hell of a day, he thought again. It had started so well, too. Stumbling on Liam and Jill like that. The tossers. He hadn't known whether to laugh or cry. He had half a mind to tell Suzy about it, to let her know just what an arsehole she was married to. But no, his first instinct had been right: leave well alone. He was having enough fun, just watching Liam squirm. The taller man had sat with his wife at the dinner table this evening, well away from John or Jill; but he'd still glanced across at them intermittently, worried John might say something in front of the others. John would keep him on tenterhooks for as long as he could. Actually, it might be a laugh to show him the photos. He didn't know about those yet. The documentary evidence. That would make Liam's eyes pop out. It would serve the bastard right. He had never treated Suzy properly. A bloody leech, that's what he was, living off her income. But Suzy loved him and John didn't want to see her hurt. Certainly not now, with everything else that was going on. Better to let the doubt gnaw away at them instead. That could prove just as corrosive in the long term.

He stretched out his arms and yawned again The cottage was as quiet as the grave. He patted his pocket. He hadn't bothered to undress when he had come to bed. *Best get it over with*, he thought. It was a bugger, having to do all this now, but he didn't really have much choice. If only money hadn't been so tight...

He pulled himself up and grabbed a couple of things from his backpack, which he had stowed under the bed. Then he moved past Twinkle's cot to the far door. His blanket was still covered in clothes and other bits of baggage. Twinkle had never been a tidy person. It was strange to see the bed empty, though.

John pulled open the door. There was no sign of anyone about. He could hear a few snores from the rooms opposite. Jill Clarke letting rip as usual. He was glad not to have to listen to that any more. He made his way quietly across the living room and through the hallway towards the front door. The beam of the lighthouse swept by periodically, lighting up the windows on each wall and catching him briefly in their beam. But there was no one around to see him.

He grabbed his coat and a pair of boots from the rack and slipped into them. He slid a second phone into the large exterior pocket. No-one knew he had that. He grinned at the thought. His own private satellite phone. Well, not his own, but one he had been lent. Adam would be livid if he knew. They weren't quite as cut off as the man thought. He had been a bit worried this evening when Adam had suggested using the flares, but luckily nothing had come of it. Thank God for the Fourth of July. The last thing John wanted was anyone contacting the mainland just now.

He left the front door on a latch and made his way out into the compound. The light from the tower helped him to navigate along the exterior wall, where the ground was fairly level. He had an app on his regular phone but he didn't want to use it until he was well away from the cottage. He ducked down as he passed Jill and Samantha's room, but the curtains were closed anyway, so there was no chance of him being seen. He stepped through the gap in the wall onto the concrete of the funicular railway. The solid path snaked down the island towards the cliff before disappearing out of view over the edge. To the south, of course, in dark silhouette, was the chapel. That was where he had made his phone call, earlier in the day; the only time he had used the satellite phone. He would have to get shot of it now. They had already found the other one in pieces at the bottom of the cliff.

He lifted up his regular phone and switched on the app, aiming the light at his feet. He didn't want to trip up on the grooves of the old rail track as he made his way across the island.

A couple of minutes later he reached the cliff edge. From there, a set of wide but slippery steps led down to the jetty, running parallel to the railway. *I must be mad, doing this in the middle of the night*, he thought. But what choice did he have? Any other time he would be seen. He paused for a moment at the top and peered down at the landing stage. A small boat had come to rest alongside the mooring post. A dim light illuminated the cabin and John could make out a dark figure sitting on the edge of the boat, smoking a cigarette. *He doesn't look happy either*, John thought. That was not a surprise. It was a bit of a risk for him, chugging about in these waters in the dead of night. But the weather was calm and there was at least a bloody great lighthouse to guide him in.

John waved a hand and began to move down the steps.

'It looks like it's not just me,' Samantha Redmond said, marching across to the breakfast table the following morning. She held out her hand and showed Adam the three miniature cameras she had discovered in the bathroom. Each one was a tiny black blob, smaller than the device she had found in her bedroom. The cameras had been imbedded in the tiles surrounding the shower. At first glance they had looked like part of the pattern. It was very professionally done; which only made it all the more worrying, so

107

far as Samantha was concerned. She had been about to disrobe when she'd spotted the first one. 'I found a couple more in my bedroom and some more in the upstairs loo.' One of the cameras had been attached to a lamp shade hanging directly above her bed. 'You were right, Adam. The whole place is wired up.'

Adam was sitting at the breakfast table with Nadia, Suzy and Liam Heigl. The married couple regarded Samantha with some puzzlement. They had got up a little later than usual and had been chatting happily over coffee and toast as she approached the table.

'What do you mean, wired?' Liam asked, wiping his mouth.

Samantha explained about the cameras. 'There are probably some in your room too,' she guessed.

'And in ours,' Nadia confirmed. Adam must have taken a look first thing. The two friends were sharing a room so it was hardly surprising that Nadia knew all about it.

Suzy, by contrast, was struggling to make sense of the news. 'Could it be some sort of joke?' she wondered, peering across at the small black cameras, which Samantha had just handed to Adam. 'Was somebody preparing a blooper reel to show at the end of the weekend?' The others shook their heads. It was not quite as daft an idea as it sounded. People falling over when drunk, people talking rubbish. It would be in bad taste, but not beyond the bounds of some members of the group. But no, it was clearly not a joke.

'Not if it's set up in the bathroom,' Liam said, with some distaste. He looked to Adam. 'Is that what the network is for, in the house?'

Adam nodded. 'Well, we assume so.'

'In that case, I think we should demand our money back.' Liam was outraged. 'We didn't agree to being filmed. I thought the place had been refurbished, not wired for sound.'

'We don't know for sure who's responsible,' Adam pointed out quietly. 'It might not be the owners. It could be anybody.' He handed the cameras back to Samantha and poured himself another glass of orange juice. 'I hate to say it, but it could even be one of us.' He took a sip of the juice and placed the glass back on the table.

That was the conclusion Samantha had came to. 'Has anyone seen John this morning?' she asked. 'He should be here. And Jill. We need to talk about this properly.'

'I think Jill's doing her exercises,' Suzy said. She had been up and out before Samantha had got up. 'John must still be in bed.'

'He's not usually a late riser,' Samantha thought.

'No, he's not,' the blonde woman agreed.

'I'll go and give him a knock.'

Adam pushed back his plate and rose to his feet. 'I'll come with you.'

Samantha made to go, but then turned back to the breakfast table. 'Do you want us to check your room as well?' she asked the married couple.

'Be our guest,' Liam said, with a casual wave of his hand; but then his expression froze. 'God, I hope they weren't filming us this morning.'

Suzy smiled sweetly at him. 'Don't worry, darling. I don't think they could have seen much.' She grabbed his hand. 'We did have the curtains drawn, after all.'

Adam followed Samantha down the stairs. 'It looks like those two have made up.'

'Yes, at long last. I am glad. It makes me so uncomfortable when they argue like that.'

'Well, you know what they're like,' Adam said. 'It's always one extreme or another.'

They reached the bottom of the stairs and headed right, towards the master bedroom. Adam pushed back the door and Samantha followed him in. It was quite a plush room, the usual mix of white walls and light brown panelling, but with just the one large bed, which had been very neatly made. Several small bottles were clustered on the bedside table – Suzy's herbal medicine – and a paperback book lay on the other side; something

109

Liam was reading. A small fluffy toy nestled between the pillows. Samantha rolled her eyes. *Some people never grow up,* she thought.

'Where should we start?' Adam was hovering by the near window.

'Opposite the bed, I think,' she suggested. Unlike Samantha's bedroom, there was no wardrobe in here, just a closet set into the near wall. But a dark picture frame hung between the two large windows opposite the double bed. It took her only a moment to spot the camera attached to the edge of the frame. She was getting good at this now. 'Here it is!' she said, pulling it off. If she hadn't known it was there, however, she doubted she would have seen it at all.

Adam was peering up at the light socket. 'I think I've found another one.' He clambered onto the bed to grab hold of the lamp shade. 'Yes. Definitely one more here.' He pulled out a penknife to detach the camera from the inside of the shade. Samantha watched him slide off the bed.

'Well, it's definitely not a tabloid sting,' she concluded, with some relief. 'Even the British papers wouldn't risk something like this. The number of laws you'd have to break. And what could you do with the footage? You couldn't publish it anywhere. No-one would touch it.'

'So it's voyeurism then?' Adam suggested, tidying up the bedsheets he had inadvertently ruffled. The cameras would have had a perfect view of the Heigls this morning. 'It might have been Twinkle after all.'

Samantha was not prepared to accept that. 'It's too elaborate for that, Adam. Or for any kind of prank. This is too professional.' She grimaced. The cameras were nothing like ordinary webcams. They were far too small. 'I was thinking about what you told me last night. About the break in.'

'Well, we don't know for certain there was a break in. It's only an inference on my part.'

'I think there must have been.' Samantha let out a breath and finally gave voice to the idea that had been praying on her mind. 'I think John Menhenick may have had something to do with it.'

'John?' Adam frowned. 'No, it's too elaborate for one of his pranks. And he's hardly a professional.'

'Even so. I have a nasty feeling he may be involved somehow.' It was the only explanation that made any sense to her. 'I think he came here ahead of the rest of us and set all this up. Perhaps with a little help from some friends. You know the kind of dubious people he hangs out with.'

Adam was sceptical. 'He couldn't have come out here. Not last week, anyway. The owner was here on Tuesday, checking up on the place, and everything was fine then. If someone did break in it had to be on the Wednesday or Thursday; and John was in London then. I spoke to him on the phone, to confirm the boat times. He caught a train to Manchester on Thursday afternoon and stayed the night with Twinkle.'

'And I suppose even if he had managed to sneak out to the island, there'd be a paper trail,' Samantha said. 'He'd need to hire a boat or a helicopter.' If John Menhenick was breaking the law, he wasn't doing a very good job of it. 'But even so, I'm sure he has *something* to do with this.'

Adam wasn't following her logic. 'Why? Why would he want to film us all like that?'

Samantha bit her lip. 'I think he wanted to film me.'

'But...'

'He may not have known which room I'd be in, but he did know I was coming here this weekend.'

Adam was taken aback. 'You told him?'

'Yes. He messaged me, a few weeks ago. After you'd told everyone I wouldn't be able to make it. Sorry, I should have told you that last night.'

'And what did he say?'

'Just that he didn't blame me. He said he was having seconds thoughts himself. He wasn't sure he could really afford it.'

'Yes, he said that to me, too.'

'I emailed him back and told him he really ought to come. We might not get another chance. I said...' She hesitated. 'I said,

"I'll come if you come." And that was what tipped it. He emailed back the next day and said "see you there!" I swore him to secrecy, though. I told him not to tell anybody about it.'

'But he knew you were coming?' Adam scratched his nose. 'Well, that does put a different complexion on things. Okay. I think it's time we had a quiet word with Mr Menhenick.' He pocketed the cameras and strode out of the bedroom.

Samantha followed him out and across the living room.

Adam knocked briefly on John's door. When there was no reply, he poked his head inside. 'No sign of him in here.'

Samantha grimaced, as the door fell back and she caught sight of the nearer of the two beds. Twinkle's bed.

Adam stepped into the room. The far bed did not look as if it had been slept in either. The blanket was crumpled, as if someone had been lying on top of it for a while. A tablet was resting on the bedside table next to an empty bottle of beer. But of John himself there was no sign.

'He always was an early riser,' Samantha said. That was the only thing he and Jill had in common.

They took a brief look around the bedroom. This time, as in Samantha's room, there was a free standing wardrobe. She perched on her tiptoes to examine the top of it. 'There's another one here,' she said. 'Another camera.' But that did not exonerate John Menhenick. He could not have known where he would be sleeping this weekend.

At that moment, a piercing scream erupted from outside the cottage.

Nadia was still at the breakfast table when she heard it.

'That's Jill!' she exclaimed, exchanging a look of concern with Liam and Suzy. They pushed back their chairs and immediately headed for the stairs.

The cry had come from somewhere outside the house. They made their way quickly out the front door. Adam and Samantha were already ahead of them, beyond the walls of the compound, moving down the rail track towards the cliff. Jill

Clarke was standing at the far end, staring numbly down the steps leading out of sight to the landing stage beyond. Nadia felt a sudden chill as she saw the expression on the face of her friend. Jill was sobbing loudly, a green exercise mat lying abandoned a few feet away from the edge of the cliff. The girl must have taken a short detour on her way back from the chapel.

Liam Heigl ground to a halt beside her and peered grimly over the lip of the cliff. 'Oh, Christ!' he exclaimed, gazing downwards.

Nadia came to a halt a second later and took in the terrible sight herself. Some small part of her had already guessed what she would see, but that did not make it any easier to behold. John Menhenick's body was spread out across a succession of concrete steps some metres below them. His arms were caught up in the metal handrail and his head was splattered with blood.

Chapter Eight

'He must have tripped up,' Liam breathed, in disbelief. John's body had come to rest halfway between the cliff top and the landing stage. His eyes were staring sightlessly up at them. 'He must have fallen down the steps. Just like Twinkle.'

Suzy Heigl clutched her husband's arm tightly. Her face was pale and her jaw slack.

Adam Cartwright, who after Jill had been first on the scene, was already bounding down the steps towards the body.

'Be careful,' Nadia called out to him, but he waved away her concern.

'Oh, my baby!' Jill sobbed desperately. 'My sweet baby!'

Nadia moved across and took the trembling woman in her arms. This was more than anyone could be expected to cope with. What on earth had John been doing out here? she wondered. And how had he come to slip like that? Had he really slipped at all? She stroked Jill's hair for a minute, attempting to calm her down, but her own mind was in turmoil too. Another death. How was that possible? This weekend was becoming an absolute nightmare.

Adam had reached the body. He bent down – Nadia could see him, over Jill's shoulder – and tentatively took in the scene at close quarters. 'I think he may have been down here for a while,' he called back.

That was not too much of a surprise. Nobody had seen John since he went to bed last night.

'You'd better not touch anything,' Liam shouted down to him.

'I wasn't intending to.' Adam took a moment to fix the scene in his mind; then he made his way cautiously back up to the others. Liam and Suzy stepped to one side to allow him back onto the top of the cliff. Adam stood silently for a moment, regarding the small group of friends. 'I'm no expert,' he said at last, a haunted look in his eye. 'I suppose he might have tripped and fallen. But there seems to have been a pretty severe blow to the side of his head. It could just be the fall, but...'

Samantha had already discounted that possibility. 'It's too much of a coincidence,' she said. 'Two people tripping up. Two people dying. It has to be deliberate.'

Suzy let out a yelp of horror. 'You don't really think...?' Her hand dropped from her husband's arm.

Samantha nodded grimly. 'I think someone pushed him. And I think someone pushed Twinkle too.'

There was a shocked silence. Samantha was only saying what everyone else was thinking, but hearing it spoken out loud like that made it seem so much more real. Could it really be true? Nadia shuddered. Could somebody have done this deliberately? She released her grip on Jill Clarke.

The red-haired woman was clutching a mobile phone in her hand. 'I found this on the grass just over there,' she mumbled, holding it up so everyone could see. 'That's...that's why I came over here. It's John phone.' The device was small and blue in colour. 'I suppose I shouldn't have picked it up, but I didn't...I didn't know....' She sobbed again.

Adam took the phone from her. 'That's okay,' he said gently. He glanced down at the screen, which was covered in dew. The device looked as if it had been outside for some time. 'It must have fallen out of his pocket,' Adam guessed.

Liam had spotted something else. 'There's a bit of blood here, too, on the track.'

That clinched it for Nadia. Samantha was right. This had to be deliberate. 'Someone must have hit him,' she concluded. 'Somebody hit him and then tossed his body down the stairs, trying to make it look like an accident.'

Jill sobbed again.

'That does seem the most likely explanation,' Adam agreed. He tapped the screen on John's mobile. 'This is locked. I can't get into it.'

Jill wiped her nose and cleared the phlegm from her throat. 'It's "Tottenham",' she said. Adam regarded her blankly. 'The password for his phone. It was always "Tottenham". At least it used to be. I suppose he could have changed it.'

He tapped the letters in and the screen lit up. '"Tottenham",' he agreed. Tottenham Hotspur, John's football team.

Jill had no interest in the phone. She glanced anxiously at the steps. 'We're not going to leave him down there, are we? My poor baby.'

Samantha put a hand on her shoulder. 'I don't think we've got a choice.' They had to leave him where he was for the time being. Unlike Twinkle, he was not in any danger of being washed away. 'We've got to wait for the police. They'll need to....examine the scene.' Jill started to sniffle again and this time it was Samantha who embraced her.

Nadia was thinking back to last night. 'Do you think anyone saw the flares?' she asked, abruptly. That was their best hope now. It was still early in the morning. If somebody had seen the light show, they might have waited until daybreak before motoring out. There was still time for somebody in authority to turn up.

Adam sighed heavily. 'Let's hope so. Because one thing is abundantly clear.' He looked up from the screen. 'Someone on this island is a murderer.'

'She's resting now,' Nadia said, returning to the upstairs room. 'I managed to calm her down a bit.' They had brought Jill back to the house and put her to bed. There was not much more they could do. 'I gave her a couple of those tablets Suzy gave me.' The blonde woman had offered up the bottle from her stock. Homoeopathic medicine. 'I don't think they'll do much good, but who knows?' Just the act of taking a pill could sometimes help to settle someone's mind.

Adam was slumped in one of the armchairs, looking ashen faced.

'You don't look so good yourself. Do you want a coffee?' she asked.

'That would be nice.'

She moved through into the kitchen to put the kettle on.

Adam jumped up and followed her in. 'What are we going to do, Nadia?' The confidence he had displayed in front of the others was now starting to collapse. Nadia had never seen him quite this stressed. It was hardly surprising. There couldn't be any doubt that John had been deliberately killed; struck hard by a blunt instrument. Adam was convinced of it, and he had seen the wound close up. The blood they had found was not just by the top of the steps, either. A few spots of it were on the trail leading back to the compound, suggesting the body had been dragged a short way before it was pushed. It was an undeniable fact: there was a murderer in their midst. Nadia was determined to keep her head, though, for Adam's sake as much as her own. Whatever was going on, she could not allow herself to give way to despair.

'Just keep calm and wait it out,' she told him, as she flicked on the kettle. 'There's nothing any of us can do right now.' She opened a cupboard and pulled out a couple of mugs. 'Do you think....do you think it was one of us, who did it?'

Adam grasped the side of his face. 'I don't know. I think it must have been. God, Nadia, one of us.'

She spooned a couple of mounds of coffee into the percolator. 'But who would want to kill John? Or Twinkle?'

Adam leaned back against the work surface and considered the matter carefully. 'I suppose Liam never liked him very much. John, I mean.'

'No, that's true.' *And with good reason*, she thought, recalling what Liam had told her in confidence the previous afternoon. The bald man had found him and Jill together, in the chapel. 'But he wouldn't resort to murder. I was thinking, though....about Twinkle.' She opened the fridge and pulled out some milk. 'About the way he died. Do you think it might have been a mistake? Somebody thought it was John standing out there and then...and then pushed him?'

Adam nodded. 'Yes, that thought had occurred to me.' With the black jacket and woolly hat, it would have been easy to mix the two men up. They were of a similar height and the heavy coat would have disguised any difference in build. 'Somebody tried to kill John, got it wrong and then had another go. That does make a kind of sense.'

'Do you think it might have something to do with all these cameras in the house? The ones Samantha found?'

'It would be a hell of a coincidence if it didn't. Someone certainly wired the place up. It could well have been John. You know he knew Samantha was coming here ahead of time?' Nadia hadn't known that. 'But it might just as easily have been Twinkle. Or somebody else we don't know about.'

Nadia shivered again. 'You think there might be someone else on the island?' The kettle was beginning to boil. She shuffled the percolator over and poured out the steaming water.

'It's always possible,' Adam thought.

'But there couldn't be, surely? There's nowhere to hide. We've been all over this island, between the six of us. And it's too cold to sleep outside at night.' Even the chapel would provide little protection from the wind. 'You certainly couldn't hide anywhere in the cottage. We'd have seen them by now.' She opened another cupboard and pulled out a bag of sugar. Adam liked his coffee sweet.

'There is one place, though,' he suggested. 'Inside the lighthouse.'

Nadia pressed the plunger on the percolator and looked across at him. 'There's nowhere to hide in there either. I've been up and down that tower four or fives time now.'

'There are a couple of rooms halfway up, aren't there? Just below the lamp room? Isn't that what you said?'

'Yes, two storerooms, one above the other. But they're locked. I tried one of the doors yesterday. I don't think they can have been used in decades.'

'But think about it,' Adam said. 'We've assumed someone broke into the lighthouse. Opened that door from the outside. What if nobody broke in at all? What if somebody was in there all along and broke out?'

Nadia's mouth fell open. That was not a happy thought.

'I've tried every variation of "Tottenham Hotspur" I can think of,'

Nadia sighed, looking across the L-shaped bedroom at Suzy Heigl. 'But none of it is working.' She glanced down at the tablet in her lap. Suzy was sitting on the other bed, going through some of Twinkle's things. It had seemed the logical thing to do, searching the room where the two boys had slept. Adam was not happy about it – he thought they should leave it for the police – but the more they found out about John and Twinkle's activities this weekend, the better informed they would be. Yes, there might be a stranger running amok, but it was far more likely that one of their friends was to blame. And if one of the group really was a murderer, they couldn't afford to wait another day for the police to arrive. At the very least – as Samantha Redmond had suggested when she'd joined them for coffee – they should try to break into John's tablet and find out if he was responsible for the webcams. Nadia had agreed wholeheartedly with that. *Perhaps he saw something he shouldn't have,* she thought. *Or perhaps he was trying to blackmail somebody.* With John Menhenick, nothing could be ruled out.

The tablet had been resting on the bedside table, plugged into the mains but not switched on. Nadia had found a couple of USB sticks, too, in the rucksack he had stashed under his bed. Maybe Adam could take a look at them later, on his laptop. But getting into the tablet was the priority now; if only they could work out the password.

'What about makes of car?' Suzy suggested. The blonde woman looked up from the magazine she had pulled out of Twinkle's rucksack. A gaming mag. 'John always loved cars.'

'I don't know. What did he drive?'

'Other people's mostly.' Suzy smiled half-heartedly.

'Are you sure you're all right, doing this?' Suzy had volunteered to help out, to take her mind off things, but sitting in John's room looking through a dead man's possessions was probably not that much of a help.

The woman nodded bravely. 'I think so. It's strange. I was so upset, yesterday afternoon, when I first thought he was dead. I was devastated. I could barely even speak. And I was so happy when I found out he was still alive. Even...even with what happened to Twinkle. But now....I don't know what to think. Murder. I'm just numb. I...I can't take it in.'

'I know what you mean,' Nadia agreed, gazing back at her. It was not an easy thing to come to terms with. 'I saw Samantha on TV, last year. Some American series. I forget what it was called. She was playing the murderer in that. The guest role. You know the sort of thing. Murderer of the week. She was really good at it. But that sort of stuff is just a parlour game. When it happens in real life...'

'I think it's karma,' Suzy said, returning the magazine quietly to the rucksack. 'I think it's retribution for past sins.'

Nadia lifted an eyebrow. 'What sins?'

'I...was thinking about what Twinkle said, on Friday night. After we watched Adam's old film. What he said about Paul.' Paul Hammond, their friend who had died in a car accident.

'What about him?'

'The fact that Twinkle felt responsible for his death.'

'He *wasn't* responsible,' Nadia said. 'Paul was drunk. He should have known better. But what does that have to do with anything?'

'I think Paul may be responsible for what happened here today.'

'Paul?' Nadia frowned, not really following. 'How can he be responsible? Paul Hammond is dead.'

'His spirit, I mean. I know you don't believe in that sort of thing. But when someone dies in difficult circumstances, their life force can often linger.' Nadia suppressed the urge to laugh, but Suzy was speaking with apparent sincerity. 'All that potential that's wasted, it doesn't go away. And us coming here together, this weekend, it may have acted as a focus for it.'

Nadia was having difficulty keeping her face straight. 'You think Paul is *haunting* us?'

'I think he may be,' the girl said, in all seriousness.

Nadia chuckled quietly. 'What, you think he's come back here to push two people off a cliff? You do realise how mad that sounds?' Suzy had always believed some pretty outlandish thing, but this was taking it to a new level.

'He's a restless spirit,' the woman insisted. 'Twinkle should have stopped him driving that day. He shouldn't have let him get into the car when he was over the limit like that. You remember? That's what he said.'

'But he was wrong. It was Paul's decision. He made a bad choice and he paid the price for it. It was awful, but these things happen. There was nothing supernatural about it. And anyway, what's any of that got to do with John? He wasn't even there. Why would Paul Hammond's spirit want to kill him?'

'The car he was driving,' Suzy said. 'Paul's car. John did the MOT on it, a month or two before he died.'

Nadia scratched her nose. 'I didn't know that. But even so..'

'It was quite a wreck, John said. The tyres were almost bald. The brake pads were worn away. But he let it through on the nod, as a favour.' That did sound like John. 'If the tyres had had more of a grip on them, then perhaps Paul might not have lost control of the vehicle. John told me that afterwards. He said the police came and talked to him about it, but as the MOT was two months before, they didn't have anything that would stick. And Paul was over the limit anyway, so they didn't bother to chase it up.'

'I wasn't aware of that. And did John feel guilty about it?'

'I don't think so. He only did what Paul asked him to do, as a favour. And he was never one to dwell on the past.'

'That's true. But seriously, Suzy. What's happened today, it had nothing to do with that accident. That was years ago. This is murder we're talking about. It's not a ghost story.' This was far too serious a business to indulge one of Suzy's flights of fancy. 'It was a human being who killed John. One of us, maybe. And it was them who dragged him across the rail road and tossed him down the steps.' On the way back to the cottage, they had seen a few more spots of blood, just outside the compound wall. 'It's a physical thing, it's not supernatural.'

'I think you're wrong,' Suzy said quietly. 'I think he's been here with us the whole weekend.' She shivered and picked up John's mobile phone. 'I would rather believe that than that one

121

of us is really a murderer.' She flicked through a few items on the phone. Briefly, she smiled.

'What is it?'

'I was just looking at a couple of photographs. There's one here of...' She stopped. Abruptly, her face paled.

'Suzy, what is it?' Nadia asked, with some concern.

Suzy stared down at the handset for a minute and then handed it across. The photograph was clear and unambiguous: Jill Clarke was up against a stone wall in the chapel, her legs straddling Liam Heigl's muscular body. The time stamp in the bottom right hand corner said Saturday 4th at 8.23am.

'Oh, Suzy!' Nadia breathed.

Chapter Nine

Samantha Redmond had never seen it first hand before. She knew Suzy had a temper, of course, and had heard the odd bit of muffled anger through the walls, but she had never witnessed the full fury up close like this. 'You had to go and do it, didn't you?' Suzy was bellowing at Jill Clarke. 'You just couldn't keep your hands to yourself, you stupid little slut.' Suzy was normally a kitten with her friends, forever smiling and upbeat. It was only behind closed doors that she allowed her anger its full rein, and then she could be every bit as ferocious as her husband. Now, however, she was letting rip in public and it was not a pleasant sight to behold.

Jill was sitting up on her bed, her jaw slack, her hands clenched together, her face puffy with tears. Suzy had not even given her time to put on her glasses. She had barrelled into the room without a moment's pause. 'I'm sorry, babes,' the girl mumbled. 'I didn't...'

'Look at you,' Suzy sneered, 'lying there with your boobs half out of your top. You're a disgrace, Jill Clarke. What could anyone ever see in you? You're forty-two years old, for heaven's sake. You're a mother. You have a husband and two children. Is that not enough? Do you have to ruin everyone else's life too?'

'It wasn't...I didn't...'

Samantha, who was sitting on her own bed, was struggling to catch up. Had something happened between Liam and Jill? Surely not. The Heigls had only just made up after their last row. But perhaps the blonde woman had discovered something new in the last couple of minutes. She was waving a mobile phone in her left hand. It was John's mobile; the blue one.

Samantha rose up from her bed, intent on making some effort to calm the situation, but before she could say a word, a shell-shocked Liam Heigl appeared in the doorway. 'It wasn't her fault,' he whispered awkwardly.

Suzy froze at the sound of her husband's voice. 'Don't you say a word!' she snarled, raising her palm to the door but not

x

123

looking at her husband. 'Don't you say a word to me!'

'It didn't mean anything!' Liam protested. 'It was just for old times' sake. We were both...feeling vulnerable.'

That was too much for Suzy. She wheeled round and turned the full force of her anger upon him. 'You are such a hypocrite, Liam Heigl. You go on and on at me. About me flirting, about me being friendly, about how I'm undermining you. Even when I'm just talking to my friends. As if I don't care a damn about you. As if I'm not devoted to our family and our children. As if I would ever do anything to hurt you. And yet what do you do, the moment my back is turned? Up against the wall with some filthy little slut, not fifty yards from the house.'

'Stop it, please!' Jill implored her.

'Don't take this out on her,' Liam snapped, stepping forward and suddenly going on the offensive. 'She's just lonely. Unhappy. This is about you and me, Suzy. About our marriage. And about respect.'

'Respect?' Suzy spat back, in disbelief.

'Do you think I don't know? Do you think I don't know about you? Your lack of fidelity.'

'Fidelity?!?' Suzy screeched. 'You don't have the first idea what you're talking about.'

'Of course not. I never do. You're the brains of the outfit. You're the creative one. I'm just the husband. I'm just meant to follow you around and bask in your glory.'

'It's never been like that,' she muttered.

By now, the raised voices had brought the entire household to the door. Nadia Kumar was hovering just outside, in the living room, with Adam Cartwright to her left. He looked utterly bewildered, but Nadia leaned in, to fill him in on the details. She would know what was going on, of course. She always did.

'You can't look me in the eye, though,' Liam continued bitterly. 'You can't look me in the eye and tell me you've never been unfaithful to me. Don't think I don't know what happened between you and John at the last reunion. And goodness knows how many times since then. Your clandestine meetings, that you never mention.'

'I haven't seen John in over two years.'

'But you have seen him?'

'We met up once or twice for coffee.'

'I bet you did. But you never mentioned it to me.'

'I didn't tell you about it because I knew you'd jump to the wrong conclusion. John and I are friends. Were friends. He's dead, for heaven's sake.' That got another whimper from Jill. 'Yes, we'd meet up for a chat once in a blue moon, when I was up in London. But that's all it was. How many times do I have to tell you?'

'But you slept with him, didn't you? In Wales. At the reunion?'

Suzy expelled her breath theatrically. 'You are such an idiot.' Her eyes were blazing now, the fury totally consuming her. 'I never slept with John, ever,' she snarled. 'And certainly not in Wales. But you won't believe that, will you? You won't ever believe a word I say.' She was losing control now, barely conscious of what she was saying. 'It wasn't John I slept with, if you must know. It was Adam. He's a much better lover than you ever were. And he is the father of your child.'

There was a horrified silence.

Oh, hell, Samantha thought. There was no going back from a statement like that. Liam staggered, as if he had been struck. Adam was standing behind him in the doorway. His hand went straight to his mouth.

Suzy stared at her husband, abruptly realising the enormity of what she had just said. 'It's not true,' she mumbled, suddenly contrite. 'I was just lashing out.'

Liam was in a daze. 'You slept with Adam?'

'I...did, yes.' Her voice was faltering now. 'You know we had a bit of a fling, at university, before you and I got together. In Wales...it was a one-off. For old times' sake. But he's not...Paul *is* your son. He really is. I was just lashing out. I'm sorry, I didn't mean to...' She moved towards him now, trying to placate him, but Liam pulled himself angrily away.

'For old times' sake,' he muttered. 'Like Jill and me.'

'Yes, just like that. I'm sorry. I'm so sorry. I do love you, I would never...'

This time it was Liam who raised his palm. 'I can't handle this right now,' he said. 'I need some air.' He turned on his heels but then pulled up abruptly at the sight of Adam Cartwright in the doorway. The other man could not meet his gaze. Liam bunched his fists together, as Adam shuffled aside; but then he marched briskly out of the room.

Suzy gave out a sob and collapsed onto the bed next to Jill. 'What have I done?' she lamented. 'Fifteen years of marriage.'

Jill was blinking uncertainly. She reached a hand across to the blonde woman. Despite everything Suzy had said about her, Jill still seemed sympathetic to her plight. 'He'll come round, babes. He always does.'

Suzy was too dazed to brush away the offer of comfort. 'I'm so sorry I said what I said,' she mumbled, looking across at her friend. 'Today of all days. I didn't mean it. I was just lashing out.'

'I deserved it, babes. I'm sorry too. I just got carried away. I don't *think*. I never do.'

And gradually the temperature in the room began to drop; but the damage had already been done. Samantha stood for a moment, trying to take it all in. Liam and Suzy had always had blazing rows. They were notorious for it. There had been dozens of flare ups and reconciliations over the years, but nothing like this. Samantha glanced across at Adam, who was slumped in the frame of the door, his face as pale as the white washed walls. She felt a pang of sympathy for him, as Nadia moved in to give him a hug. *As if this weekend couldn't get any worse*, she thought.

Adam was focusing all his attention on the lock. He had wanted to get away from the cottage and Nadia was happy to provide the excuse. They had tromped up the lighthouse's spiral staircase and stopped on a curve opposite the first wooden door.

'You really think you can open that?' Nadia asked, with

126

some scepticism.

'I'm not sure. But it's worth a try.' He pulled out his Swiss army knife and flicked open a couple of useful tools. 'It's a fairly basic lock, but it's been a while since I last did this.' An escapologist friend of his at the Edinburgh Festival had given him a couple of lessons. Adam's work there brought him into contact with all sorts of bizarre people.

Nadia gazed across at him as he set to work. 'Of course, you have actually checked the door is locked?' she teased.

Adam refused to rise to the bait, but she could see the half smile on his face as he replied in the affirmative. He inserted a small lever to steady the barrel of the lock and then set to work with the pick.

Nadia was trying to keep everything light and breezy. 'I don't know why you didn't do this on the other lock, when we opened up the winch room.'

'That was a padlock. Different sort of mechanism.'

'Well, I'll be suitably impressed if you do manage to do it.'

'Thank you. That makes it all worthwhile.'

Despite the casual banter, Nadia knew just how distressed Adam was at Suzy's unfortunate reveal. For him, their brief night of passion was a dim and distant memory, a mistake he'd long since put behind him. He had not expected it to resurface like this, in such a destructive manner.

Whenever Adam was really stressed, he would throw himself into some mad task or other, and today was no exception. He would take out his frustration on the lock and when he had calmed down they would discuss the matter quietly. That was his way. For now Nadia would stand back and let him get on with it, throwing in the occasional light comment as an added distraction.

It was bound to come out eventually, she thought. That moment of madness. They had all known about it, apart from Liam. *I'm surprised it took so long.* There had been lots of bed hopping that weekend at the castle. Suzy had slept with Adam. Jill had slept with Paul Hammond. Even Samantha and Twinkle had disappeared off together, though Nadia wasn't sure if anything

127

had happened there. And of course John Menhenick had tried it on with her. God, that had been embarrassing, trying to dampen down his drunken ardour. But he had at least taken no for an answer. And now he was dead, and Twinkle too.

Nadia could make no sense of it. Events were skidding out of control. Perhaps Adam was right and there was a stranger on the island, bunked out somewhere in one of these rooms. That was a far more palatable proposition than the alternative, that one of her friends was really a cold-blooded killer. But after witnessing the venom on display over the last couple of hours, she could not dismiss the possibility entirely. The bitterness and anger of decades might well have spilt over into violence.

Liam Heigl certainly had good reason to want to harm John Menhenick. He wouldn't have wanted the man blabbing about his tryst with Jill Clarke. Had he lost his reason and pushed Twinkle off a cliff, mistakenly thinking it was John? It seemed unlikely. Killing the bald man would not have prevented Suzy from finding out the truth. These things had a habit of coming out eventually, as Adam had just discovered.

What about Suzy? Could she have killed John and Twinkle? She hardly fitted the mould of a calculating killer. Too ditzy by half. And in any case, she and John were good friends. But maybe he had threatened to tell Liam about her and Adam, and about the child. Or perhaps he had just joked about it, in his usual cavalier manner – even though anyone with an ounce of sense could see that Liam really was the father – and Suzy had taken him at his word. But to kill him like that? Suzy certainly had a monstrous temper – as did her husband – but could that spill over into bloody murder?

And then there was Jill Clarke. The ginger-haired woman had always had a love-hate relationship with her one time husband. So far as Nadia knew, there had never been any actual violence there, but John had a way of deflecting attention, of covering up what he did with jokes and exaggerated winks. Who knew what kind of psychological harm he may have inflicted on his wife over the years. Maybe even – Nadia shuddered to think – physical harm. Jill, of course, had been fond of Paul Hammond.

She had shagged him in Wales, while John was trying it on with Nadia in another room. Could she have held John responsible for Paul's death? She must have known about the dodgy MOT. But that seemed pretty thin as a motive for murder.

Nadia's thoughts kept coming back to Twinkle. What if it wasn't a case of mistaken identity? What if John Menhenick had killed him, before he himself had died? Twinkle might have set up those webcams, for reasons of his own. What if John had found out about it? She could just picture the glee on his face, discovering Twinkle's dirty little scheme, knowing he had something juicy dangling over a friend's head. John's business hadn't been doing well, by all accounts. What if he decided to try a little blackmail? And then things had gone horribly wrong. Or, conversely, what if John had set the cameras up and Twinkle had found out? Perhaps John had pushed him over the cliff, knowing that everyone would think it was an accident; and maybe someone had seen him do it. Samantha Redmond perhaps. She had always been very close to Twinkle. How would she react if she had witnessed his murder first hand? Was it possible she had found out about the filming and had decided to take matters into her own hands?

There was one other possibility: perhaps the cameras had recorded something they shouldn't have, something that would incriminate one of the group. But something worthy of murder? Nadia shook her head. She was drowning in motives. Far better if it was someone else, a mad stranger rushing about. Then at least she did not have to suspect some of her oldest friends.

'Well, I think I've done it,' Adam announced, with a satisfied smile. The lock clicked in gentle confirmation. Adam had been fiddling with the mechanism for the better part of two minutes.

Nadia regarded him thoughtfully. Adam, of course, had organised this whole reunion. She had helped out in the day or two running up to it, but before that Adam had been working alone. He lived quite close by, relatively speaking, and he had known exactly who would be coming this weekend, which Nadia had not. He had a laptop with him, too, which could easily have been connected up to the webcams, though he wasn't particularly computer literate. She shook herself, embarrassed even to consider the possibility that her closest friend might be involved in any of this. But she could not rule out the idea entirely. The red haired man would have had ample opportunity to set everything up; and, as he had just shown, he did know how to pick a lock.

Adam pushed back the door of the storeroom and gestured theatrically for Nadia to step inside.

'Oh, no,' she said, with a grin. 'After you.'

Liam Heigl was sitting on the remains of the altar. There was a slight drizzle in the air but the wind dropped a little as Samantha Redmond moved into the ruins of the chapel. She had needed a bit of fresh air, away from the house, and Liam had evidently had the same idea.

Back in her bedroom, Suzy and Jill were talking quietly together and Samantha thought it was best to leave them to it. She had stepped outside for a minute and then seen Liam heading away from the compound.

Samantha had never been particularly good at dealing with confrontation. Seeing Liam and Suzy at each other's throats like that had been deeply upsetting, even if both of them had good reason to be angry. As an actress, Samantha had developed a fairly thick skin when it came to the critics and the newspapers – she could barrel through a bundle of reporters without the slightest hesitation – but a stand up row between friends was a different matter. How could you live like that, screaming at somebody one minute and then making love to them the next? Some people seemed to thrive on it. This time, though, things had gone too far.

'How are you doing?' she asked Liam sympathetically, pulling herself up onto the altar next to him. The stone was roughly hewn – or at least, heavily worn by the elements – and it was noticeably chilly, even through the thick fabric of her trousers.

Liam acknowledged her arrival with a nod. 'I've had

better days,' he admitted.

'It'll blow over,' Samantha assured him, trying her best to strike a positive note. 'You'll forgive her. She'll forgive you. You've done it a thousand times.'

'I know. It's just...I never thought.' He dropped his head into his hands. 'I know I've always worried about....well, things like that. But I didn't ever believe she would really do it.' He lifted his head. 'And with Adam, of all people. I suppose everyone knew, did they?'

Samantha looked away. It was true, they had all known. And not just about Adam. A lot of people had behaved badly that weekend. That was partly why Samantha did not feel inclined to judge Liam too harshly this time. That and the fact that she had always liked the man. Indeed, at university she had had something of a crush on him. 'Probably best not to ask,' she replied quietly.

Liam gazed across at her then, the wind whistling through his cropped brown hair, his puppy-dog face as forlorn as she had ever seen it. 'You've all been laughing at me, haven't you? All these years. And no one said a word.'

'No-one's laughing, Liam.'

'It did cross my mind, at the time, that something might have happened. But there was no real evidence, so I put it out of my mind. But then, at Jill's wedding last year.' He sat himself upright. 'She was talking to me about whether or not there would be another reunion. Whether Adam would organise anything. And she said I ought to make sure I was there this time. She even made a joke about keeping an eye on Suzy.' That had not been very tactful, Samantha thought. But then, Jill had never been the most tactful of people. 'I didn't think anything of it at the time, but afterwards I couldn't help thinking back. Could it have been more than a joke? Had something really happened at the castle after all? And once the idea took hold, I couldn't get it out of my head. But if something *had* happened, I was sure it would be with John, not Adam. That idea never even occurred to me.'

'Don't be too hard on him,' Samantha said. 'Or Suzy. They were both drunk that night. We all were.' It had been like their graduation party all over again. 'I know that's no excuse.

131

But they were just feeling sentimental. There was nothing more to it than that.'

'But you knew about it?' Liam asked.

Samantha nodded regretfully. 'We all knew. But it wasn't our place to say. Look Liam, Suzy was just lashing out. She didn't mean what she said about Paul. He's definitely your son. He has your eyes and everything. Your hair, your youthful complexion.'

Liam managed a smile at that. 'You're right. I know you're right.' He stretched out his legs. 'Look at me, sitting out here, wallowing in self pity, when two people have died. Two of our friends. What does anything else matter?' He sighed. 'Do you think Adam is right? Do you think there might be somebody else here on the island?'

'I don't know,' Samantha said. 'It's a pretty remote place. It's not at all easy to get to. My PA had quite a job sorting out the flights.'

Liam raised an eyebrow. 'You've got a PA?'

'Yes, I'm afraid so.' She looked down in embarrassment. 'I don't have a husband to do all the paperwork and make all the phone calls for me.'

Liam grinned at that. *He has such a lovely smile,* she thought.

'I do sometimes feel more like a PA than a husband,' he admitted. 'But you could have just hopped on a boat like we did. Isn't that what all the stars do? Put on a pair of sunglasses and blend into the crowd?'

Samantha shook her head. 'That's a bit of a myth. It doesn't really work. But that's what I mean. If there were someone else on the island, and if they came here to cause mischief or even to...to kill someone, there would be some kind of record of it, surely? You hire a boat. You stay in a hotel. They would know that. As soon as the police started looking, they'd find you. You'd never be able to get away with it. And if you couldn't get away with it, why would you take the risk? Going to all this trouble.'

'Always assuming that was the intention,' Liam said. 'I don't think logic necessarily comes into it where murder is concerned.'

'No, that's true.' Samantha sighed. 'That's why....that's why I think it must be one of us.' It was a horrible conclusion to draw, but it was the only one that fitted the facts. That was another reason she had wanted to get away from the house. 'I don't think it was planned. I can't believe anyone came here with murder on their mind. I think something must have happened after we got here. Something horrible that triggered it all off. There have certainly been enough arguments this weekend. Not just you,' she added, hastily.

Liam sat in silence for some moments. 'I hope you're wrong,' he said at last. 'If it is one of us then that'll be the end of our group. It'll tear us apart.'

'I know,' Samantha said. Even Adam Cartwright wouldn't be able to hold them together after this.

The room was bursting with equipment, most of which looked like it hadn't been used in decades. Abandoned machinery was propped up against the walls, there were cardboard boxes full of odds and ends, and on a table by the window a large radio transmitter. Nadia's eyes had lit up at the sight of that, but the device was not connected up and there was no sign of a battery. 'Do you think we could make it work?' she wondered. 'If we took it downstairs? Maybe fiddle with the wiring?' She had visions of calling up the Coast Guard and getting a boat out.

Adam was dubious. 'I don't think so. This must be fifty years old. There's no plug socket that I can see. We'd need to get the back off it and wire it up to the mains. I wouldn't know where to start.'

'What, you mean you've never represented a radio engineer at the Edinburgh Festival?' Nadia teased.

'Strangely enough, no.' He pushed the transmitter away. 'John might have been able to do something with it, or Twinkle, but I wouldn't have a clue.'

Nadia shrugged, dismissing the idea. 'Oh well. Can't be helped.' She peered out of the grated window. She had to pull herself up on tip-toes to see anything more than the line of the horizon. She ran a finger absently across the metal sill, on the other side of the table. There was quite a bit of dirt there. 'Is just me?' she asked, turning back to Adam and gesturing to the room as a whole. 'I'd have thought it would be dustier in here.'

Adam glanced around. 'You know, you may be right.' There were certainly plenty of cobwebs in the corners and layers of dust on the table, but not quite as much as you might have expected, if the place had been locked up for decades. 'This room certainly hasn't been abandoned for fifty years.' He crouched down to examine one of the cardboard boxes. He pulled back the flap and peered inside. 'Look at these.' He pulled out a thick black volume. 'A set of log books. They must go back decades.' He flicked through the first one. 'Maybe when they refurbished the cottage they dumped all the old stuff up here, to get it out of the way.' He smiled suddenly, returning the book to the box and rifling through some of the others. 'There's a couple of novels in here too. From the sixties.'

Nadia chuckled. 'For the long winter evenings.' She moved back from the window. 'But no sign of recent life. No intruder.'

'No, not that I can see.'

The second room, higher up, proved a little more interesting. 'It's not even locked,' Adam observed, pulling on the handle and opening the door.

'I didn't try that one,' Nadia admitted. 'I just assumed they were both shut up.' The chamber was situated directly below the lamp room. It seemed darker than the first room, even though the window was in the same position.

'Well, someone's definitely been in here,' Adam remarked, moving into the darkened chamber. There was an old mattress lying across the floor, next to the usual array of crates and boxes.

Nadia eyed it up with some interest. 'That could have been here for decades too.'

'Possibly.' Adam stamped a foot on it. Nadia half-expected a cloud of dust to engulf him, but there was barely more than a gentle puff. 'Or possibly not,' he added.

Nadia drew her scarf around her neck. 'Any other signs of life?'

Adam flicked a switch by the door, to see if the main light was working, but on close inspection it turned out there was no bulb in the socket. 'There's a lamp on the table,' he observed. He crouched down in front of it. 'There looks to be some oil in it.' The glass was fogged but not dusty. 'I think this has been used sometime recently.'

Nadia's eyes widened. 'So there is someone here.'

Adam was not entirely convinced. 'Well, there has been, but not necessarily in the last few days. It could be weeks or even months ago.'

'But the front door, when we arrived...'

'I know. And yesterday, the door to the tower being open.' Adam bit his lip. 'It's not completely impossible. But if someone *were* creeping about here, where could they be hiding? I mean, right now? They're not in the tower. And they'd be seen if they were wandering around the cottage.'

'There's the chapel,' Nadia suggested.

'Yes, but people nip out there all the time. That's where Jill does her exercises.'

'And Liam,' Nadia added, mischievously.

'Well, there you go.' Adam stood up. 'So where could our mysterious stranger actually hide? Where could he be right now?'

'Or she?'

'Or she.' Adam pushed against the oil lamp. 'I don't know if this makes things better or worse.'

'At least it's food for thought.'

'I think we'd better take a full inventory of everything in this room. See if our imaginary friend has left anything incriminating behind.'

'What, like a signed confession?' Despite the seriousness of the situation, Nadia was having difficulty stopping herself from laughing. She would often get a fit of the giggles at the most inappropriate of times.

'I think that might be expecting a bit much,' Adam

135

responded dryly.

'A murder weapon then?'

'Not much chance of that. Whoever did this, they wouldn't leave anything behind for us to find. Whatever they used to thump John with, they'd have got rid of it by now. Maybe thrown it out to sea. You know, if we're lucky, it might not have carried too far, if it was something heavy. The police might be able to find it.'

'When they get here.' Nadia bent down to examine one of the other cardboard boxes. She lifted the flap and gazed inside. There was a heavy object at the top, wrapped up in an old copy of the Daily Sketch, a long defunct newspaper. The paper was sticky and heavily stained. Nadia frowned and pulled back the edges. She froze, catching sight of the object within. 'Adam,' she breathed. 'You're not going to believe this.'

He leaned across. 'What is it?'

Nestling inside the newspaper was a heavy wooden mallet. Its head was stained with blood.

Chapter Ten

Adam Cartwright was taking charge of the situation with a renewed vigour. Bizarrely, the discovery of the murder weapon had proved something of a relief, to him and to Nadia. Back at the cottage, the group gathered together and listened calmly as Adam outlined what they had found up in the tower. He kept the details light, just the fact that they had stumbled upon a recently bloodied mallet, but that was enough to clinch the matter, so far as everyone in the house was concerned. There was somebody else here on the island with them; or at least, there had been until last night. Nadia could see the relief in their eyes. None of them were responsible for what was happening this weekend.

'Assuming they're still around,' Adam said, 'there aren't many places they can hide. So I suggest we make a systematic search of the island. We'll check the cottage and the lighthouse first and then fan out across the island. If everyone's in agreement?' There were nods across the table. 'If there *is* someone here, we'll find them.'

Before the meeting, Nadia had spent a few minutes in the kitchen with Samantha Redmond, preparing some sandwiches so that everyone could have a bite to eat. The dark-haired woman had taken the news of the discovery with her usual calm. Nadia had never been that close to Samantha and occasionally found her a little difficult to read. She could sometimes seem a bit aloof, although in reality she was probably just shy. That was rather ironic, considering how famous she was. But Samantha had never been above mucking in with the rest of them, and she had happily buttered up the bread and grated a bit of cheese from the fridge.

Out in the dining room, Liam and Adam had exchanged a few tense words before they got down to business. Adam had tried to broach the subject of the Wales reunion, in a misguided attempt to clear the air, but Liam had not wanted to hear it. 'I don't want to know,' he insisted. 'For the moment, we're all in this together. But when it's over, Adam, I'll tell you this: I don't ever want to see or hear from you again.'

Adam had not known what to say to that. 'Fair enough,' he agreed, sadly.

The mood brightened a little when Nadia and Samantha brought out the sandwiches, and once Adam had explained everything an air of calm descended upon the group. They munched away and considered his plan.

Liam voiced an obvious fear. 'What if this guy's armed?'

'I don't think that's likely,' Adam said. 'Not if he's using a mallet as a weapon. And there are more of us than there are of him.'

'He might still be carrying a knife,' the other man thought.

'Maybe we should do the same,' Nadia suggested. 'There are loads of sharp knives in the kitchen.'

'Well, I think we ought to search the house first, before we start worrying about that,' Adam said. 'I suggest we split into two groups. One group can run up the tower. The other one can check out the cottage. Once we've examined every little nook and cranny here, we can lock the place up and check the outhouses. Then maybe one group can circle north and the other one head down south. We need to check the cliff edges in particular. Are there any other beaches or access points? There might be a boat tied up out of sight somewhere.'

Samantha did not think that likely. 'We'd have seen it, surely?'

'Not if it was down south. Has anyone been down there, beyond the chapel?' That question provoked an uncomfortable silence. The chapel was still a sore point.

'I'll go with Suzy and Nadia,' Liam suggested. He met his wife's eye briefly. 'If there's a maniac on the loose, I don't want to let you out of my sight.'

Suzy nodded her agreement. 'Better if we stick together.'

Adam was happy with that arrangement. It limited the chances of any friction. 'So that leaves Jill, Samantha and me. We'll check the lighthouse while you three do the cottage.' He grabbed another sandwich. 'Just as soon as we've polished these off.'

Jill Clarke had been very quiet at the dinner table. It was unlike her, Samantha thought, but not surprising in the circumstances. The loss of her ex-husband had devastated the woman and the row with Suzy had scarcely helped. Her self esteem was probably now at an all time low. Suzy Heigl had calmed down enough to realise this and the two women seemed to have come to a fragile rapprochement. A couple of glasses of vodka had doubtless helped to oil the wheels. The same could not be said for the men, however, and Liam was sensible in suggesting he and Adam kept well apart for the duration.

Samantha accompanied Adam and Jill across to the lighthouse. Jill had gone back to her room first to pick up a pair of flat shoes. Samantha had suggested that might be more practical for her if they were to go walking around the island later on. 'All right, babes,' the woman agreed. 'You're the boss.'

The view from the top of the tower was spectacular. This was the first time Samantha had seen it. She did a quick circuit of the balcony, peering out across the island. It was an impressive if rather desolate place. There was certainly no sign of life down there; no mysterious stranger creeping about. Not that Samantha had expected there to be. *It's a fantasy*, she thought. *There's not going to be anybody else here.* Even after the discovery of the murder weapon, it had seemed an unlikely proposition to her. But at least the possibility had served to distract them all and brought the group back together, albeit temporarily.

'This is where we found the mallet,' Adam told her, as they made their way back down the stairs from the lamp room.

Jill shuddered, staring at the open door. 'I don't think I want to see.'

Samantha poked her head inside. There were crates and dusty equipment but the mallet was tucked away out of sight in one of the cardboard boxes. 'So John got up in the night, went out of the cottage and then somebody thumped him from behind?'

'Well, that seems the most likely sequence of events,' Adam agreed.

'My poor baby,' Jill mumbled. Adam gave her shoulder a

gentle squeeze.

'Do we know what he was doing, up and about at that hour?' Samantha asked. John had always been a night owl, but only when he was sharing a drink with his friends. She doubted he would sit up boozing on his own.

'Nothing good, I imagine. Perhaps he had the same thought as we did, wondering if there was somebody else here. He might even have known who it was.'

'Perhaps he was going out to meet somebody,' Jill suggested.

That was not impossible, Samantha thought, as she closed up the storeroom door. The stairwell was a bit of squeeze for three of them and Adam moved down a step to free up some space. But it still didn't make any sense. Why would anyone creep up here to hide a murder weapon, when it could be disposed of much more easily outside? And if there was a stranger lurking about, where had they disappeared to afterwards?

Liam, Suzy and Nadia had completed their search of the main house and were waiting in the hallway as the three of them emerged from the tower.

Adam threw a questioning look at Nadia. 'Not a whisper,' she told him.

They filed out the front door and Adam turned back to lock it up behind them.

Samantha pulled out her phone to check the time. It was just gone half past ten. It felt like a lot later.

'Right,' said Adam. 'We'll do a quick circuit of the compound and then move up to the head of the island.' The northern heights, where they had recovered Twinkle's body. He gestured to Nadia and the two Heigls. 'I suggest you three head down to the tail and work your way back up. Check out the landing stage too, if you don't mind. If you find anything, give us a shout. Don't take any risks and be careful with the cliffs. There's a bit of a breeze brewing up.'

'Yes, dad,' Nadia replied, with a grin. 'Don't worry, we'll be careful.' And with that she and the others headed off towards the rear of the compound.

Adam and Jill remained behind, momentarily lost in thought. They were an odd pair, Samantha thought, regarding them now. Jill had always been fond of Adam. He was something of a father figure for the group. Even now, he had shown particular consideration for her feelings, getting the others to check out the landing stage, making sure Jill didn't have to see the body of her ex-husband a second time.

Adam became aware that Samantha was staring at him. 'What is it?' he asked. 'Is everything all right?'

'Yes, sorry, just thinking,' she said. 'Shall we check the winch room first?'

In other circumstances, Nadia might have found it quite amusing. Liam and Suzy were on their best behaviour. The sight of John Menhenick's body – their first port of call, lodged halfway down the steps – could not help but be a sobering one. The married couple were putting aside their anger for now, to concentrate on the task at hand. If there really was a madman prowling about, then they needed to stick together. But it was obvious that this would only be a temporary truce between them. Liam had suggested they start here, checking out the landing stage. It was better to get it out of the way. Nadia saw the look of horror, though, on Suzy Heigl's face as she reached the top of the steps and took in the body of her dead friend a second time.

'Do you want to wait up here?' Nadia asked, with some sympathy. They didn't need three people to go down to the jetty.

Suzy shook her head. 'We should stick together.'

The small group began its descent. Liam led the way, with Suzy following behind him and Nadia bringing up the rear, watching her feet every step of the way and grasping the handrail as tightly as possible. The wind was whistling heavily and Nadia felt the cold through her thick coat and her jumper, even in the direct light of the sun, which was peeping occasionally through the clouds.

They stopped for a moment as John's body loomed, his eyes still wide and staring. It felt disrespectful to leave him like that, all tangled up.

Suzy regarded her dead friend for a moment, wiping a tear from her eye, then stepped forward and crouched down in front of him.

'Better not to touch him,' Nadia whispered, as the woman reached out a hand.

'We don't want to disturb anything before the police get here,' Liam said.

'I should close his eyes, at least.' Suzy's fingertips brushed the dead man's face and she gently pulled the lids closed. Then she kissed her fingers and touched them to his forehead. Nadia watched sadly as Suzy rose to her feet and Liam quietly enfolded her in his arms. The couple broke apart a moment later and Suzy wiped her eyes again. 'I'm sorry,' she said, glancing across at Nadia in embarrassment.

'That's all right.' She allowed the woman a moment to regain her composure.

Liam had had a gruesome thought. 'Do you think...do you think we ought to photograph him? For the police, I mean?'

Suzy recoiled at the idea. 'That's horrible!'

It was a rather grim suggestion, but not without some merit. 'It's a thought, I suppose,' Nadia said. 'If it helps the police find out who did it.'

Suzy took a deep breath. 'Yes, you're right,' she agreed, doing her best to put a brave face on it.

Liam patted his pockets, searching for his mobile. 'Damn. My phone's back at the cottage.'

That left it to Nadia and, when it came to it, she could not bring herself to take the photograph. Not on her own phone. It was too creepy.

Suzy was already moving off, heading down the last of the steps towards the small jetty at the base of the cliff.

Nadia exchanged a look with Liam and the two of them followed her down.

The landing stage was a concrete platform not much higher than the level of the sea. A couple of heavy duty posts were welded into the concrete, with a hoop for tethering the mooring lines. The platform was wet with the spray of the sea and any evidence of anyone moving about down there had long since been swept away. There were certainly no boats. A few tufts of grass and weed speckled the sides of the lower steps and here Nadia found a couple of cigarette butts, wedged into a crevice. She pointed them out to Liam but he just shrugged. They might have been there for days or weeks.

'John did smoke like a chimney, though,' Nadia reminded him. 'You never know. He might have come down here to meet someone. A boat even. And then somebody clobbered him on the way back up.'

Liam scratched an ear hole. 'Maybe. But his phone was up at the top, wasn't it? So he must have got that far at least. And wasn't there some blood outside the compound too?'

'Yes.' It was all rather confusing. *Nobody would have followed him all the way back up to the compound just to thump him and then toss him back down the steps,* she thought. *They'd have clobbered him down here and thrown him into the sea.* She put her hands in her pockets. So perhaps he hadn't been meeting anyone after all.

Liam was taking one last look around. 'There's nothing here,' he concluded.

They had better luck at the chapel, back up top. There were more cigarette butts and, in a clump of grass by one of the walls, an old beer bottle.

Nadia had humped all the crates of beer up to the cottage herself, with a little help from Adam. 'That's not one of ours,' she said, eyeing up the bottle in Liam's hand. It was a different brand. The glass was broken in half and the jagged edge looked rather brutal. There were lots of footprints scattered about too, inside the chapel, and the impression of a mat where Jill had laid out her exercise roll. But it was all inconclusive. Any of the things they had found could have been here for months.

They headed downhill to the lowest point of the island. Nadia hadn't been this far south before and the wind was particularly ferocious. She pulled her scarf around her neck and tried to stop her teeth from chattering. *I should have brought my hat.* The wind chill here made it seem much colder than the north side of the island. The cliff edge was much lower, however, and there were enough jagged edges that somebody could probably climb up it. Samantha would be able to, anyway. There were no steps this time, but there was a small beach, not unlike the one to the north. It was doubtful you would be able to moor a boat there, however, and – like the beach where Twinkle's body was discovered – the place was being constantly pummelled by the sea.

They turned away and began to move back up the island, combing the remaining cliff edges and crossing east to west periodically to make sure they didn't miss anything. But there was nothing to miss. No little caves unmarked on the map. No little boats quietly moored. Unless Adam and the others had had more luck, there was nobody else on the island.

It's just us, Nadia realised grimly. *And that means one of us is a murderer.*

Samantha's group had not found anything of interest either. There was nothing in the winch room or the other small storage huts; and there were so many footprints on the grass to the north of the compound that it was impossible to tell one set of prints from another. They had all been shuffling about out here yesterday afternoon, organising the recovery of Twinkle's body. All that remained to do, therefore, was circle the fringes of the island, meet up with the others and then head back to the cottage. 'If there was anyone out here,' Adam suggested, 'they must have left last night, after John was killed.'

Samantha did not believe that for a minute. Nothing she had seen this morning had altered her view: there was nobody else here. As the search progressed, she found herself reflecting, morbidly, on which of her friends might be to blame instead. Try as she might, she could not picture any of them as a murderer, except perhaps John Menhenick, and he was already dead. Yet one of them had to be responsible.

The three friends were making their way around the west

side of the compound now, following the line of the wall and examining the turf as they went. Adam was sticking close to the cliff edge, peering over the side at every opportunity, in search of any clues.

'Be careful, babes,' Jill Clarke said, watching his feet nervously as he skimmed the verge.

Adam flashed her a warm smile. 'It's all right. The wind's blowing inland at the moment. I'm not likely to be blown off.'

'No harm in taking care though,' Samantha told him.

Adam stopped for a second and dropped down onto his knees. It was one thing to peer, but to get a complete view over the edge you needed to poke your head a little way beyond the rim.

The sun was peeking briefly through the clouds, as it had been doing intermittently for the last hour or so, and a warm glow momentarily bathed the trio. Samantha turned away from the glare and caught sight of the other group, huddled together on the far side of the chapel. Suzy Heigl was gesticulating broadly at some feature of the terrain, but it didn't look as if they had found anything either. As Samantha had feared, this whole expedition had been a fool's errand from the start.

Her eyes came to rest on a blackened patch of grass a little closer to hand. The sunlight had illuminated it briefly, catching her attention. She frowned and strode across, leaving the other two back near the compound wall. She crouched down. A small patch of grass barely wider than a grapefruit had been flattened and scorched. 'Adam, come and look at this,' she said. Her voice barely carried the distance, but he saw the gesture and rose to his feet.

'What have you found?'

Jill Clarke adjusted her glasses and followed him over.

'I'm not sure,' Samantha admitted. A small area had been blackened and burnt. There was soot too, nestling in the blades of grass leading from there to the cliff edge, less than a metre away. 'It looks like there's been a fire,' she said.

Adam crouched down next to her. 'A very small one,' he agreed. He ran his hands across the grass. 'It's still warm. I suppose that could just be the sun.'

'But somebody has definitely been out here.' Samantha was taken aback by that. She really hadn't expected to find anything at all.

Adam pursed his lips, trying to gauge the significance of the find. 'So, somebody burnt something and then kicked the embers over the edge.' He shuffled across the grass.

Samantha glanced back at the compound. The terrain between here and the wall had been flattened by dozens of footsteps, some more recent than others. There were no identifying marks that she could see. Their own footsteps just now had already muddied the scene and, anyway, most of the group had walked around here at some point, although perhaps not quite this close to the edge. She looked back at Adam, who was now spread out on his belly, his head once again dangling over the cliff top. 'Can you see anything?' she asked.

'I'm not sure.' His hand was out of sight, exploring the terrain below. 'Something's definitely been shoved over the edge. There's a bit of soot down here. One or two embers. Hang on a minute.' He looked back. 'There is something else, caught up on a clump of nettles. A fragment of something. Can you grab hold of my legs? I'm going to try to edge down and grab it.'

The two woman exchanged doubtful glances. 'Be careful, babes,' Jill warned. But Adam was not to be dissuaded. Samantha crouched down next to him and the two women took hold of a leg each. Jill flashed a grin, alive to the absurdity of the situation, but then regarded Adam anxiously as he shuffled his torso forward and twisted his upper body over the edge of the cliff.

'Nearly there,' he wheezed, stretching out his arms.

'That's far enough, Adam,' Samantha said, holding his leg as tightly as she could. 'We're not going to dangle you right off the edge.' She was damned if they were going to lose a third person that way.

'It's all right. I think...' He let out a slight groan. Samantha could feel the tension as he extended himself as far as he could go. 'That's it. I've got it.' He paused for a second and then stifled a nervous laugh. 'Now how the hell do I get back up?'

That was a rather more awkward manoeuvre. Adam had to shuffle himself backwards with one hand clasping whatever it was he had found. They flipped him over at the last moment and he wormed his upper body clumsily back onto level ground. Jill started to laugh and Adam grinned up at her. 'You look like a beached whale!' she said.

'God, I wouldn't want to do that again.' The two of them chuckled for a moment, a welcome relief of tension. Once Adam had recovered his composure, Samantha helped him to sit up. Quickly, he scrabbled onto his knees.

'So what did you find?' she asked.

Adam opened his hand. 'A bit of fabric. A corner piece, I think.'

Samantha peered at it. It was some kind of cotton-like material, scorched and black, except the tip which was a solid lump of green and white.

'I don't think it's clothing,' he added.

Samantha took it from his hand. 'It's not clothing,' she agreed. It had a slightly rougher feel than that. 'It's a towel, I think. From the bathroom. It must be one of ours.'

Adam was none the wiser. 'Green and white. Who has a green and white towel?'

Samantha looked across at the bespectacled figure of Jill Clarke. 'This is yours,' she said, in disbelief.

Chapter Eleven

Nadia Kumar only became aware of the problem as she returned to the compound. Adam was chatting calmly to Jill Clarke a little way out from the white stone walls, but the woman herself was gesticulating wildly. 'I didn't do nothing,' she protested. 'I loved him, the stupid bugger. I wouldn't harm a hair on his head.'

'Nobody's saying that you did,' Adam reassured her. His voice was measured and unthreatening. 'But this is your towel?'

'Anyone could have nicked it. It was hanging up in the bathroom.'

Samantha Redmond was standing back, holding a small piece of fabric in one hand. She looked gratefully to Nadia as the other woman stepped onto the rail track and interrupted the conversation. 'What's going on?' she asked. Suzy and Liam Heigl pulled up behind her and Adam quickly filled them in on what they had found. Samantha held up the fragment of towel for them to see.

'I didn't do it,' Jill said again, tears streaming down her face. 'I loved him. I always loved him.'

'I know you did,' Nadia agreed, coming forward. 'Come on, let's get you inside.'

There were grim faces everywhere as they gathered in the living room. It appeared, after all their efforts to prove the opposite, that one of them really had killed John Menhenick. Nobody else would have had access to the bathroom last night. But could it really have been Jill? Nadia found that very hard to believe.

'We should search her room,' Liam suggested quietly. 'See if there's anything in there that might incriminate her.'

Jill looked up sharply from the sofa, as if she had just been slapped. 'You don't really think I did it, do you? Liam?'

The man threw up his hands. 'I don't know what to think.' It was clear from his expression that he was seriously entertaining the idea. 'I wouldn't blame you if you had.'

Jill let out a low moan and gazed down at her lap, pulling

self-consciously on the hem of her skirt. 'I don't want anyone going through my things.'

Nadia exchanged a look with Adam. They didn't really have much choice. 'We'll be very circumspect,' she said.

'And we'll search all the rooms,' Adam declared. 'Not just yours.'

'We should probably have a look at her mobile phone as well,' Liam added.

That was going too far for Jill. 'You all think I did it, don't you?' She gazed up at them in horror. The whole group was gathered awkwardly around the sofa where she was sitting. 'You really think I could do that? That I could kill John, of all people? And Twinkle too? It's bonkers. I've never hurt no-one.'

Nadia was inclined to believe her. Jill had always been a larger than life figure and she certainly liked her drink, but she was never malicious. Nadia could not see her lashing out at anyone, less still pushing someone off a cliff.

'We ought to have a look at her phone, though,' Liam insisted quietly. He held out his hand.

Jill was not happy. 'There's private stuff on there,' she protested, grasping the mobile tightly to her chest. 'Babes, I swear, there's nothing on here about John.'

'Just let us have a look,' Liam said patiently, bending over to take the phone from her hands. She pulled it away from him sharply and sprang to her feet, causing the others to step back in surprise. 'Leave me alone,' she moaned, pushing her way through the group and darting across to the bathroom at the far corner. The door slammed shut behind her and the lock clicked into place.

Nadia made to follow her, but Adam raised a hand. 'Maybe leave her for a minute?'

Nadia shook her head. 'It's better to talk.' She did not like to see Jill upset like this, especially when there was no real proof against her. Anyone could have grabbed that towel. Adam relented and Nadia moved across to the bathroom door. She took a breath and knocked gently.

'Hey, Jill,' she called through the door. 'Look, no-one's accusing you of anything. But Liam's right. We should take a look at everyone's phones.'

'You're all ganging up on me,' Jill called back miserably from the other side of the door.

'Honestly, we're not. Well, I'm not, anyway. I think there's been a mix up somewhere and we need to get it sorted out. It's not just you. We're going to look at everyone's phone. We should have done it before. So why not let me have a quick look at yours, eh? If there's anything embarrassing on there, I promise I won't show it to the others.'

There was another plaintive moan from behind the door but a few seconds later the phone was slid under the bottom. 'Just you, babes,' Jill mumbled through the keyhole.

'Just me,' Nadia agreed. 'Thanks, Jill.' Her heart went out to the woman. To be accused of the murder of her ex-husband, only hours after she herself had discovered the body. If Jill was innocent, that would be like a dagger to her heart. She bent down to pick up the mobile. 'We'll get this sorted out, I promise.'

She returned to the others. Liam was still intent on searching Jill's room, and Samantha and Suzy were happy to help out.

Once they were gone, Nadia sat down next to Adam and flicked on the mobile. It was a bright orange smart phone. 'I'm pretty sure she didn't do it,' Nadia said quietly, glancing across at him. Adam looked tired, his face as grave as she had ever seen it. 'Why on earth would she? This is Jill we're talking about.' The sofa was far enough away from the bathroom door for them not to have to worry about being overheard. 'She's not a killer. And any one of us could have grabbed that towel.'

Adam was not ready to pass judgement either way. 'Perhaps. But she does have a pretty good motive. Her divorce from John was pretty messy, you know. And think of the damage to her current marriage, if John had showed her husband those photos he took yesterday morning.'

Nadia bit her lip. 'That still doesn't seem like much of a motive to me. That kind of thing is bound to come out, no matter what you do. And why would she kill Twinkle? Assuming she killed both of them.'

Adam shrugged. 'Who knows? Perhaps that was a case of mistaken identity. Jill was very fond of Paul Hammond, back in the day. Seeing him in that film the other night, and hearing what Twinkle said about the accident, it might have brought it all back for her.'

'Yes, but not to the point of murder.' Nadia was skimming quickly through the phone as she spoke. 'And why burn the towel? What was she trying to cover up?'

'Well, that's the really interesting question,' Adam said. 'There wasn't that much blood on John's head that I could see, but there was some. If he was struck from behind, there might have been a fair bit to start with.'

'We saw some blood on the track,' Nadia pointed out. 'There was even a few spots of it near the compound wall.'

'Well, that's it. If he was hit some distance away from the place where he ended up, then someone must have carried his body over there, or dragged it. How do you do that in the middle of the night without getting blood on your clothes? At least, a little bit.'

Nadia grimaced, picturing the scene. 'I suppose if it's just the head, you'd find something to cover it over with.'

'Well, exactly. Like a towel. But what happens afterwards? You've tipped the body down the stairs but you wouldn't be able to wash the towel. You'd have to dispose of it somehow.'

'By setting light to the thing?' Nadia was sceptical.

'And tossing the embers over the side of the cliff.'

'It all sounds a bit messy.'

'It wasn't very well thought through,' Adam agreed. 'They must have been making it up as they went along. Which makes it sound a lot more like Jill than some masked intruder.'

That was true enough. 'But how would all that tie in with the webcams? And the lighthouse doors?'

Adam sighed, stretching out his legs. 'I wish I knew. Have you found anything on that?' He gestured to the phone.

Nadia shook her head. 'Just a few photos. There's a really bad one of you.' She chuckled. 'Oh, you should have a look at my phone, by the way.' She reached into her bag, which was resting on the coffee table. 'I promised we'd all check each others.'

Adam grinned, waving it away. 'It's all right, Nadia. I trust you.'

'That's as maybe,' she joked, 'but I'm not altogether sure I trust you.' She placed the phone on the sofa between them. 'Besides, I quite fancy having a look at yours. See if you're as perfect as you always try to make out. Oh, and I should take a look at your laptop as well.'

'Oh god!' Adam shuddered theatrically. The computer was resting on the table, next to Nadia's handbag. He leaned forward. 'I'd better just delete my browsing history first.'

Nadia was busily skimming through Jill's device. 'A couple of dating apps on here,' she observed.

Adam looked across in amusement. 'For a married woman?'

'You're hardly in a position to judge.' She grinned. 'Some...er...some rather dodgy websites she's got bookmarked.' Nadia stifled a laugh. Jill had something of a liking for athletic looking men, judging by her browsing history. Nothing wrong with that, of course. 'Oh, one or two slightly more embarrassing photographs she must have downloaded from somewhere.' A few close ups of some very well proportioned individuals. Adam raised an eyebrow, but Nadia didn't think she should let him see those.

'Any text messages?'

'A few.' Nadia was already scrolling back through them. 'The last one was on Friday morning. From a work colleague.' A slightly joky message. 'Telling her to behave herself this weekend.'

Adam smiled. 'Not much chance of that, was there? What about from John?'

'I'm just searching.' She tapped in the name. 'One about three weeks ago, arranging to pick up the kids. Nothing much else that I can see.' Nadia switched off the phone. 'I don't think there's anything on here.'

Adam was looking down at his laptop. A sudden thought

occurred to him. 'She knew the password for John's mobile. She might know the password for his tablet as well.'

'She said she didn't. Why, do you think she might have sneaked into his room and taken a look?'

'It's possible,' Adam said. 'Maybe she found something on there that she didn't like...'

'Something bad enough she'd want to kill him?'

Adam shrugged. 'Who knows?'

At this point, Liam Heigl popped his head around the far door, interrupting their conversation. 'Guys, I think we may have found the smoking gun,' he announced solemnly. In his hand he was holding a gold cigarette lighter.

Nadia and Adam rose to their feet. 'Where did you find that?' Nadia asked.

'In Jill's handbag. It's definitely John's. Look, it's got his initials on it.' The lighter was a chunky affair and had the letters "JM" stencilled on the side. 'She must have grabbed it out of his pocket last night,' Liam guessed.

Nadia closed her eyes, not wanting to believe the evidence of her own eyes. But Liam was right. It was pretty damning.

'We should bring her out here,' he declared. 'Confront her with this. Get her to confess. Then we can lock her up and wait for the police to arrive.'

Nadia did not like the idea of a public inquisition. Jill was still innocent until proven guilty. 'Let me have a word with her,' she said. 'On the quiet. Just...leave us alone for ten minutes. Let me talk to her. If she is guilty, she'll know the game's up, when I show her the lighter. I'll...I'll try and persuade her to do the right thing.'

Nadia had brought a bottle of beer for herself and the dregs of the vodka for Jill. The two women were sitting opposite each other in the bathroom, Jill squatting on the loo, with the lid down, Nadia propped up on the side of the bath. Nadia could recall similar heart-to-hearts in the past – boyfriend trouble at university, all the usual things – but nothing had ever been quite this grave. That was why Nadia had brought the booze. She knew it would help to steady Jill's fragile nerves.

The bathroom wasn't large but a fair amount of light filtered in through the one frosted window. Jill was gazing down at her lap, the vodka in her hand. Her glasses were drooping slightly on the bridge of her nose and her red hair was looking more straggled than usual.

It hadn't taken much effort to persuade her to unlock the door. 'I've brought you a drink,' Nadia had called out as cheerfully as she could manage 'You could probably do with one. I've had a look through your phone. There's a really dreadful photo of Adam on there from Friday night, but nothing incriminating.'

Jill had opened the door without another word. Nadia slipped the catch back on when she stepped inside, to make sure the two of them were not disturbed.

'Oh, babes,' Jill mumbled, pouring out the last of the vodka into a glass and draining it gratefully. 'What a mess, eh?'

Nadia nodded, nestling the beer bottle in her hands. 'Not what we signed up for,' she agreed. Jill placed her now empty glass down on the tiled floor and an awkward silence descended. Nadia was not really sure how to begin this conversation. An outright accusation might make Jill clam up completely. Better just to get her talking. 'Adam's tearing his hair out,' she said eventually. 'His big weekend ruined. He was hoping we'd have such a good time.'

Jill managed a smile at that. 'Bless him. It's not his fault. He's always so calm, ain't he? Whatever happens. Always in control of everything.'

'He likes to create that impression,' Nadia agreed, with a sly grin. 'But it's only on the outside. It's funny, we've all known each other for such a long time. It's so easy to slip back into the old relationships. But something like this, it makes you realise just how little we know each other, really. All the things that are going on under the surface.'

'Not me, babes,' Jill said, seriously. She leaned back against the cistern and wiped her mouth with the back of her hand. 'What you see is what you get.' She gazed down at herself, the short skirt and orange strappy top looking rather the worse for wear after the morning's activity. 'Look at me. What a mess, eh? Forty-two years old and still dressing like a teenager. Mutton, that's what John said I was. And he was right.'

'That's rubbish,' Nadia told her firmly. 'Jill, you shouldn't do yourself down. You look great.'

Jill shook her head. 'I look awful. I'm such a stupid bitch. I act like a tart and drink like a fish.' She gazed down at the empty glass regretfully. 'And I'm a lousy mother too.'

'Rubbish,' Nadia insisted again. 'You're a great mum.' Jill was getting maudlin now and that would not help the situation. Nadia took a swig of beer and marshalled her thoughts. *Best get down to business*, she decided. 'So tell me about John. Did you see much of him, after the divorce?'

Jill shrugged. 'Just picking up the kids. Once a month, that's all. He always put on a bit of a show for them.'

'You didn't row?'

'No, not in front of them. And Nathan – my husband – he kept well out of the way. He knew what John was like.'

'And how did you feel, him coming here this weekend?'

She scratched the side of her face. 'I don't know, babes. I thought it would be all right. We're adults. But he kept needling me. Making sarky comments. You know what he's like.'

'I suppose that must have got under your skin?'

'A little, yeah. It wasn't as if I ever expected him to behave like a saint. I'd always hoped...I don't know.' She sighed. 'I always thought somewhere, deep down, he still cared for me. You know? Just a little bit. But this weekend...I realised what a total prat I'd been. I'd thought....I don't know, I'd thought we might hook up. Just one last time, for old times' sake. Like Adam and Suzy.'

'I don't think that was ever likely to happen.'

'No, I know. I was deluded. He didn't give a toss. I'm not sure if he ever really loved me. So I thought, what the hell. I don't want him anyway.'

'And you started making eyes at Adam? And Liam?'

155

'Yeah. I don't know why. I suppose I thought he might get jealous. It was mad. I didn't know what I was doing. And Liam...God, babes, what a stupid thing to do. I never stop to think, do I? It was all me. I threw myself at him. Didn't give him a chance. And now Suzy hates my guts. She's only holding back because...' Jill gestured vaguely. 'Because of all this. And John....even after all he'd done to me, even knowing he didn't give a toss, I still...I still wanted him. I still loved him.'

Nadia nodded sympathetically. 'You were married a long time. But the divorce, it was quite acrimonious, wasn't it?'

'Yeah.' Jill stared sightlessly at the tiled walls. 'He caught me shagging his best mate. I thought he was going to kill me.'

Nadia hesitated. 'Did he...hit you?'

'No.' The response was a little too emphatic. 'Well, not then, anyway. He just packed his bags and left.'

"Not then". Nadia didn't like the sound of that. 'Did he ever hit you? When you were married, I mean?' It was an awkward question, but in the circumstances it could hardly be avoided. John had never been a violent man, so far as Nadia was aware. Oh, he had a cruel sense of humour, but that was not the same thing at all. He had always claimed to be good with his fists, though. Nadia had assumed that was just male bragging. Behind closed doors, however, things might have been very different.

'We argued. He did sometimes give us a whack.' Jill looked down at her lap in embarrassment. 'It was my fault, babes. I shouldn't have provoked him. I'd drink too much and say something stupid. And he'd get angry. Of course he would. Who wouldn't?'

'And he hit you?'

Jill met her gaze then, trying to convey her point as forcefully as she could. 'It was just his way. It was nothing serious. I provoked him. He lashed out. I was never badly hurt.'

Nadia was appalled. 'That's not the point, Jill. He had no right to hit you. Nobody does. God. Didn't you ever...call the police? If Richard thumped me I'd be straight on the phone. No-one has the right to do that to you. Not a husband, or a father or anyone.'

156

'But it wasn't his fault, babes. If I hadn't been such a disappointment to him...'

Nadia was emphatic. 'It was never your fault. If he hit you, he was the one to blame. You should have walked out the first time it happened.'

Jill shook her head sadly. 'Oh, babes. We're not all like you. I loved him, don't you understand? He was my baby. I could never have left him. It was my own stupid fault it all fell apart.' She swallowed hard, her mind flipping back to the events which had led to the divorce. 'The kids were away with mum and dad that weekend. John had said something hurtful and stormed out for the evening. I got drunk. His best mate happened to call by, a bloke from work. And I threw myself at him. He'd always fancied me. And we ended up in bed together. John came back and caught us at it. He just walked out. He wasn't even mad. He just didn't want to be with me any more. And that was that. Seven years of marriage over. But I'd have gone back, babes, any time, if he'd offered.'

'And Nathan? Your new husband. He's a decent man?' Nadia had not been at the wedding last year. She had not had the chance to meet him.

Jill nodded firmly, wiping her eyes. 'I don't deserve him. He does everything right. But he has to work long hours. And the kids are at school now. I get so lonely. I didn't kill him, babes,' she added quietly. 'I would never have hurt a hair on his head.'

Nadia met the other woman's gaze and, strangely, she believed her. 'What about the towel?' she asked gently.

Jill had no answer to that. 'It's mine, babes. I don't know how it got out there.'

'You didn't notice it was missing this morning?'

'No, I didn't. But then, look at me. I ain't even had a shower yet. I do my exercises first, don't I? Exercises, then shower, then breakfast. I was just coming back here when I...' Her face fell. 'When I found him.'

Nadia glanced around the room. There were several towels on the rack, of varying colours. The blue one was probably Liam's. There was a small pot by the sink, with various toothbrushes, and marks in the grouting where the webcams had been removed. 'Is there anything else missing from here?' she asked, out of curiosity.

Jill looked around. 'No, nothing. Nothing that I can see.' She swung her head and peered at the ledge underneath the frosted window. There were a few bottles on top of it: aftershave, roll on deodorant. 'I think there might have been an aerosol there. Hair spray. Samantha's, not mine. She probably took it back to the room.'

Nadia inclined her head. 'I'll ask her about it.'

'She'd have heard me, wouldn't she, if I'd got up in the night?' Jill thought suddenly. 'You know how much I clomp about.'

That was a point. They all shared rooms. How could any of them have got up without the other person hearing?

'We shared a room, back at Uni. Samantha and me. Think about it, me shacked up with a film star.' She chuckled. 'Who'd have thought it, eh?'

'You shared with Twinkle too, didn't you?'

'Yeah. Well, not a room, but the apartment. Student digs. He was such a lovely bloke. He doted on Samantha.'

'Yes, I know. You were never tempted to sleep with him?' Nadia enquired mischievously.

'What Twinkle?' Jill grinned. 'Nah. Poor bleeder. He was sweet, a real teddy bear, but you could never fancy him. Not with that face.' She laughed. 'He was good fun, though, on the quiet. Would stay up drinking all night.'

'You didn't feel resentful, later on?'

Jill frowned, not quite following. 'Resentful? About Twinkle?'

'About what happened to Paul Hammond.'

Jill hesitated. She knew all about the accident, of course.

'You were quite fond of him, weren't you. Of Paul?'

The woman nodded sadly. 'I should have married him. Not that he would have had me. I was so upset when he died. We slept together, that weekend, at the castle.'

'I remember.'

'And then on Friday, seeing him again...'

Nadia suppressed a chuckle. 'Yes, I don't think it was the best idea Adam's ever had, showing that film.'

'But Twinkle weren't to blame for what happened to him. Yeah, he should have spoken up. But we've all done it. Had a skinful and thought, well, it's only a couple of miles, what does it matter?'

'And John? Did you know about the car? The MOT?'

'Only afterwards.' Jill looked away. 'He shouldn't have done that neither. Oh, babes, it was all such a mess. But it weren't as if either of them wanted him dead. It was just an accident. That's what the police said. Could have happened to anyone.'

'I know. I'm just clutching at straws,' Nadia admitted. 'Trying to work out why anyone would want the two of them dead.'

Jill wiped her mouth again. 'It's obvious, init? Them cameras.' She gestured to the gaps between the tiles. 'Someone was getting their rocks off, filming us all. One of us found out and blew their top.'

'Do you think John might have set them up?'

'I don't know, babes. He's seen most of us with our kit off at one time or another. Why would he bother?'

'Twinkle then?'

'I suppose. He always kept himself to himself. But I wouldn't have thought he was that desperate.'

'No, neither would I. Were you there when Samantha found the first camera?'

'Yeah. I thought it must be some sort of joke.'

'And what about the network connection that Liam found? Did you notice that, when you were playing with your mobile?'

'No. Adam said there was no wi-fi, so I had it off most of the time. Except when I was taking a few snaps.'

'Yes, I saw those.' Nadia chuckled again. 'I think one of them was even in focus.'

Jill gave a weak grin. 'I've never been much cop at that sort of thing.'

'So you had no idea anything strange was going on until

Samantha found the first camera?'

'No, nothing at all.'

'And last night. Did she get up at all? Samantha?'

Jill shrugged. 'I wouldn't know. As soon as my head hits the pillow, that's me for the night. But any one of us could have nicked that towel, couldn't they?'

'Yes. That's the bizarre thing. We were all sharing a room. Liam and Suzy. Adam and me. You and Samantha. If one of us was creeping about, surely somebody would have noticed?'

'You'd have thought so. John must have been up, though, if he went outside. But he weren't sharing with no-one. Not last night, anyhow.'

'No.' Nadia grimaced. But if one the group was responsible for his death, then they must have been wandering about in the early hours as well.

Jill adjusted her glasses. 'What are you going to tell the others? I didn't do it, babes. Honestly. I never hurt no-one. You do believe me?'

'Yes, I believe you,' Nadia said. And she did, genuinely. 'Look, I'll speak to the others. But I don't think they're going to believe me.'

'Why not?'

'They...searched your room.' Jill frowned at that, then boggled as Nadia pulled the cigarette lighter out from her trouser pocket. 'And we found this in your handbag.'

'That's John's lighter,' she breathed, as Nadia handed it across. 'That ain't possible. This was his pride and joy.' She nestled it in her hands. '18 carat gold. He wouldn't let anyone borrow it.'

'It was in your handbag,' Nadia said again. If Jill really was as innocent as she claimed to be, then how it got there was the most disturbing question of all.

Samantha Redmond had been taking another look at John's tablet. She had grabbed hold of the device and sat herself down on his bed. If anything was the key to all this, she reasoned, it would be the contents of John's computer. There were a couple of USB sticks on the bedside table as well, which might supply a few answers, but it was the tablet that would provide definitive proof: had John set up the webcams, or was somebody else responsible?

Samantha was pleased to have something straightforward to think about. She had not felt at all comfortable rifling through Jill's belongings earlier on. A proper search needed to be conducted of all the rooms, but she was happy to leave the rest of it to Adam and the others. Even with the evidence of the lighter, Adam was sceptical of Jill's guilt and Samantha was inclined to agree with him. She had known the woman for years, on and off, and she could not believe that Jill was capable of anything like this. Liam Heigl felt otherwise, however, and it was right for him and Adam to complete the search together, despite the understandable tension between the two men. If there was any more evidence to be found, they would be the ones to uncover it. Samantha, meantime, would focus on the tablet.

If it's not his football team, she thought, gazing down at the device in her lap, *it must be a name of some sort.* She remembered Twinkle telling her once how predictable people's passwords often were. Names of relatives. Names of cats. That was assuming they didn't just go with "password" or "password1". She had already tried all the obvious combinations, though. She picked up John's mobile and began scrolling through the contacts list. It was then that another option presented itself. She tapped the word in on the tablet and the device lit up. *Bingo!*

Samantha didn't waste any time congratulating herself. She went straight for the folder marked "video_files". Actually, there wasn't much else on the tablet, just the usual default apps. The device appeared to be factory fresh, with no customisation at all; but it was connected up to the house network, as Adam had suspected, and the video files were not encrypted. So it looked like John had been responsible for the webcams after all. But what had he been hoping to see?

She clicked on the most recent file, which John had named "final". According to the time stamp, it had last been altered shortly after midnight. Samantha's heart sank as she saw an image of herself pop up on the screen; but in all honesty she could not pretend that she was surprised. It was a shot from the wardrobe cam; her getting undressed on Friday night. The video cut to the same image from a different angle. And then a third. She watched the video play out quietly, her mind struggling to come to terms with it all. There was nothing particularly pornographic about the footage, just a momentary flash here and there as she peeled off her underwear and put on her night things. The picture quality was pin sharp, however, and it still felt like a violation. It was the next scene, though, in the shower, which really made her cringe. The same sequence, on Saturday morning, from three different angles. And this time everything was on display, in graphic detail. Samantha gripped her hands together angrily and paused the film. She took a deep breath and closed her eyes for a moment. There was no point getting upset about it. John was dead. She couldn't shout at him now. But even so, it made her queasy to think of footage like this being posted online. Oh, sure, it was pretty tame stuff by the standards of the internet. A woman washing herself in the shower. It might get a thirteen year old boy excited, but it was hardly anything hard core. Even so, this was her body they were talking about, with all its embarrassing imperfections. Nobody had any right to put that on public display.

She calmed herself and clicked once again on the play button, determined to see if anything worse was to come. But the next scene was even tamer than the first. She was trying on her costume for the cabaret. She smiled suddenly at the sight of herself in her schoolgirl outfit. It was barely even risqué. She'd been planning to dress up as a sixth former, in a straw boater and a pleated skirt. She even had the hockey stick to go with it. Nobody could get turned on by that, she thought, watching herself attaching the silk stockings to her suspender belt. *John must have been hoping for far more*. Perhaps he'd been expecting her to hop into bed with someone. After Wales, that would not have seemed completely impossible. She had disappeared off with Twinkle for the night, after all, even if nothing had actually happened. Maybe John had been hoping for a reprise. Perhaps that was why he had left the cameras in place in his own bedroom.

The video file came to an end and Samantha clicked a couple of the others. There were three files for each room, each capturing the stream from a particular camera. All of them came to an abrupt end at 23.26 on Saturday evening, according to the log. The last shot on the bathroom camera was of her brushing her teeth, just before she went to bed. *Another moment to wow the teenagers*, she thought. A woman in her early forties getting ready for bed.

It was her fame that made the difference, pure and simple. A movie star in the shower. That's all it was. Somebody somewhere would pay good money to see it. And somebody else would profit from it. It made Samantha sick to think of it. And it wouldn't be the raw footage. It would be carefully edited. The images were crystal clear, in high definition. They would be able to zoom in and artificially pan up and down her body as she soaped herself. They might even improve the footage, adjust her shape, like the magazine editors did with their cover shots.

John must have really needed the money to sink this low, she thought. But could this really have been what got him killed? And had he been acting alone, setting up all the cameras? It did not seem likely. He was a mechanic, not an internet whiz. He would have needed a friend or two to sort all this out. And presumably they would have expected to receive the footage at some point. Had he managed to pass it on to them before he died? The word "final" suggested he might have done, which was a worrying thought. He could not have sent anything out over the internet, however, not from here. The only way John could have delivered the material was if his friends had come to collect it in person. Perhaps Adam was right after all and there was somebody else on the island, or had been. Maybe they'd arrived last night, to pick up the footage, and had then killed John as he was heading back to the house. But for what reason? Or perhaps they had been in hiding in the tower all the time, then bumped John off in the early hours and left, taking the footage with them. But again, if that was the case, why on earth would they need to kill him? For all the humiliation Samantha felt, she had to admit that none of the footage she had seen was a matter of life and death. There had to be more to it than that.

She clicked on another file and saw John and Twinkle's bedroom. The cameras must have had motion sensors as the footage jumped from one set of people to another. She whizzed through the stream quickly but then stopped and wound back.

Twinkle was on his own. He had entered the room furtively and then moved across to the wardrobe. This was late on Saturday morning, according to the time stamp. He stared up at the camera thoughtfully for a moment, then went over to John's bedside table, where the tablet Samantha was now holding was being charged up. He grabbed it and sat on the bed, tapping away at the screen. Samantha wondered how long it would take for him to guess the password. By the looks of it, less than a minute. He sat for some time on the bed, skimming through the files, his expression grave. *So he did know,* Samantha thought. But did John know that he knew? Perhaps that was the reason Twinkle had been killed.

She skipped on through the next bit of footage, then wound back in surprise as she saw Liam Heigl enter the same bedroom. He was on his own and moved straight across to Twinkle's bed. He looked to the door briefly, then opened the rucksack lying on the mattress and began rummaging around inside. Samantha checked the time stamp. It was a little after midday. What on earth was he doing in there?

Chapter Twelve

'Can I have a word?' Adam asked, sticking his head around the kitchen door.

'Of course.' Nadia had come upstairs to get herself a glass of water. Jill Clarke had been coaxed out of the bathroom and was now resting on her bed, under the watchful eye of Samantha Redmond. 'How did the search go?' she asked.

Adam was looking a little unsettled. 'There was nothing in any of the bedrooms. Nothing of any consequence, anyway.' They had given the entire house a thorough going over. 'Look, have you got a moment? There's something I want you to see.'

'Sure.' She drained the glass and followed him out of the kitchen. They tripped down the stairs together and into the corridor leading across to the lighthouse. Adam came to a halt in front of the main door. He glanced nervously back, to make sure there was no-one else around.

'What is it?' Nadia asked, intrigued.

Adam took a moment to collect his thoughts. 'Samantha managed to break into John's tablet. I've just been talking to her about it.'

'And?'

'It was like we thought. John *was* spying on us.' Nadia raised an eyebrow. 'Well, not us,' Adam clarified. 'He was making a video of Samantha, soaping herself in the shower. Getting undressed. That sort of thing.'

'What, for his own...?

'No, I don't think so. I'm pretty sure it was just for the money. You know how badly his business was doing. Perhaps he was meeting someone last night. Getting paid off. But that's not the curious thing. Samantha found something else on there. Something incriminating.'

Nadia's heart quickened. 'Something to do with Twinkle?' Perhaps now they were getting to the heart of the matter.

'Yes. Twinkle and Liam Heigl.'

Nadia did not try to conceal her surprise. 'Liam??'

'He was in Twinkle's bedroom, just after lunch on Saturday. He was caught on the webcam, looking through his things. Searching for something.'

'And you think Liam might have...?'

'I'm not sure what to think.' Adam expelled a lungful of air. 'But that's not the only thing we discovered.' He gazed across at the archway leading back into the cottage. 'Before I spoke to Samantha, I came out here. I thought, as we were searching everywhere, I might as well have a look at the coat rack.' He indicated the line of outdoor clothes hanging from the hooks in front of them. 'This is Liam's jacket here. The blue one.' He grabbed one of the sleeves and lifted it up. Nadia peered at it, but for the life of her she could not see anything odd about it. Adam stuffed his hand into the sleeve and pulled the insides partway out. The fabric inside was stained a deep red. Blood red. Nadia boggled at the sight of it.

'That's not the only thing,' Adam said. He dug into the side pockets and pulled out a pair of gloves. They were thin and, like the coat, dark blue in colour. He held them up and Nadia fingered them briefly. The woollen tips were coarse and immobile.

'That's blood too,' she said, unable to disguise her shock. 'Dried blood. You don't think...?'

Adam folded the gloves up in his hands. 'I don't know what to think. But Samantha says Liam was the one who found John's lighter, in their bedroom. He could easily have slipped it into Jill's bag, to sow suspicion.'

Nadia scratched the side of her head. 'But if he used the lighter to burn the towel last night, why wouldn't he burn the gloves as well, if they were covered in blood?'

Adam shrugged. 'I don't know.'

Nadia gestured to the footwear lined up on the mat beneath the coat rack. 'What about the boots? Have you checked those?'

'Yes. Nothing there that I can see. But, look, you've got to admit, Liam has been behaving pretty oddly the last day or so. And he was very quick to pin the blame on Jill.'

'He's probably feeling guilty about yesterday. I suppose he did have good reason to dislike John, though.'

'Well, exactly,' Adam said. 'And now it looks as if there might have been something going on between him and Twinkle. Perhaps his death wasn't a case of mistaken identity at all. Maybe it was deliberate.'

'And then John found out what Liam had done and had to be silenced?' Nadia's mind was whirling with the possibilities.

'It could be. Look, I'm going to have to talk to Liam, confront him with all this.'

'Do you think that's wise?'

'I don't see that I have much choice. Don't worry. There's nothing he can do to me in a house full of people. But I think it might be better if we get Suzy out of the way first. That's where I need your help. There's no telling how she might react, if we start accusing her husband.'

'What about Jill?' Nadia asked.

'She'll be all right if we leave her in her room.'

'Okay.' She gazed out of the window. 'Leave Suzy to me.'

'Good news,' Nadia announced loudly as the two of them returned to the living room. 'We've seen a boat.' That got the attention of everyone. Strictly speaking, it was not even a lie. She had spotted a dot somewhere off in the distance, through one of the windows in the entrance hall.

'How far away is it?' Liam asked her, rising to his feet.

'A fair way,' she admitted. Far too far for anybody on board to take notice of the island. 'I don't think they're heading our way. But I was just saying to Adam, if there are any flares left, we might be able to attract their attention.'

Liam was dubious. 'In broad daylight?'

'They're a bit more powerful than your average firework. Isn't that right, Suzy?'

'They're blinding,' the blonde woman agreed.

'It might be worth having another go, if you're up for it?'

'Oh, definitely!' Suzy rose to her feet. 'I think it's worth a try.'

'The sooner we can get somebody out here, the sooner we can get all this sorted,' Adam said.

'You don't think anyone saw the flares last night?' Liam had not given up hope of that.

Adam glanced at his watch. 'It's midday now. If someone had seen something they'd be here by now. Where's Samantha?'

Suzy jerked a finger at the far door. 'She's in with Jill.' The blonde woman hesitated for a moment, her eyes flicking between Adam and Liam, wary of leaving the two men alone together. 'Are you all right, staying here?' she asked her husband.

Liam pursed his lips. 'I'll be fine. We were going to check each other's phones weren't we?' he suggested. Adam nodded and reached down to his pocket.

'We won't be long,' Nadia said. She and Suzy moved out of the living room.

Suzy was still thinking about the discovery of Jill's towel. 'Liam seems pretty sure she's guilty,' she said, as they made their way out into the corridor and across to the lighthouse door. 'I hope it's not just because of me. Not that he blames her. But I can't really see it myself. Jill's even scattier than I am.'

'And that's saying something! You're right. I can't see it either.'

Suzy grabbed the handle of the door. 'And anyway, if Jill was responsible, then how did she get in here, into the lighthouse?'

'That's a good question.' Nadia moved through into the basement. The crates were laid out across the lower room as before. 'There was more than one box of flares, wasn't there?' They had just grabbed the first one they had seen last night.

'Three or four, I think,' Suzy agreed. 'Plenty to be getting on with. We had a good hit rate last night, didn't we?'

'Yes. Just a shame about the competition.' Nadia moved across and crouched down in front of the nearest crate. 'I suppose we don't actually have to climb all the way up the tower. We could do it outside, on the cliff top, couldn't we? They'll see it just as well from there as anywhere.'

Suzy wasn't having that. 'Oh, but it'll be much more fun to do it up top. And if they've got binoculars they're more likely to see us waving at them from up there.'

Nadia rolled her eyes good-naturedly. 'All right, up top then.' Another exhausting ascent to the heavens. She didn't really mind. Setting off the flare was the least of her concerns right now. Her thoughts floated back to the cottage. She didn't like the idea of leaving Adam alone to confront Liam Heigl, but at least Samantha would be on hand in the adjacent room. If Liam was the killer – and it was a big if – he might be capable of anything.

Samantha Redmond was not about to let Adam confront the man on his own.

When she had first seen the footage of him moving about on John's tablet, her instinct had been to give Liam the benefit of the doubt. There could easily be an innocent explanation for his behaviour. Samantha had always been fond of Liam and she simply could not picture him as any kind of killer. But when she'd shown the footage to Adam and he had told her about the gloves, she had been forced to reconsider. The evidence, this time, was very strong. She hated confrontation, but if Adam was going to talk to him, it was better there was somebody else there, providing him with a bit of moral support.

She left Jill listening to some music on her phone and moved out into the living room. Adam threw her a grateful smile as she closed the door and came across to sit next to him on the sofa.

Liam was sitting on one of the armchairs, at right angles to the fireplace. 'I can't believe Jill is still denying the truth,' he said, gazing across at the far door. 'After all the evidence Nadia showed her.'

'Perhaps she's innocent,' Samantha suggested. 'The evidence is pretty circumstantial. And I really don't think Jill would be capable of something like this.'

Liam sucked in his cheeks. 'I don't know. By the sounds of it, John treated her pretty shabbily, over the years.' That was

169

something of an understatement, if what Nadia had told them was true. 'You could hardly blame her if she finally lost her rag.'

'But what about Twinkle?' Samantha asked.

'Yes, that is more difficult to explain. But we always thought that might have been a case of mistaken identity. I'm sure the police will work it all out, one way or another, when they finally deign to turn up.'

There was an awkward pause. 'I've been doing a bit of detective work myself,' Adam volunteered, leaning forward. He glanced briefly at Samantha. 'Actually, we both have. I had a look at the coat rack out in the hallway. All the boots and stuff.'

Liam was not surprised. 'Did you check Jill's shoes?' She did not have any boots with her, but she did have a pair of flats alongside a couple of pairs of stilettos.

'Yes. I checked Jill's and mine and Samantha's. And yours,' he added pointedly.

Liam frowned. 'What *about* mine?'

'Not the boots.' Adam carefully pulled out the pair of gloves and placed them on the coffee table. 'We found these in your coat.'

Liam gazed down at them. 'My gloves. What about them?' He smiled briefly. 'They've not been a lot of use this weekend. I should have brought some thicker ones.' He reached forward and picked them up.

'We noticed there's a bit of blood on them,' Adam observed quietly. 'On the fingertips.' His eyes flicked awkwardly to Samantha and then back to Liam.

'So?' Liam shrugged. Then he looked up and stifled a laugh. 'You don't think I....? Oh, for Christ's sake.' He dropped the gloves back onto the table and lifted up his hands. 'Look at them.' He waggled his fingers. 'It was that cable yesterday afternoon. They're absolutely raw.'

'The cable?' Samantha had not considered that possibility. His hands certainly did look a little ragged, though there was no sign of any blood on them now.

'I was the one feeding it out. And then hauling it back up here, when Twinkle was attached to it. It was all right for the rest of you. You all had proper thick gloves. But these...' He gestured to the woollen mittens on the table. 'They were no use at all. I practically cut myself to ribbons. That's where the blood came from. Not from John, if that's what you're thinking.'

'That isn't our only reason for bringing it up,' Samantha said.

'You were the one who found the cigarette lighter,' Adam pointed out.

Liam was starting to bristle now. 'Oh, and what, you think I planted it there, in Jill's handbag?'

'Did you?' Adam asked.

'No, I bloody didn't.' He gazed across at the two of them. 'You think I killed John? And Twinkle?' He growled. 'That's crazy. I wouldn't lay a finger on either of them. And if Jill *didn't* kill them, then it's far more likely to be one of you, if you ask me. Look at you both, sitting there, accusing me, with no real evidence. Maybe John set up the webcams, to film Samantha here. Our big Hollywood star.' Liam was guessing about that – he had not been told about the tablet as yet – but it was an easy conclusion to draw. 'You realised what he was up to and tried to put a stop to it.' Liam was getting angry now. He glared at Samantha.

'But why would I kill Twinkle?' she asked. 'He was one of my closest friends.'

'You might have mistook him for John, because of that jacket. And what about you?' He rounded on Adam. 'You organised this whole farrago.' Liam gestured to the cottage. 'You knew where it was going to be held months in advance. You knew Samantha would be coming here but you lied to the rest of us about it.'

'That wasn't his fault,' Samantha put in, but Liam was not about to be interrupted. He was in full flow now.

'You had every reason to hate both of them. Paul Hammond was your best friend, wasn't he? He was the best man at your wedding. You blamed them both for killing him. And you showed us that stupid film of yours, just to rub our noses in it.'

'That's ridiculous,' Adam said.

171

'No more ridiculous than accusing me. And what evidence do you have? A bit of blood on my gloves, after letting out that cable for God knows how long. And the fact that I found John's cigarette lighter.'

'That isn't the only evidence,' Adam said.

'Oh, there's more? I can't wait!'

Samantha picked up the tablet. 'We finally managed to hack into this,' she explained, flicking on the screen. 'It *was* John who was filming us. I've been scrolling through some of the videos he left on here.' She clicked the relevant file and found the point where Liam entered the bedroom. She twisted the tablet around and showed him the footage: him rummaging through Twinkle's rucksack. Liam stared at it, nonplussed.

'What were you doing in his bedroom?' Adam asked.

Liam looked from the screen to them, a half smile on his face. 'You really are clutching at straws. If you must know, I was looking for a belt, for the cabaret. I mentioned it to you yesterday at lunch. Don't you remember?'

Adam nodded, reluctantly. He did remember.

'The trousers I'd brought didn't fit properly. I thought I'd brought a belt with me but I must have left it at home. Twinkle said he had one I could borrow. He told me to go and grab it but I couldn't find the damn thing. I was going to ask him again, but of course that was the last I saw of him.' He regarded the image on the screen a second time. 'And you can see how annoyed I am there. And the fact that I haven't taken anything.' Liam settled back against the cushion. 'Well, if that's the best you've got, probably better you don't join the police force any time soon.' He gestured to the tablet. 'Is there any footage of the bathroom on there? Then you can see me cleaning the blood off my hands on Saturday afternoon as well.'

'I...haven't looked at all the footage,' Samantha admitted.

Adam slumped back into his seat. 'Okay,' he said. Liam, it seemed, had an answer for everything. Some of it might even be true.

The other man raised his arms above his head. 'Christ, would you look at us all. It's ridiculous. This suspicion is driving

172

me crazy. The sooner we get this over with the better for everyone.' In that at least they were all agreed. Liam drew a breath and regarded Samantha thoughtfully for a moment. 'So what was the password? For the tablet?'

Samantha smiled shyly. 'Oh, I found it on his contacts list, on John's phone.' She hesitated. 'You're not going to like it, I'm afraid.'

'What was it? "Liam Heigl is a twat"?' He chuckled.

'No, nothing like that.' Samantha looked away. 'It was "princess".'

In the end, it was a simple mistake that revealed the truth.

Suzy Heigl had slotted the cartridge into the flare gun. 'Is that where the mallet came from?' she asked, looking down at the crate where the flares had been stored.

'One of these boxes,' Nadia confirmed. 'There's lots of random stuff in there. Adam and John went through them yesterday evening.'

'What I don't understand is why somebody would take a mallet from here, kill John with it and then bring it back.'

'It does seem a bit daft,' Nadia agreed.

'And why not just leave it down here? Why clomp all the way up to the second floor?'

'It does seem like overkill. Have you seen the storerooms upstairs?' Nadia asked.

'No, I haven't.' Suzy looked down at the pistol in her hand. 'Too busy playing with this last night!' Her foot brushed against some loose paper on the floor. 'Oh, look.' She bent down. 'They must have had a subscription.' She lifted up the paper.

'Subscription?'

'The Daily Sketch.' She beamed. 'This must be where they got it from.'

Nadia frowned, not quite following her.

'The newspaper. To wrap the mallet in.'

'Newspaper?' Nadia grimaced, looking down at it. 'Who said anything about a newspaper?'

'Adam did, didn't he?' Suzy blinked. 'He said he found it in a box, upstairs, wrapped in newspaper.'

'No, he didn't,' Nadia replied cautiously. 'He said he found it in a box in the lighthouse. He didn't say anything about a newspaper.' She felt a sudden chill. 'And he certainly didn't mention the Daily Sketch.' In fact, he had deliberately kept the details of the discovery as vague as possible.

Suzy was momentarily disorientated. 'I'm sure he said something about that. Maybe later, I can't remember.' She placed the paper back on the floor.

'He didn't say anything about it at all,' Nadia insisted. Her heart was beating furiously now. 'The only way you could have known about that is if...is if you put it there yourself.' She stared at the woman in horror. No, it wasn't possible. Not *Suzy*. But how else would she have known? Nadia swallowed hard. She had brought the woman out here to protect her from danger. It hadn't occurred to her that Suzy might *be* the danger.

'Oh, nonsense!' the girl exclaimed, brushing the matter aside with a flick of the hand. 'Nadia, this is me you're talking to. I'm not a murderer. I write children's books. And anyway, we've been friends for years.' But her voice was not quite as confident as her words implied; and as she was speaking, she was edging slowly back towards the door.

Nadia regarded her warily. Could it be true? Could Suzy really be behind everything that had happened? 'You've always been a terrific actress. That much I do know.'

'What, and you think I murdered John. And Twinkle? That's mad. Why on earth would I?'

'You tell me,' Nadia said, not taking her eyes off the woman. 'Or better still, tell the others. I'm sure they'll be interested to hear the explanation. They want to discover the truth as much as I do.' Her voice was sounding firmer than it had any right to be.

'Oh, Nadia,' Suzy sighed, finally allowing the mask to slip. 'I never wanted to hurt anyone. Least of all you.' She slid her free hand into her pocket, pulled out a key and turned briefly to the door. 'But now you've given me no choice,' she said.

Chapter Thirteen

Nadia lunged forward, but Suzy was too quick for her, grabbing her arm and twisting it behind her back. Abruptly, Nadia felt hard metal pressing against the nape of her neck. 'Don't make a sound,' Suzy said. 'If you want to live.' The loaded flare gun was jammed up against the back of her neck.

'Suzy, listen to me,' Nadia breathed. 'This is madness. You can't get away with this. When the police come....'

'When the police come, there won't be anything for them to investigate. The mystery will already have been solved.' Despite the confidence of the assertion, Suzy's voice was now wavering desperately. 'If it's not an intruder, or Jill, then I'm afraid it has to be you...' She released her grip and shoved Nadia forward onto the floor. Nadia hit the concrete with a heavy thud and, while she recovered her senses, Suzy finished locking up the door. 'I'm so sorry, Nadia. I really didn't want it to end like this.' Her voice was cracked and apologetic.

Nadia had flipped herself over and was now sitting on the floor, gazing up at her friend in disbelief. 'What...what are you going to do?'

Suzy stared back at her, momentarily lost for words. It wasn't entirely clear if she had any kind of plan. She could not have anticipated being found out like this. 'I think we should head upstairs,' she decided at last, briefly regaining her composure. 'Adam and the others are expecting a couple of flares. They'll get suspicious if they don't see them. Come on. Up you get.' She waved the pistol.

Nadia rose warily to her feet, using the nearest crate to balance herself. Had Suzy gone completely mad? Nadia could make no sense of it. *Suzy, of all people.*

The woman gestured to the stairs, keeping the flare gun level.

'You do know that's not a proper gun?' Nadia said.

'Maybe not. But at point blank range the effect will probably be the same.' She grabbed Nadia by the arm once again, twisting her around and propelling her towards the stairs. For all her faltering words, Suzy's grip was alarmingly strong. What was she intending to do? Nadia's mind was in a whirl, trying to make sense of it.

Suzy let go of her arm as she stepped onto the spiral staircase, but kept the flare gun pressed against her back. Slowly, they began to climb the stairs. Nadia was struggling to control her panic. She had no choice but to do as she was told. It was difficult enough, coming to terms with the fact that Suzy Heigl was holding a gun on her. And the woman was right, fired at close range that pistol would almost certainly kill her. Was Nadia going to be the next victim? Had Suzy completely lost her mind? One thing was certain: the girl was not any kind of master criminal. She had made far too many mistakes already. But that was of little comfort right now. Nadia had seen the determined look in her eyes. Suzy would not hesitate to shoot her if she didn't do exactly as she was told. 'Keep climbing,' the woman ordered briskly. 'Let's get this over with.'

'What...what are you going to do?' Nadia's heart was pounding in her chest and she almost lost her footing on one of the metal steps.

Suzy prodded her again. 'I don't know. Just keep climbing.' They passed the storerooms and continued on up to the summit.

Only when they reached the top of the staircase did Nadia risk turning back to look at her friend. 'Suzy, this is madness. Whatever you've done, we can talk about it. I'm sure...I'm sure you had your reasons.'

Suzy gestured to the door and Nadia opened it up, moving through into the lamp room. A sturdy metal railing surrounded the large circular column containing the acetylene lamp. *What is she planning to do? Push me off the balcony?* Nadia backed herself up against the railing and grabbed hold of it tightly. She wasn't going to let that happen. Whatever Suzy said, she had no intention of being dragged outside.

The blonde woman closed up the inner door behind her, her expression grave. Nadia edged around the central column, keeping as much distance as she could between herself and her friend. Suzy did not attempt to follow her; instead she remained at the door, apparently lost in thought. The pistol drooped slightly in her hand. *Perhaps I can rush her*, Nadia thought desperately. The gun was no longer being held at close range. But Suzy was a lot fitter and faster than she was and Nadia did not fancy her chances. The woman had already bested her once. Suzy caught her gaze and levelled the pistol again. 'This is such a mess,' she declared, her voice crumbling once more into despair.

'What happened?' Nadia asked. Despite her fear, she felt an overwhelming desire to understand. What had happened to drive Suzy to all this? More than anything now, Nadia just wanted some answers.

'I...I don't really know,' Suzy admitted. 'I never intended for any of this to happen. It's all been such a nightmare. I was so looking forward to coming here this weekend, seeing everybody again. I thought it would be so cool. And then...and then...' Suzy was not really looking at her now. Her eyes were speckled with grief.

'You didn't intend to kill anyone?'

'No. Why would I?' Suzy shook her head emphatically. 'I didn't intend for anyone to die. I came here to see some old friends. To catch up with everyone, to have a few drinks and play a few games. That's all I wanted. I never intended for anyone to get hurt.'

'So what happened?' Nadia asked again. Had it all been a terrible accident?

Suzy took a deep breath. 'It was John,' she declared bitterly. 'It was John who ruined everything. The plans he had for this weekend.'

'You mean, the webcams. Filming us all?'

'Yes. I didn't know anything about it, beforehand I mean. It was all his idea. He wanted to make a bit of money. I suppose I can't blame him for that. His business really was in dire straits. He might have lost everything.'

'He thought he'd earn a bit of easy cash by filming Samantha?'

177

'That's right. He knew she was coming here. They'd exchanged a few emails, apparently. Not that I knew anything about that before this weekend. But I did know about his financial problems. If I'd known about the cameras, I'd have tried to talk him out of it.'

'So what was the plan?' Nadia was genuinely curious. 'He was going to video Samantha and sell the footage?'

'He'd already sold it. He had a friend who operated a few dodgy websites. Celebrity porn, on the dark web. Not a very nice man. But they got talking and hatched the plan together. As I understand it, he knew all about the cameras and the technical side of things, which John didn't. And they weren't going to be ordinary webcams, they were professional spy cameras. The sort that governments use. Well, you've seen. He told John they'd make a fortune selling footage of an A list movie star. Even just video of her in the shower. But John thought he could do better than that. He remembered what happened last time, in Wales. All that bed hopping. He was hoping Samantha might end up shagging Adam or Twinkle. He even thought about trying it on himself, he said, just for the hell of it. I think he may have been joking. But that kind of footage would be worth a fortune.'

'In High Definition.' Nadia shook her head. The things some people would pay for. 'And he came out here, earlier in the week, to set it all up?'

'No, not John. This friend of his. He was the technical one. Like Twinkle. He came out to the island last week. He had his own boat.' A rather successful pornographer, by the sounds of it. 'He ran up the coast in it. It wouldn't have been difficult. And there was nobody here on the island. He broke into the cottage and set it all up. The cameras. Fitted them into the walls. It was all very professionally done. John kept well away, in London. Keeping his hands clean, he said, in case anything went wrong.'

'And how did he get into the cottage? This guy?'

'I don't know. He must have had a set of keys. What do they call them? Skeleton keys. He'd done time in prison, apparently. John said he was a career criminal. So he would know how to pick a lock.' It seemed to be quite a common skill, Nadia reflected ruefully. 'And then, when he got here, he found a genuine key in one of the drawers. A rusted old thing that opened up the lighthouse. John said the guy couldn't resist having a look round. He even thought he might set up a camera or two up top, but he decided against it. The place was out of bounds anyway, so Samantha was unlikely to come up here.'

'And when did *you* find out about all this?'

'Not until Saturday morning. Everything had been set up by then. The recording had already started. There was a hub attached to the underside of the TV in the living room. A tiny little thing. When John arrived, he was able to link his tablet up to the network and start recording straight away. There were cameras in all the bedrooms as well as the bathroom. They didn't know which room Samantha would be in so they covered all the bases. And once the party started, it was anyone's guess where we'd all end up anyway.'

That's true, Nadia thought. That must be why John had left the cameras running in his own bedroom. In case Samantha had finally taken pity on Twinkle or in case he had got lucky himself. And if his bald head had popped up in the footage – carefully edited, of course – then no-one would ever have suspected he was behind it. Though what his new girlfriend would have thought was anyone's guess.

'But one of the cameras wasn't linking up properly, he said. The image was flickering a bit. He had to sneak in and correct it. That was how I found out about it all. We were all upstairs playing cards. You remember? I went bust early on, so I came down to find John. I thought he might like to join us. I hadn't seen him that morning. But as soon as I got downstairs, I found him creeping about in my bedroom. He'd got the cameras running, even in there, but the one on the picture frame wasn't working properly. He tried to make a joke of it, but he was standing on a chair.' Suzy smiled briefly at the memory. 'I knew he was up to something and I insisted he show me.'

'You saw the camera?'

'It was a tiny thing. Well, you saw them. He said it was just a dummy, a practical joke, but I knew better. I insisted he tell

179

me the truth. And so he came clean. He told me everything. The plans. The money. The footage.'

'And how did you react?'

'I was upset. Disappointed in him. It felt like such a betrayal. This was meant to be a private weekend, a friendly get together, not a money making opportunity. And having cameras in my room as well, with Liam and I. That was such a shock. But he said he wasn't interested in that. It was just Samantha. No-one else would be involved. He'd delete the rest of the footage.'

'And Samantha?'

'He said it would be good publicity for her. He said she had her face plastered all over the tabloids every day anyway, so what did it matter? And he really did need the money.'

'What did you say to that?'

'I told him he was mad. There was no way he could get away with it. There'd be all kinds of repercussions. He'd end up in jail. And what would happen to his business then? But he didn't think that was likely. He was always a bit of a gambler, John. He had everything sorted, he said. It was a dead cert. Nothing could be traced back to him. His friends weren't planning on releasing the footage straight away. They'd leave it a couple of months before they put it online and, by that time, the trail would have gone cold. There'd be no way of proving his involvement.'

'We would probably have guessed the truth,' Nadia thought, 'when the footage came out.'

'I think he realised that. But it couldn't be helped. He thought he'd probably be able to talk me around, at least.'

'And did he? When you found out?'

'No. I told him straight: he had to stop. It was utter madness. But he wouldn't listen to me. He wasn't prepared to give it up. He'd already taken half the money, he said. Five thousand pounds up front. He had to provide something in return. I tried to insist, but he wasn't having it. He'd made a deal and he was going to stick to it. He could be so pig-headed sometimes.'

'So what happened next?'

'We left it there. I didn't have a choice. I could see I

wasn't going to be able to persuade him. I needed to get back upstairs anyway, in case Liam started to get twitchy. And I couldn't expose John to the rest of the group. You'd never have forgiven him. But he did at least agree to switch off the cameras in my bedroom.'

'Judging by what Samantha found on his tablet,' Nadia said, 'I don't think he did.'

'No. He lied about that.' Suzy grimaced. 'He lied about a lot of things. Maybe he thought....I don't know...that Liam might end up...' She shuddered, not wanting to finish the thought. 'It's strange, but when John first told me about all this, I actually felt sorry for him. I know that sounds daft, but we were always such good friends and I hated to see him reduced to this. I was quite calm about it. I didn't lose my temper or anything. But it was so sordid. He really was that desperate. If his business failed, he'd lose his house. So I thought...I thought okay, I'll drop it for now and then maybe talk to him later, on the Sunday. Have another go at trying to persuade him. But then, with everything that happened after that, on Saturday afternoon, I didn't get the chance.'

'And Twinkle? What happened there? He found out about it too, didn't he?'

'Yes. That same morning, I think. He was up later than the rest of us. But he must have stumbled across the network at some point. Or perhaps he discovered the hub attached to the television set.' Twinkle had been fiddling with the TV on Friday night, when they had been preparing Adam's film show. 'It wouldn't be easy to see. It was made to look like a part of the aerial, apparently. But if anyone could find it, it would be Twinkle. Anyway, however it happened, he found out. He discovered one of the webcams and traced the signal back to John's tablet.'

Nadia nodded. According to Adam, there were video footage from John's bedroom of Twinkle breaking into the device and viewing the recordings.

'He saw what John was up to and he was absolutely horrified. You know how fond Twinkle was of Samantha.'

'Yes. Yes, I know.' No wonder the mood had been so sour at lunchtime.

'They had an awful row, the two of them. Twinkle waited until after lunch, when John was outside having a cigarette, and then he confronted him. I don't know exactly what was said. But I did…I did see a part of the argument, from up here. Well, not from here, but from one of the storerooms.'

Nadia's eyes widened. 'So you did come up here before? Into the lighthouse?'

Suzy nodded. 'It was me who unlocked the door. John showed me where the key was. He was trying to change the subject, when we were talking earlier on. He knew how disappointed I was that the tower was out of bounds. He showed me the key. And later, when the house was quiet, I borrowed it and came to have a look around.'

'This was on Saturday morning?'

'No, it was in the afternoon. After lunch. I went up to the second floor. I needed some time to think. The storeroom door was already open for some reason. I popped my head inside and had a look out the window. It was such a gorgeous view. Then I looked down and saw Twinkle and John on the cliff below, just outside the compound. It was quite windy and they were both in their black coats, standing together close to the edge. Even from up here, I could tell they were having a serious argument. I couldn't hear what they were saying, of course – the wind cuts everything dead – but I guessed straight away what it must be about. Twinkle had a phone in his hand. The satellite phone. He must have brought it out from the kitchen. John grabbed it from him and threw it over the precipice. Twinkle rounded on him then. It was horrible. I was worried they were going to come to blows. And they were standing so close to the edge.'

'So what happened? Did he fall? Or did John push him?'

'No. I didn't see what happened next. But John didn't do anything. I rushed downstairs as fast as I could. By the time I reached the front door John was already heading back into the house. He was in such a mood. He said it was all over. Twinkle had found out what he was up to and was threatening to call the police.'

'What time was this?'

182

'An hour or two after lunch. You were all upstairs playing cards, I think. John headed back to his room. He must have been going to grab his tablet. He was probably thinking of destroying the evidence, of wiping it all. And I was left standing there, in the hallway, not knowing what to do. There was no sign of Twinkle. I assumed he was still on the cliff top. I thought, maybe I should go out and have a word with him, try to calm him down. Perhaps I could persuade him to let it go, for old times' sake.'

'And did you? Speak to him? He was still alive at this point?'

Suzy nodded numbly. 'He was alive. He was standing there, on the edge of the cliff, with his back to me. I don't think he heard me coming.'

'And you spoke to him?'

'Yes. He was startled when I popped up suddenly behind him. But we talked. He was very upset. He wasn't shouting or screaming – that was never his way – but he was furious all the same. I had never seen him like that. There were tears in his eyes. It was such a betrayal of trust, he said. I tried to calm him down. I told him I would speak to John, I would get him to stop, make him delete the footage. But Twinkle said it was too late for that. The damage was already done. He shouldn't be allowed to get away with it, he said. There was no reasoning with him. He was even more stubborn than John. He just wouldn't let it go. He was going to call in the police, tell Samantha, bring it all out into the open, even if it meant John ended up in prison. And all of us ended up in the newspapers.'

Twinkle had been deeply in love with Samantha Redmond. Nadia was not surprised that he would react that way. 'And what happened then?'

'I...don't really know. He was waving his arms about and he...and he must have lost his footing, somehow. There was a gust of wind. He slipped on the grass.'

'And he fell?'

'No. Well, not...he was just standing there, unbalanced. He reached out a hand to me, like this.' Suzy mimicked the gesture. 'He was tottering on the edge, trying to recover himself. But he couldn't find his balance. I could see he was going to fall. I...I could have helped him. I could have saved him. But I didn't. I didn't do anything.'

'You froze?'

'No. That's the strange thing.' Suzy's eyes were wide, almost childlike. 'I didn't freeze at all. I felt so calm. I met his eye. And in that...in that moment I...I didn't want to help him. It's difficult to explain but...he was being so unreasonable. I don't know what came over me. I...I didn't do anything. He reached out at the last minute, trying to grab my hand, trying to save himself. And I stepped backwards, deliberately, putting myself out of reach. And then...he fell. Just like that. He disappeared from view. Oh God, Nadia, I could have saved him, but I didn't. I let him die. In that instant....I...I can't explain it, but at that moment, I *wanted* him to die.'

Nadia regarded her friend in bewilderment.

'You'll think I'm mad, but...afterwards, standing there, it seemed to me that...that it was meant to happen. My angel...my Guardian Angel, he spoke to me. He tried to calm me down. He told me everything would be all right. It had happened for a reason, he said. It was karma. My hand had been guided by another. An old friend, a dear friend. And he was right. I was standing there, with the wind flitting through my hair, and I did...I did feel a presence nearby.'

Nadia was not following this at all. 'A presence? You mean, another person?'

'No. At least, not in the way that you mean. It was...it was Paul. He was there with me on the cliff top.'

'Paul Hammond?' Nadia boggled.

'Yes.' Suzy's eyes were barely focused now. 'I know you won't believe me, but he was there, and I think it was him who stopped me from helping Twinkle. He held me back. He...he wanted Twinkle to die.'

Nadia gazed at the woman in disbelief. 'Suzy, you must know how crazy that sounds.'

'I think he's been here with us this whole weekend,' Suzy said. 'In spirit. Just waiting for his chance. And at that moment, he took possession of me. Twinkle had to fall. He had to pay the price for what he had done, all those years ago.'

Nadia was having difficulty making any sense of this. Suzy had always been a bit dappy, but this was insane. Could she really believe any of what she was saying? 'Look Suzy. You're letting your imagination run away with you. Twinkle tripped and fell, that's all. You froze. Okay, if you hadn't hesitated, he might have survived. And that's dreadful. But there was nothing mystical about it. It was an accident, pure and simple. Perhaps you were partly to blame. Maybe you could have helped him. But all this nonsense about angels, the spirits of the dead. It's just crazy. You do know that, don't you?'

Suzy let out a gentle sigh. 'I wouldn't expect you to understand. Nadia, this was meant to be. It was so clear to me then. I was the instrument. I killed Twinkle and it was what was meant to happen. I...I can't explain it any other way.'

Nadia drew in a breath. Suzy had always been a bit eccentric, but not to this extent. Nadia had never taken her talk of angels or spirits seriously. Lots of people believed in the spirit world. Often, it was just a way of coping with everyday life; helping to give people a sense of purpose. Nadia had never felt the need for it, but she understood why people were attracted to the idea. It had never occurred to her, though, that Suzy really did hear voices in her head. It appeared that there was something seriously wrong with the woman. *Best not to challenge her,* Nadia thought. *Better to keep calm and let her talk.* 'So, what happened next?' she asked.

'I just stood there. I felt numb. But my angel, he comforted me. He told me what to do. I came back to the house and went into the bathroom. I just...' She smiled sadly. 'I just sat on the loo. I don't know how long for. Ten, fifteen minutes maybe. And we talked, my angel and me. He helped me to pull myself together. He warned me of the danger. I had to keep everything under wraps, he said. I couldn't afford to break down, to let anyone discover the truth.'

'But what did you have to worry about?' Nadia wasn't following her train of thought. 'Nobody knew you'd even been

185

out there. And even if they did, it was just an accident. Twinkle fell. No-one could prove any different.'

'But it wasn't an accident. Don't you see? I killed him deliberately. And if I...if I let myself go to pieces, if I broke down, babbled out the truth, then everyone would know. And they'd think I was crazy, like you think I'm crazy.' Nadia did not respond to that. 'And that would be the end of everything. Not just for me, but for Liam and the kids. It would be a disaster. So I did what my angel recommended. I pulled myself together. I put the whole thing out of my mind, as if it hadn't even happened. It was an acting exercise, like the ones we did at university. Do you remember? Living the role. I put myself into that mind set. It was an ordinary day. I was preparing for the cabaret. I had no idea that Twinkle was dead.'

'And so when I discovered the body...?'

'I was as surprised as anyone. I convinced myself I had no idea what was going on. And when everyone thought it must be John who had died, I thought it must be John too. I submerged myself in the role. That was the only way to protect myself. If I believed it, then it had to be true. And I *did* believe it.'

Suzy had always been a first class actress, Nadia knew. She had the ability to give herself up to a role completely, to compartmentalise each character in her mind's eye. And that, perhaps, was the heart of the problem.

Nadia forced her attention back to the story. 'And what did John think, when he realised Twinkle was dead?'

Suzy's face fell. 'I don't really know. We spoke about it afterwards, when we'd broken into the winch room. He...seemed confused.'

'It must have been a bit of shock, everyone thinking he was dead like that. And then to discover the man he had just been arguing with had fallen off a cliff.'

'Yes, I suppose it must have been. He pretended to be amused, of course, but that was just his way. And I was doing the same, playing the role, pretending to be relieved, happy he wasn't dead. But part of me...part of me...I don't know why, but I couldn't put my whole heart into it. And I wasn't sure how

186

convincing I had been. I started to wonder...to wonder if John suspected the truth. I had walked straight out of the compound, just after he had told me about the argument. What if he'd followed me? What if he had seen what I had done?'

'That doesn't sound likely.'

'No, but it *was* possible,' Suzy insisted. 'More than possible, in fact. And I couldn't get the idea out of my head. John seemed so distracted. Oh, he was making a joke of it, but I could tell he was worried.'

'We'd just found out Twinkle was dead. We were all worried.'

'Yes, but there was more to it than that. The way he looked at me. What if he had seen the two of us argue? What if John had seen Twinkle fall?'

'Did he ask you if you'd spoken to him?'

'No. I don't know what I would have said if he had. But Liam popped up at the window so we didn't get the chance to talk any more. And then there was all that activity, hauling Twinkle's body up from the beach. I didn't get to speak to him again for quite some time. I watched him, though, that afternoon, as we all beavered away. And there was an odd look in his eye. He kept avoiding my gaze. I could tell he was worried about something. And it had to be more than just the argument he'd had. It seemed to me, somehow, that he must know what I had done. I can't explain it any other way.'

'Perhaps he was worried *you* suspected him,' Nadia thought. 'He was the last person to see Twinkle alive, so far as he was concerned. And you knew the two of them had rowed. Perhaps he was worried you thought *he'd* killed Twinkle.'

'I...I suppose that's possible.'

'And even if John had known what you'd done, he wouldn't have blamed you. He certainly wouldn't have said anything to anyone else. You were his princess. He would never do anything to hurt you.'

'No. He did always put me on a pedestal.' Her eyes flicked downwards sadly. 'Even when I slept with Adam that time, in Wales. He never judged me for that. He hated Liam so much he didn't care.'

'Did you speak to him again, last night?'

'Yes, briefly. Before he went to bed. He told me he was going to cut his losses. He knew there'd be an enquiry into Twinkle's death and he didn't want anyone to know what he had been up to. Better to shut everything down, he said, and pretend it had never happened. He'd collect up all the cameras tomorrow, on the quiet. And he'd call his friend to tell him it was all off. He had a satellite phone with him. His own one.'

Nadia boggled. 'He kept that quiet! I wonder what happened to it.'

'I don't know. It wasn't...it wasn't on him when he died. He must have thrown it into the sea. Or given it back to his friends.'

'But he decided to call the whole thing off?'

'That's what he said.'

'Did you believe him?'

'No. No, I didn't. There was something shifty in his face when he said it. But what could I do? He swore blind he was going to delete all the footage. He'd collect up all the cameras as soon as he could. He even promised to show me the tablet in the morning, so I could see for myself. He had a special program, he said, on one of his USB sticks, that would wipe the whole thing. Something his friends had provided him with. But he couldn't meet my eye when he said it. I've known John a long time. He's not an actor. He tries to cover things up with jokes but he could never really hide things from me. I knew he was up to something and I knew it was something I wouldn't like.'

'You think he decided to hand on the footage anyway?'

'I think he must have done. He hadn't got any of the sex scenes he wanted, but he'd got shots of Samantha in the shower and getting undressed. He must have thought that would be enough. But there was more to it than that. I was lying in bed, later on, thinking about it. I couldn't sleep. It must have been two or three in the morning. Liam was dead to the world. And I couldn't stop thinking about what had happened. About John and about Twinkle. About what I had done. And then I started to think about Paul. About his restless spirit. And at that moment....I know you won't believe me, but...I felt his presence. He was in the room with me. Paul. As clear to me as you are now. He didn't speak – at least not to begin with – but I could feel him there. And I could feel his restlessness. He hadn't found his peace. Even with Twinkle dead. That wasn't enough.'

Nadia felt a cold shiver descend her spine.

'Twinkle wasn't the only one to blame for what happened to him, you see. It was John too. If he had done his job properly, there wouldn't have been an accident that night and Paul might be alive today.'

'Suzy, that's ridiculous. You can't think like that.'

'But it wasn't me, don't you see? It was Paul. I could feel the anger, radiating out of him. His hatred, his desire for revenge.'

'You...spoke to him?' Nadia asked carefully. She did not like where this seemed to be heading.

'No. Well, not exactly. But I knew what he was thinking.' Suzy shuddered. 'He wanted *revenge*.' In some dark corner of her mind, the memory of Paul Hammond had come to life and interacted with her. But it was not the Paul Hammond that Nadia knew. 'I was horrified, of course. John was one of my oldest friends. But Paul was adamant. He had to pay the price for his actions. Like with Twinkle, there had to be a reckoning. I tried to protest. I told him John wasn't really to blame. You asked him to do it, I said, to let the car through, knowing the state it was in. But Paul wouldn't accept that. John didn't have to go along with it, he said. He just wanted the money. He was out for himself, as always, and to hell with the consequences. "John hurts everyone he comes into contact with. Jill and me, and now you," he said. "He doesn't deserve your pity. He's already lied to you. And if the police find out what you did, he won't lift a finger to help you."' Suzy gazed down at her hands sadly. 'And I knew he was right.'

Nadia's voice was a hoarse whisper. 'So what did you do?'

'I lay there for a long time, thinking it over. What was I supposed to do? John had been a good friend to me for so many years. He wasn't a bad man. Selfish, yes, but not malicious. But

Paul...his anger was so strong. He couldn't rest...he couldn't find peace without some kind of payback. And it was down to me. I had to find a way to...to convince him to let it go, to accept responsibility for his own death. Blaming John like that, it was madness. Somehow, I had to convince him that he really wasn't to blame for anything.'

'And how did you think you would you do that?'

'I thought...I thought, maybe I should go and talk to John.' Suzy's eyes lit up at the memory of the idea. 'I'd go and talk to him and Paul could eavesdrop. I'd ask him about the accident and let Paul hear his side of the story. I was sure John would show some remorse for what had happened. He hadn't wanted Paul to die, after all. We could thrash everything out – about Twinkle, about Paul, about the cameras. We could clear the air, just the two of us. And Paul could listen in and he would see that John wasn't an evil person, that he hadn't intended any harm, and that he didn't deserve the kind...the kind of retribution Paul was after. And then, maybe, Paul would be satisfied and he would be able to move on.'

Nadia was struggling to follow the woman's line of reasoning. The layers of delusion Suzy had enmeshed herself in were difficult to comprehend. As far as she was concerned, Paul was not just a voice in her head, a vague presence. He seemed to be as real to her as a living human being. *She's lost it completely,* Nadia concluded. *She's living in a fantasy world.*

'Paul accepted the challenge,' Suzy continued, without pause. 'He knew how fond I was of John and he was willing to give me the chance to speak to him, to let him defend himself. Better that, I thought, than...than the alternative. So I slipped out of bed and we went to his room.'

This was in the early hours of the morning, of course.

'What about Liam?' Nadia wondered suddenly. 'Didn't he hear you get up?'

'No, he's always been a heavy sleeper. He's used to me getting up in the middle of the night. We have three children. It would take a stampede of elephants to wake him up.' Despite herself, Nadia could not help but smile at that. 'I snuck across to

190

John's bedroom. There was no light under the door. I was just about to knock when another light flashed outside. The beam of the lighthouse. It lit up the living room windows. I froze. I was standing in the middle of the room. John was outside. He had a phone in his hand. I saw his face when the beam came round.'

'He didn't see you?'

'He wasn't looking. And the room was in darkness. He passed by, heading out of the compound. With the phone. I thought it must be the satellite phone. I couldn't work out what he was up to. But then I realised: he must be calling his friends.'

'Like he said he would?'

'Yes. But not to cancel anything. Not at that time of night. He was going ahead with it all, just like Paul said he would. And then I thought....what if it's more than that? What if he's running out on me? What if he's afraid of being blamed for Twinkle's death? What if he's running away? Why else would he be up and skulking about at that time of night?'

'I....I decided to follow him. I got as far as the front door. I was going to grab a coat and then I thought...what if he gets angry? What if I confront him and he won't listen to reason? And then I thought about the crates in the lighthouse where we found this.' She wiggled the flare gun in her hand. 'The spanners. The hammers and mallets. I crept into the tower and grabbed the nearest one. I don't know what I was intending to do with it. I wasn't really thinking. It was as if...as if Paul was guiding me, as if he knew what was going to happen next. I took a coat from the rack by the front door and slid the mallet inside. I wasn't intending...I don't know what I was intending. All I could think of was how Paul had been right. John was trying to save his own skin, putting himself first, not caring about anyone else. Not caring about me. I felt so angry, so hurt, so betrayed. I tip-toed outside and moved to the edge of the compound.'

'And where was John?'

'He was disappearing down the steps towards the landing stage. I crept after him. I didn't dare use a torch or even the light from my phone. But the beam from up here...' She gestured to the lamp. 'It gave me the lie of the land and I was able to navigate down the rail track to the cliff edge. I crouched down on my knees then. I didn't want to be seen even in silhouette, if anyone looked back.'

'And what was John doing at the landing stage?'

'There was a boat there and two men. His accomplices. He must have called them in, even though he'd promised he wouldn't. He'd lied to my face, just like Paul said he would. He'd phoned them up and summoned them here, to rescue him. He was clearing out, before things got too hot.'

'Hang on a minute. When did John call them? It must have taken a while for the boat to get out here.'

'I think it must have been that afternoon, perhaps even before John found out Twinkle was dead. You remember, he disappeared off on his own to the chapel? And we were all looking for him in the house? He'd argued with Twinkle and I think he must have slipped away then to call up his friends, to let them know what had happened. But not to cancel anything. To hand things on, to complete the deal. Twinkle knew what John was up to, so I suppose he thought he had to act quickly.'

'He arranged for the boat to come out here in the dead of night to collect the footage?'

'That must have been the plan. He'd have copied it all onto a USB stick and handed it over. But after Twinkle died, he thought again. At least, that's how it appeared to me, watching him heading down to the jetty. He knew how bad it looked, Twinkle dying like that. He may even have suspected I had something to do with it.'

'Or was worried that you suspected him.'

'I...I suppose so. But whatever the truth, things were getting too hot for him. He was running away, cutting his losses, like he always did when things got difficult. And, worst of all, he was leaving me behind to take the blame.'

'You can't be sure of that.'

'Why else would he be sneaking about in the middle of the night? He was running away. He lied to my face and now he was betraying our friendship. Paul was right. He couldn't be trusted. It was so obvious. He was leaving me behind to suffer the

192

consequences. It made me so angry. I couldn't believe it. We had been so close for so many years. And now he was abandoning me, stabbing me in the back. Saving his own neck and leaving me to fend for myself.'

'But...he *didn't* leave, surely?'

'No. That was the strange thing. He was in the boat for ten, fifteen minutes perhaps. I kept expecting to hear the engine start up and see it pull away. But then he stepped back onto the jetty. I thought, he must have left something behind. Something that will incriminate him. Not the cameras. There was nothing he could do about them. But something else that might link him to it all. The hub perhaps.'

'Or the tablet?'

'He would have wiped that already. At least, that's what I assumed. But I didn't really have time to think about it. I was terrified he might see me. I had to scrabble back up to the house as quickly as I could, while he was climbing the steps. I knew I wouldn't have time to get out of my jacket and boots, so I ducked down behind the wall of the compound. I was going to let him in, find out what he had forgotten, and then, when he came out again, I'd confront him.'

'And did you?'

Suzy shook her head numbly. 'He stopped, just outside the wall. I could hear his breathing. I suddenly thought, he must have seen me, he must know I am here.'

'Why didn't you step out and talk to him? You could have spoken to him. Accused him of deserting you. Even if he got angry, there's no way he would ever hurt you.'

'But he was running out on me, don't you understand? He was leaving me to take the blame. My life would have been in ruins. My family. My children. I was so upset, so angry. I just wanted to hit him. He was trying to ruin my life, just like he had ruined so many other lives.'

'But...'

'I was enraged, don't you see? I wasn't thinking straight. I was so hurt. And so I...I slipped the mallet out of the coat. And as he walked through into the compound I hit him as hard as I could.' She stopped, picturing the scene in her mind. 'It only took one blow. He didn't even cry out. He just slumped to the ground. I looked down at him and all the anger just evaporated. It was my friend lying there. I couldn't believe what I had done. I don't know what had possessed me.'

'Oh, Suzy.'

'But I didn't...I didn't panic. I felt a strange calm wash over me. Like before, on the cliff top. I didn't break down. I didn't freak out at all. And then I saw the boat leaving.' Her eyes flashed with an echo of surprise. 'The light bobbing up in the sea. I couldn't understand it. They were leaving without him. And then I realised,' she sobbed. 'They had been planning to leave all along. John wasn't running out on me at all.'

'He was just handing over the footage?'

Suzy nodded miserably. 'I felt like such a fool. But there was nothing to be done. John was dead. I couldn't bring him back. And perhaps...perhaps anyway it was meant to be. It wasn't about me at all. It was Paul. He had been there with me all along. He had guided me to this and now I could feel him slipping away, letting go. And I could feel his gratitude. I had done what he wanted me to do and now he was leaving, moving on to the next life, as he should have done all those years ago.'

Nadia suppressed a shudder. It was clear Suzy believed every word she was saying. 'And what did you do then?'

'My angel brought me back to reality. He spoke to me, helped me to focus. I needed to act quickly, he said. So I went back to the house. I slipped off Jill's shoes and tip-toed over to the bathroom. The cameras wouldn't be filming any more, but I kept the light off anyway, just to be sure. I grabbed the nearest towel from the rail. Then I went back out to...to deal with the body.'

'You wrapped his head in it, to staunch the blood?'

'Yes, that was the idea. There wasn't that much blood really, but I didn't want it pressing against my clothes, even wearing someone else's coat and shoes. And I thought, when the police get here, they'll be really confused anyway. The forensics people, I mean. There won't be anything to connect this to me.' Despite the madness of her actions, Suzy seemed to be able to

194

think rationally enough when it came to covering her tracks. She might be deluded, insane even, but she was clever too. 'I didn't want to drag the body across the grass. Better to use the railway line, I thought. So I shifted him over to the steps. It wasn't easy, but I managed it somehow. I could have rolled him over the cliff anywhere on the island, but I knew he was unlikely to end up in the sea whatever I did. He'd get caught up in the rocks somewhere.'

'So you shoved him down the steps and let him come to rest in plain view?'

'Yes. It didn't matter. I was never going to be able to cover up the fact that he had died and I didn't think anyone would believe he had simply tripped up. Not with Twinkle dead too. But a boat had visited the island and not just once, but twice. The first time, to set up the cameras. So I thought, maybe I could pin the blame on them.'

'And once you'd dumped the body?'

'Well, first I had to get rid of the towel. It had a bit of blood on it and goodness knows what else. I couldn't just throw it over the edge of the cliff. It was bound to snag on something. Better to burn it, I thought. Luckily, I'd already grabbed the lighter from John's pocket. I knew I would probably need it. I went over to the far cliff and...and I set light to the towel. It was more difficult than I thought it would be, but I got it to burn eventually. And once most of it was gone I kicked the embers over the edge of the cliff.'

'And what time was this?'

'I don't know. About half past three in the morning. A quarter to four maybe. I had to hurry. It looked like it might start getting light soon.'

'Why didn't you throw the mallet over the edge as well? A solid object like that. It would have been easier to get rid of than the towel.' Less air resistance.

'That was the plan,' Suzy agreed. 'But if I was to stand a chance of getting away with this, I needed to shift the blame onto John's two friends. My angel helped me to think it all through.' He did seem to be the brains of the outfit, Nadia reflected ruefully. 'I had no doubt the police would find out who the men were, once they discovered the webcams and what John had been up to this weekend. But how could I prove they had been on the island? What evidence could I plant to incriminate them? And then it occurred to me. Adam already believed there was somebody else here. I mean, apart from us. He had seen the open door of the lighthouse and the cottage door when you first arrived. Maybe I could use that to my advantage, hide the mallet upstairs somewhere in the tower. If the murder weapon was found up there, people could easily believe there were strangers on the island. The police would believe it. So I came back here, with the mallet. I'd wiped the handle clean with the towel before I burnt it and I made sure not to get any fingerprints on it afterwards. I found some old newspapers downstairs. The Daily Sketch.' She sighed, remembering how that fact had tripped her up. 'And I brought it up to the storeroom on the second floor. I slipped inside, cleared away a few of the cobwebs.' She screwed up her face. She had never been a fan of creepy crawlies. 'And placed the mallet in one of the boxes, where it could easily be found. I even lit a lamp, to help suggest somebody had been up there. And then I came downstairs and went back to the bathroom. I had a quick wash and made sure I wasn't too dirty. And then I went to bed. And Liam was still fast asleep, just where I had left him, the poor lamb, completely oblivious.'

'What about the lighter? Why didn't you get rid of that? Or plant it with the mallet?'

'I was going to. But then I thought, what if nobody believes it *was* an intruder? What if everyone convinces themselves it was one of us? I decided to wait and see how people reacted in the morning. Maybe I would get lucky and someone would find the mallet. If everyone decided a stranger was behind it, then I could easily throw the lighter away. But if not...'

'Then you could plant it on one of us. Put it where we would be bound to find it and then blame the whole thing on them.'

'That was the idea.' A useful contingency plan. Despite her delusions, Suzy could be quite calculating when she put her mind to it. 'And when Adam found the bits of towel this morning...' She shuddered. 'I had hoped no-one would find that...but when he did and he realised it belonged to Jill, then she became the easy target.'

'And after what she did with your husband yesterday morning, you weren't going to feel too guilty about that.'

'That wasn't the reason. I didn't really blame her for that. She didn't know what she was doing.'

'You didn't pick her towel deliberately then, when you grabbed it from the bathroom?'

'No. It was dark. I just took the first one I could lay my hands on. As I say, I wasn't intending for anyone to find it.'

'But when they did, you were willing to let Jill take the blame.'

'It was her or me. She had a credible motive. I slid the lighter into her handbag when no-one was looking and Liam found it there a few minutes later.'

'So you were happy to let Jill take the blame for everything?'

'Not happy. But yes, I would have let her go to prison, in my place. For the sake of my children. And for my family.'

Nadia shook her head. 'It wasn't for their sake at all. You were saving your own skin.' Suzy had not been thinking about anyone else at all. 'My god, Suzy....you need help. You really do. You're not well.'

'I never intended to hurt anyone. Don't you see? Everything just ran away with itself. And when it did, I...I had to protect myself and my family. And it was all for the best in the end. Paul got the resolution he deserved. But you finding out about all this...' She grimaced. 'It's ruined everything. That stupid newspaper. You'll tell the others the truth and that'll be the end of me. I have no choice now, Nadia. You do understand? There's only one course left open to me.' She moved across to the glass door leading out onto the balcony and slowly pulled it back.

Nadia's jaw dropped. 'You're not going to...?'

'I'm sorry, Nadia. I really am. I've always liked you. But I have no choice. It's you or me now.'

'What are you...?'

Suzy pursed her lips together and waved the flare gun. 'You have to step outside, onto the balcony.'

Nadia regarded her in horror. 'Suzy, there's no way I'm going out there.'

'Only one of us can leave here, Nadia. I can...I can tell them you confessed it all to me. I can say you were behind everything.'

'You're mad, Suzy. No-one's going to believe that.'

'They will. I can say you argued with John. You found out what he was up to. You saw him kill Twinkle and then you spotted him trying to slip away in the night. And you couldn't let that happen. So you hit him. You didn't intend to kill him, of course, but he died anyway. And then you tried to cover it up.'

'Suzy, that's nonsense. No-one will believe that.'

'They will. They'll believe me. People always believe me. Why would I lie?'

Nadia gripped the handrail behind her. 'Suzy, you don't have to do this. You can end this now. We can find someone to help you...'

'It's too late for that, Nadia. You have to step outside.'

Nadia shook her head firmly. 'You're going to have to shoot me, Suzy, because there's no way I'm stepping out there.' She stared defiantly at the other woman. 'And if you do shoot me in the head, nobody's going to believe you were acting in self defence.'

'You're right,' Suzy agreed sadly. 'But if you don't do as I say then I'll have lost everything anyway. I'll spend the rest of my life in prison. Or in a psychiatric hospital. They'll think I'm mad, like you do. I couldn't bear that.' She aimed the pistol. 'So I might just as well shoot you anyway.'

Somehow, Nadia found the courage to stand her ground. 'I'm not stepping outside. If I'm going to die, then you're going to have to kill me right now. Look, Suzy, you're not well. You're not thinking rationally. The things you've done....okay, Twinkle, maybe that was an accident. Maybe you're misremembering it, over dramatising it somehow. But you killed John deliberately.

You murdered him, Suzy. It wasn't Paul Hammond who told you to do it. It wasn't your angel or anything supernatural. You did it yourself. You made that choice. And one way or another, you have to pay for that. You have to be held to account.'

Suzy Heigl was trembling now. At some level, she had to know Nadia was right, but she was not prepared to admit it, even to herself. She advanced slowly, the pistol raised and Nadia flinched as she felt the nozzle press against her forehead. They stood there for a moment, the two of them, but Suzy could not hold the gun steady. Her whole arm was shaking. Her finger was wrapped around the podgy trigger, but she was barely managing to keep the weapon straight. It was one thing to attack someone in the dark, from behind, it was quite another to look them in the eye as you did it.

'Damn you!' she muttered at last and, abruptly, struck Nadia hard across the face with the barrel of the gun. The impact took Nadia by surprise and, without thinking, she let go of the rail behind her. Suzy dropped the pistol and grabbed the other woman by the shoulders, hurling her towards the open door. Nadia stumbled, her head banging against the metal frame. That disorientated her further. Suzy grabbed her arm again and suddenly she felt the wind on her face as she was propelled out onto the narrow metal balcony.

'Suzy, no!' she cried, fearfully. But Suzy was beyond any reason now.

Nadia stumbled and for a brief second Suzy lost her grip. Nadia wriggled sideways and attempted to regain her footing, then looked around, terrified, and saw Suzy stomping towards her, her arms outstretched. She tried to recover her feet, tried to move out of the way, but there was no escape. Suzy grabbed her by the throat and began to squeeze it tightly. Desperately, Nadia took hold of her shoulders and tried to push her away; but Suzy's grip was too strong. Struggling for breath, she dropped a hand and tried to punch the woman in the stomach, but the blow had no effect. Then, in desperation, she smacked her head against Suzy's forehead. There was an unpleasant crack and, momentarily disorientated, Suzy released her grip.

Nadia made the most of the opportunity, hitting the other woman square in the jaw. Suzy staggered backwards but, before Nadia could follow it up, Suzy had lowered her head like a bull and barrelled into her.

This time the momentum carried Nadia backwards and up, against the protective railing. The top of the rail was barely waist height and Suzy had her hands on her face now, pushing against her, bending her body slowly over the top of it. *This is it*, she realised. There was no way back. The railing began to creak and stretch under the pressure. It was a hundred years old and was not built to withstand this kind of assault. With a horrifying crack, it came away behind her.

Nadia's legs smacked down onto the balcony, but there was nothing to support the rest of her body. Her head fell back over the edge and her legs, carried by the momentum, began to whip up and over.

Suzy had been leaning over the top of her and had even less support than Nadia. She fell forward, knocking away the unconnected railing, and with a cry fell out into the open air. In an instant, she was gone.

Nadia was already half on the way to joining her, but a dying kick from Suzy's legs knocked her against the supporting rail to the left and, as she skittered across the edge of the balcony, some last minute reflex enabled her to grab hold of the awkwardly jutting pole. She hung there for a moment, her head and chest just above the lip of the balcony, but her legs dangling below.

I'm not going to die, she told herself forcefully. But the wind was whipping her whole body left and right. Her hands grasped the rail as tightly as she could. At least this one did not look as if it was going to come away. She took a moment to marshal her resources, then with a super human effort, she pulled her upper body forward and onto the balcony. She paused a moment there, and at last scrabbled her legs back onto the safety of the metal walkway. Finally, she rolled over onto her back and lay for some time, breathing heavily, her mind completely blank, the adrenaline surging but her brain unable to re-engage.

Gradually, even through the breeze rustling through her hair, she could hear noises coming from below. Urgent voices. Slowly and very carefully, she pulled herself to her feet, keeping as close as she could to the glass wall of the lighthouse. She pressed against it for a moment and then, gathering together the last of her courage, she stepped forward to the edge of the balcony, lowered herself to her knees and gazed down over the edge.

Suzy's body was lying in the grass, some eighty feet below, her head and legs at an obscene, impossible angle. She had fallen out beyond the compound, to the west side of the lighthouse. Already, some of the others were racing out from the cottage.

For a moment, Nadia closed her eyes. She was alive. But her mind was too fogged over to encompass the enormity of what had just happened. Would anyone even believe her?

Jill Clarke was looking back up at the top of the lighthouse, pointing at her. Nadia managed to raise a hand, albeit half-heartedly, just to let them know she was okay. But Liam Heigl, she could see, was not paying her any attention. He was crouching by his dead wife, cradling her body in despair.

Nadia pulled herself up and made her way back into the lamp room. *It was all so stupid,* she thought. Nothing that had happened here needed to have happened at all. Suzy had lost her mind and given way to fantasy. One pointless, stupid mistake and then everything had fallen apart.

A flock of seagulls fluttered overhead. The sea was calm and a handful of wispy clouds did nothing to obscure the view. Nadia lifted a hand to her brow and screwed up her eyes. The mainland was visible now – the Isle of Lewis, in the distance – and down in the water, chugging towards the island, was a chunky red motor boat. It was too far away to make out much about it, but it was not dissimilar to the one she and Adam had arrived on. Maybe somebody had seen the flares after all. Whoever it was, they were certainly heading in the right direction. But it was far too late for them to help.

Nadia returned to the lamp room and found the flare gun

201

Suzy had dropped. There was a small amount of blood on the barrel. Her blood, she realised. Her face was bleeding, where Suzy had struck her. She checked the cartridge and then stepped out one last time onto the balcony. Calmly, she lifted the pistol into the air and pulled the trigger. A bright light flared high above Flaxton Isle.

Chapter Fourteen

The men and women of the press were keeping a respectful distance, for a change. Even they knew not to intrude too far on a day like this, though the odd discreet photograph would still appear online after the mourners emerged from the hall at the end of the service.

Nadia Kumar barely noticed them. She wiped a tear from her eye and shot a sad smile at Samantha Redmond as the two of them made their way slowly around the concrete building to the garden of remembrance. 'It was good of you to come,' she said, taking Samantha's arm as they walked along the parade of flowers and peered at each motto in turn. 'After everything that happened.'

'How could I not?' Samantha said. She crouched down to read one of the cards. "TWINKLING FOREVER. REST IN PEACE BABES. LOVE JILL"

'He'd be pleased at the turn out,' Nadia thought. Twinkle had a lot more friends than he had realised. People who loved him. Clients, internet friends. His mates from the pub. And all the well wishers who had read about what had happened and sent flowers in his memory.

Samantha rose up. 'It's a shame Jill couldn't come.'

'She couldn't face it. I spoke to her yesterday. She's going to have to go to John's funeral next week, now that they've released the body. She thinks she owes it to him. And the kids have to go, of course. She sends her love, though.' Nadia frowned, pausing briefly in their walk. 'What a mess. So many lives ruined.'

They stopped for a moment to read another card.

'Oh, I got an email from Jim Peterson a few days ago,' Nadia said. 'You know, the owner of the cottage. Poor sod. He spent a fortune upgrading the place, before we arrived.'

'I suppose no-one will want to rent it now.'

'No, just the opposite, actually. He's had dozens of enquiries. You know what the say, all publicity is good publicity.

The place could easily be booked out until next summer.'

Samantha pursed her lips distastefully. 'People can be so ghoulish, sometimes.'

'He was going to turn them down. Said he felt a bit uncomfortable about it. But I told him to go for it. He might as well make a bit of money out of it.' Nadia nodded her head to the journalists hovering at the edge of the car park. 'Everyone else has.'

The press had had a field day, of course, though they had been slightly torn about the focus of the story. Hollywood star caught up in a series of murders or popular children's author kills two friends and then dies in roof top struggle. *They must have thought it was Christmas.*

Nadia had missed the worst of it, though. She had spent the two days following their rescue at the local police station being questioned. It had been quite a gruelling experience, but she did not blame the police for that. They had to be thorough. They only had her word about what had happened at the top of the lighthouse. But the testimony of the others and the forensic evidence had backed up everything she had said; and all that Suzy had told her about the other deaths. Nadia had been released without charge forty-eight hours later.

Jim Peterson had got to the island ahead of the police. It was his boat Nadia had seen heading towards them. It was almost funny. He hadn't actually noticed the flares on Saturday evening; but a neighbour had mentioned them to his wife at church the following morning, and asked if they had rented out the cottage to a bunch of Americans. Fourth of July and all that. Peterson suspected his neighbour was probably mistaken, but he had placed a call through to the island anyway and – when there was no response from the satellite phone – he thought he had best come out to check in person. The first thing he saw when he arrived was the body of John Menhenick hanging from the handrail. He radioed the coast guard at once and got a message through to the police. The authorities arrived an hour later.

After Nadia had been released, she flew straight back to Dubai to be with her husband. It was a relief to see him. Richard really was her rock. But as soon as she had been given a date for the funeral, she had booked her ticket back. Samantha Redmond had been braver, staying in the UK for the duration, despite the press camped out on her mother's doorstep and the despair of her producers in LA. It was the right thing to do, she'd said.

The police had arrested John's accomplices. A fisherman had already reported some suspicious activity in the waters off Lewis and they had quickly followed it up. The video footage had been impounded and would never see the light of day. It had taken police experts some time to decrypt the files. Samantha would not be staying around for the trial, which was slated for the end of the year. 'It's good that Liam came today,' she said.

'Yes. He's aged ten years in the last two weeks, the poor thing.' The press had presented Suzy Heigl as the villain of the piece – not without reason – and there had not been much sympathy to spare for her husband. 'Fending off the press, looking after three kids. And no money coming in.' Suzy had been a fairly rich woman, but she had never been afraid to spend the money she had earned. There was some left in the pot, but not a huge amount; and there would be nothing more to come. Her books had already been withdrawn from sale. 'And he's too proud to accept any money from Suzy's mum and dad.'

'I thought of offering to help out,' Samantha said. She had always had a bit of a soft spot for Liam. 'Do you think he'd be offended if I suggested it? I don't want to tread on any toes.'

'I don't think he'd be offended. It's a nice thought. But I don't think he'd take it. You might be able to do something for the kids, though.'

Samantha nodded. 'I'll text him in a month or two, when things have settled down.'

Adam Cartwright appeared at the far end of the garden, with his other half. He waved a hand and Nadia smiled back. 'He's looking a bit stressed as well,' she said.

'He doesn't look any different to me.'

'Trust me. I can tell. Still, he got off fairly lightly compared to some of us.'

'We all got off lightly, compared to you,' Samantha

reckoned. 'Fighting for your life up there.'

Nadia had done her best to put that out of her mind. She had been offered counselling, but she had decided not to bother. She had always been a self reliant person. And besides, her husband was there to help her through it. Him and their gorgeous little girl.

'Was she mad, do you think?' Samantha asked. 'Suzy?'

'In the end, I think she must have been.' Nadia had been thinking about that a lot. 'We all laughed about her little quirks. But when it came to it, she got so caught up in her own world, she couldn't find a way out. It was so sad. So *pointless.*'

They had reached the end of the flowers. 'Are you coming back to the house?' Nadia asked.

Samantha shook her head. 'I don't think so. I'll pay my respects to Twinkle's mum and then head off. My flight's booked for tomorrow. I don't think I'll be coming back to the UK for a while.'

Nadia gave her a hug. 'We'll miss you.'

'I'll miss you too.'

Nadia smiled warmly. 'See you in another ten years,' she said.

The Scandal At Bletchley
by
Jack Treby

"I've been a scoundrel, a thief, a blackmailer and a whore, but never a murderer. Until now..."

The year is 1929. As the world teeters on the brink of a global recession, Bletchley Park plays host to a rather special event. MI5 is celebrating its twentieth anniversary and a select band of former and current employees are gathering at the private estate for a weekend of music, dance and heavy drinking. Among them is Sir Hilary Manningham-Butler, a middle aged woman whose entire adult life has been spent masquerading as a man. She doesn't know why she has been invited – it is many years since she left the secret service – but it is clear she is not the only one with things to hide. And when one of the other guests threatens to expose her secret, the consequences could prove disastrous for everyone.

www.jacktreby.com

The Red Zeppelin
by
Jack Treby

"You'll never get me up in one of those things. They're absolutely lethal."

Seville, 1931. Six months after the loss of the British airship the R101, a German Zeppelin is coming in to land in Southern Spain.

Hilary Manningham-Butler is an MI5 operative eking out a pitiful existence on the Rock of Gibraltar. The offer of a job in the Americas provides a potential life line but there are strings attached. First she must prove her mettle to her masters in London and that means stepping on board the Richthofen before the airship leaves Seville. A cache of secret documents has been stolen from Scotland Yard and the files must be recovered if British security is not to be severely compromised. Hilary must put her life on the line to discover the identity of the thief. But as the airship makes its way across the Atlantic towards Brazil it becomes clear that nobody on board is quite what they seem. And there is no guarantee that any of them will reach Rio de Janeiro alive...

www.jacktreby.com

The Pineapple Republic
by
Jack Treby

Democracy is coming to the Central American Republic of San Doloroso. But it won't be staying long...

The year is 1990. Ace reporter Daniel Parr has been injured in a freak surfing accident, just as the provisional government of San Doloroso has announced the country's first democratic elections.

The Daily Herald needs a man on the spot and in desperation they turn to Patrick Malone, a feckless junior reporter who just happens to speak a few words of Spanish.

Despatched to Central America to get the inside story, our Man in Toronja finds himself at the mercy of a corrupt and brutal administration that is determined to win the election at any cost...

www.jacktreby.com

The Gunpowder Treason
by
Michael Dax

"If I had thought there was the least sin in the plot, I would not have been in it for all the world..."

Robert Catesby is a man in despair. His father is dead and his wife is burning in the fires of Hell – his punishment from God for marrying a Protestant. A new king presents a new hope but the persecution of Catholics in England continues unabated and Catesby can tolerate it no longer. King James bears responsibility but the whole government must be eradicated if anything is to really change. And Catesby has a plan...

The Gunpowder Treason is a fast-paced historical thriller. Every character is based on a real person and almost every scene is derived from eye-witness accounts. This is the story of the Gunpowder Plot, as told by the people who were there...

www.jacktreby.com

Printed in Great Britain
by Amazon